BY HONOUR BOUND

BY HONOUR BOUND

VALERIE GRAY

St. Martin's Press
New York

c.1

Library of Congress Cataloging-in-Publication Data

Gray, Valerie.
    By honour bound / by Valerie Gray.
        p. cm.
    ISBN 0-312-02174-7
    I. Title.
  PS3557.R3337B9   1988
  813'.54—dc19   88-12013
                                                CIP

First published in Great Britain by Robert Hale Limited.
First U.S. Edition
10 9 8 7 6 5 4 3 2 1

Map artwork by Larry Fink

Contents

Prologue: Home from the Wars 11

There Was a Fair Maid Dwelling 23

Reunion of Two Friends 38

The Shopping Expedition 51

Local Society 65

Mr. Pontefract Pursues His Quarry 78

Anne Escapes 90

In Which Mr. Pontefract Is Temporarily 99
    Vanquished

Natherscombe House 113

London Bound 128

Delights of the Metropolis 142

Further Developments 159

The Spectre of Newgate 172

Anne and Mortimer Go Sightseeing 184

A Lady's Sense of Honour 197

Resolution 210

Epilogue: All's Well That Ends Well 221

Dedication

To my parents, Frances and Fred Deakins, of Worthing in Sussex with my love and thanks for all their help and encouragement.

To my daughter, Antonia, who really prefers science fiction to romance.

And to Colin, as always.

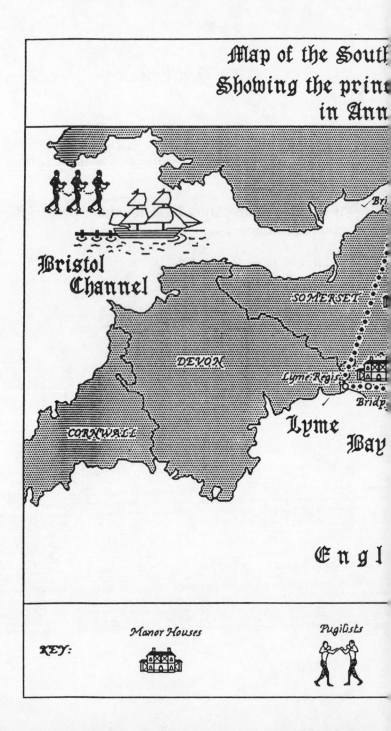

Map of the South
Showing the prin
in Ann

Bri

Bristol
Channel

SOMERSET

DEVON

Lyme Regis

Bridp

Lyme Bay

CORNWALL

Engl

KEY: Manor Houses   Pugilists

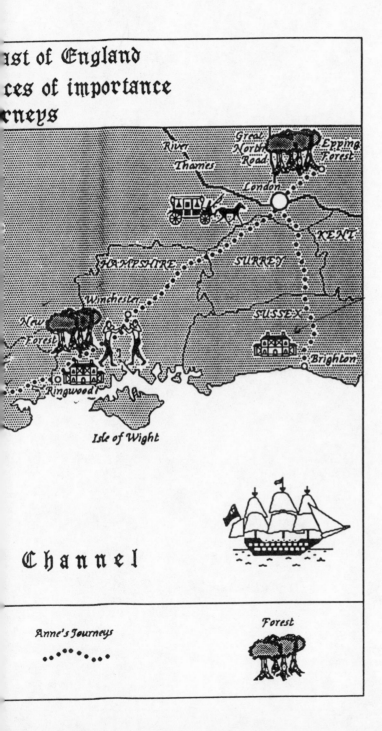

Young and attractive orphan flees from
an unwanted marriage to Dorset where
she falls in love with a veteran of
the Peninsula War.

Prologue: Home from the Wars

'It's of no use, Hester, I can't forget her!' exclaimed Sir Mortimer Vane, fixing his sister with an imploring gaze.

The lady thus addressed glanced with concern at her companion as they stood together in the Throne Room at Carlton House, awaiting their turn to be presented to the stiff little old Queen Charlotte and her son's guest of honour, the Czar of All the Russias.

'My dear, not now,' muttered Hester, through clenched teeth. 'We are next. I think my hair is about to fall down. Do walk very slowly.'

With small, deliberate steps and head held high to balance her nodding plumed headdress, Hester advanced towards the canopied throne. Mortimer paced slowly beside her, resplendent in the full-dress uniform of an aide-de-camp to the Duke of Wellington. Sonorously their names were announced. Hester sank into a deep curtsey.

Queen Charlotte managed the tiny, tight-lipped movement which normally passed for a smile on the part of this prim, some said tyrannical, royal lady. She certainly insisted on the rigid etiquette of the petty German court of her youth. Hester moved on, leaving Mortimer to make his bow. Again she curtsied low, but this time she was assisted to rise by the Saviour of Europe himself.

On this evening in June 1814, the Emperor of Russia

11

was regarded by Englishmen, and more particularly by
English ladies, as a hero of the first magnitude. Since
Napoleon's ignominious retreat from Moscow, Czar
Alexander and his peoples had stood high in the
estimation of their allies. Now the monster Bonaparte
was safely imprisoned on the island of Elba and the
Czar's visit to England, accompanied by the King of
Prussia, had prompted a national outburst of almost
hysterical enthusiasm and rejoicing. Czar Alexander
greatly enjoyed the adulation, but tonight was becoming
a trifle bored with the seemingly endless procession of
ladies in low-necked, high-waisted satin dresses,
attended by sworded, white-stockinged gentlemen in
formal court attire. He greeted Hester's familiar face
with a smile of relief.

'My Lady Montfort, again we meet, such a pleasure.
My compliments to your esteemed husband.'

He spoke in rapid French and seemed inclined to
prolong the conversation, but the pressure of the line
was inexorable. Hester murmured a polite reply and
moved aside. The Czar continued to amuse himself by
quizzing the younger and prettier women, while Hester
and Mortimer sought relief from the intense heat of the
Throne Room in the Conservatory.

Hester perched precariously on a low wall just outside
the west door and surveyed the wide lawn and
weeping-willow trees.

'How tranquil it is. I vow if that ordeal had been
prolonged five mintues more, I should have fainted
away. Did you observe Prinny's face when he presented
the Marchioness of Hertford and the Emperor barely
acknowledged her? Such a slight to our host. Oh dear,
my court feathers are wilting at last. You would not
believe the number of pins which I have penetrating my
head at absurd angles – I am nothing less than a
porcupine. Poor unfortunate creatures! But observe,
Tim dearest, the peacocks, are they not handsome?' She

indicated with her fan several fine specimens prome-
nading solemnly towards the shrubbery.

Her brother regarded the birds in question with a
jaundiced eye. 'If you say so, m'dear. For myself I find
them entirely appropriate in this setting – a blend of fine
feathers and small intellects.'

'You are too severe. Or, perhaps, the light is too dim to
do them justice.' Hester hesitated, then added gently, 'Is
that indeed how you see us, all outward show and
frivolity? London must seem very heedless to you after
all you have seen and suffered. You have changed so
much I hardly know you anymore. Ten years ago you
went to join Sir John Moore's Light Brigade an eager,
hopeful boy and now ...' Her voice tailed away and she
made a small sound, halfway between a sob and a sniff.

Mortimer glanced down at her bent head, bearing the
eloquent, drooping feathers. In a trice his bitter, disdainful air vanished. He squatted beside her and clasped one
small, gloved hand in his own.

'I'm a a a brute to distress you so. Not fit company to be
taken about in polite society. Not your fault. It's just that
all I fought for, all my dreams for after the wars, ended
when I heard Stephanie was married and after that I
could not come home, I wanted to die in Spain. Nothing
mattered to me or made sense. You were happy and
well-cared-for with Hugo and my nephews – no real
responsibilities – so I fought wildly and recklessly,
nothing heroic about it! Of course, that was years ago,
before Corunna. After I recovered from my wounds I
felt cold, numb. When I joined the Duke's staff I became
ruthlessly efficient, a war machine. When the peace came
it caught me unprepared. The life of a soldier is the only
one I know. How can I settle down at Shawcross as a
country squire – alone? No, no, I shall sell up my
commission and persuade Hugo to oversee the estate in
trust for my nephews. I plan to return to the Continent as
soon as possible. There's always a little war to be found

somewhere in Central Europe.'

Hester listened silently to this tirade. Her gray eyes, dark with sympathy, rested thoughtfully on Mortimer's profile. The lights from the Conservatory harshly illuminated the cruel, deep scar, which ran from his cheekbone to his right ear, a legacy of the assault on Ciudad Rodrigo two years earlier. After a moment, she shook her head decidedly, and said lightly, but firmly, 'Well, my dear, wallow in self-pity if you feel you must, but I think you would be wrong to rush away and offer your services to some foreign princeling too quickly. Hugo writes from Paris that there is still much unrest. We may not have heard the last of Bonaparte. I wish you would remain in England, at least for a few months. Who else will serve as my escort while my husband does his duty at the Peace Conference, if not my Peninsular hero?' She finished on a pleading note, and sat back assuming a wistful expression.

Suddenly Mortimer grinned, his deep-set hazel eyes glinting with amusement. 'Doing it rather too brown, Hester. You know as well as I that if Hugo goes on to Vienna he will summon you to his side as soon as it can be arranged. He positively pines without you.'

'But my poor boys. Then they would run wild without their stern uncle to instill some discipline in my absence,' protested Lady Montfort, clutching at straws.

More people began to drift out onto the terrace and Mortimer pulled Hester to her feet. She smoothed her crushed skirts, gave her hair an encouraging pat, and placed her hand on Mortimer's arm as they reentered the vast Gothic Conservatory. For several minutes they were preoccupied by the necessity for acknowledging various acquaintances in the crowded chamber, but eventually they reached a clearing at the upper end, beneath a splendid medallion bearing the initials G.P.R. Here they paused to survey the colourful scene and Hester gave vent to a stifled giggle.

'Whatever will he think of next?' she whispered. Mortimer followed her gaze, observing the traceries on the ceiling, more appropriate to a cathedral than a room designed to house plants. The walls were lined with rich hangings of pink and silver, punctuated at intervals by tall mirrors and shelves bearing an assortment of bright golden ornaments.

He shook his head and responded in an undertone, 'I cannot imagine. However, I will say I find it somewhat more tasteful than that oriental folly in Brighton. Wasteful, but tasteful! Even the household servants' dark blue livery is less ostentatious than I would have expected, knowing, as I do to my cost, our host's strong interest in military uniforms.'

'You are thinking of the Field Marshal's attire which he recently designed for himself and the Duke?' queried Hester mischievously.

Mortimer scowled, then grinned reluctantly. 'Did you read of it in the *Chronicle*? My dear, it was incredible. The whole was made up according to His Highness's own instructions. Not only the cuffs, but also the front of the coat and the collar were embroidered with unexampled generosity. The embroidery was two inches wide, at least. It taxed all my powers of tact and ingenuity to prevent Wellington from sending it back with a sharp note on the subject of man milliners.'

'Despite his extravagance and his treatment of his wife, which has aroused such hostility against him, I do have a soft spot for our Prince. Do you remember him ten years ago, so happy by the sea with his parades and music and Mrs. Fitz? 'Tis a great pity that he was obliged to make such an unfortunate dynastic marriage.' Hester shook her head and sighed.

Less tenderhearted, her brother reacted briskly. 'We have all changed a great deal in ten years. But we have not all run to seed through gross over-indulgence.' He glanced about him disdainfully and continued, 'Don't you think we have done our duty for tonight? I find the atmosphere in here quite stifling.'

Tacitly Hester acquiesced to his suggestion. They began to thread their way slowly through the throng, traversing in turn the Golden Drawing Room, the Blue Velvet Room, and the Rose Satin Drawing Room. They did not speak again until they had made their farewells and were comfortably ensconced in the darkness of Lady Montfort's town carriage, clattering over the cobblestones of the metropolis. It was still quite early for the fashionable West End and the bright gas lamps revealed many people of all descriptions hurrying about their business. After a few moments, Mortimer moved restlessly, his dress sword clanking awkwardly at his side. The vehicle swung into St. James's Street, heading for Piccadilly and Park Lane, as he peered through the gloom at Hester's averted profile.

'Forgive me, I have quite ruined your evening. I did not mean all that I said. You have scarcely changed at all since you married Hugo. If anything, you have improved in looks since I went away.'

Unable to resist the pleading note, Hester responded warmly, 'Oh, Tim, there is not the least necessity for you to be so remorseful. I enjoyed my evening very much. I had hoped to make you known to one or two of my friends, particularly Jane Dartington and her daughter, but there will be another opportunity quite soon, I have no doubt.'

Uneasily Mortimer inquired, 'And how old, pray, is Miss Dartington?'

'She is twenty. A charming young lady, with decided manners and a strong sense of the ridiculous, which is why I fancy she has already been out two seasons ...' Suddenly aware that she had been trapped, Hester gasped, and continued hurriedly, 'but you need not be so suspicious. I am not matchmaking! I just want you to indulge in a little gaiety and frivolity after so much grim soldiering. Why, even the Duke himself will be merry-making in London next month and will take part in the celebrations for the Centenary of the House of Hanover.'

Mortimer snorted, 'Bread and circuses ... and a bevy of insipid young females. Such inducements do not tempt me. 'Pon my soul, I begin to hanker for the peace of the countryside.'

Hester began to feel dizzy. At one moment she was talking to the easygoing, good-natured young man she remembered and the next she found herself seated beside a cold stranger who threw up an invisible, impenetrable shield to discourage any form of intimacy. Not for the first time, she longed for the support of her husband, with his cool good sense and deep affection for her brother. Lady novelist and observer of human nature though she was, sometimes Hester felt that she did not understand men at all. Stung by Mortimer's last remark concerning 'insipid females', she was about to accuse him of arrogance and pomposity, and then she recalled he was disappointed in love, so she bit her tongue and gazed instead at the dim, shadowy trees in Hyde Park.

They had arrived almost at the door of her elegant town mansion in Portman Square when Hester ventured to say, 'Tim dearest, Stephanie is married – quite happily, I believe. You are moping and pining to no purpose. You have had so few opportunities on campaign to take time to look about you and form a rational connection and so it is only natural that you have cherished the memory of Stephanie. But now, with the peace, I hope you will seek and find a lady who will value you as you deserve.'

Sir Mortimer smiled bitterly, tapping the scar which disfigured the right side of his face. 'I am twenty-eight years old, battle-torn and disillusioned. What young female of sense would spare me more than half a glance?'

Hester would listen to no more. Laughingly she protested, 'You goose! Do you not realize what a romantic creature you have become? Have you not heard of Lord Byron? Many ladies of exquisite sensibility (I do not say sense, for that does not enter into the case) would be in transports of delight if you would but offer them the slightest encouragement. Your very aloofness makes you irresistible.'

Acutely uncomfortable, Mortimer retorted gruffly, 'Stuff and nonsense. You are merely trying to provoke me. Ah, thank heaven we have arrived. Allow me to assist you.'

The carriage steps were let down, but before Mortimer could move, Hester had flung open the door and leapt out into the arms of a tall gentleman who was waiting on the pavement to receive her. He was still wearing a many-caped traveling coat.

'Hugo, oh my dear one, I have been wanting you so much. But why are you here, is anything amiss? Are you much fatigued?'

Lord Montfort enfolded his chattering wife in a close embrace, then with one arm still encircling her waist, he reached out to grip his brother-in-law's hand in a warm clasp. 'Come inside, my dears, and all will be revealed.' So saying, his lordship ushered them up the steps and into the spacious well-lit hall. Unobtrusively Giles, the butler, relieved them of their coats and wraps. Hester bespoke light refreshments in the drawing room and led the way into that apartment, pulling out pins to remove her court feathers as she sank down on a low sofa. Giles set a taper to kindle the small fire of wood and coal laid ready in the grate. He then withdrew, but reappeared almost immediately with a tray of sandwiches and little cakes, followed by a maid bearing pots of coffee and hot chocolate. Finally he placed a decanter of sherry wine at Lord Montfort's elbow, bowed to his master, and retreated on tiptoe, closing the door softly behind him.

Mortimer grinned, observing, 'I do like a well-ordered household.'

Smiling as she poured the coffee, Hester responded, 'Yes, you would never guess from his demeanour that poor Giles was quite vexed. You see, he feels it to be his duty to serve and hand round the refreshments, but after an evening like this evening I need a little informality. Are you both quite comfortable? Good. Now, Hugo, pray do tell your patient but curious wife, why you are here and not in Paris. Could you not have sent word, so that I might have had the pleasure of anticipating your coming?'

'Your pardon, my love. It was a sudden decision. There were dispatches to be delivered and I felt that my usefulness in Paris was at an end. Besides, I hankered for a sight of you and my two young rascals. But I apologize for appearing in your drawing room in all my traveling dirt.' Hugo glanced ruefully at his mud-splashed top boots.

Hester leaned back in her chair with a sigh of satisfaction. She sipped her coffee meditatively and surveyed her dark, handsome husband with approval. "Tis no matter. You look very well. I trust you will not be leaving us again in the near future?'

Reassured on this important question, Hester chattered on about family affairs and described in loving detail the latest escapades of their two sons, Dickon and Harry. Hugo inquired about the progress of her new novel and listened attentively as Hester described the detailed ramifications of her plot, his green eyes glinting with pleasure as they rested on his wife's animated countenance. Then, in his turn, Hugo sketched the situation in Paris and deftly included Mortimer in the conversation, canvassing his views on the prospects for a lasting peace. The younger man exerted himself to respond intelligently, but when the talk drifted again to domestic matters, he yawned and rose to his feet, drawling, 'Think I'll leave you two lovebirds together, if you'll excuse me, m'dear. Good night to ye both.'

At the door Mortimer paused and looked back.

Wistfully he observed the two heads close together, oblivious of all else in the happiness of their reunion. Quietly he ascended the stairs and sought his solitary bechamber.

The next morning dawned fair and Mortimer felt distinctly more cheerful when he appeared at the breakfast table. He was the first one down and was engaged in reading his correspondence when Hester joined him. She immediately observed her brother's improved spirits and the healthy appetite with which he was tackling a substantial plateful of kidneys and ham. He greeted her with an airy flourish, waving a letter in his hand.

'Good news?' she inquired, smiling in return.

Mortimer nodded and pushed aside his plate. 'From Jack Davenport. You remember he was wounded beside me in '12 and came home with a musket ball in his knee. He's still lame and staying down in Dorset with his aunts, Miss Ippolita Prawne and Miss Letitia. They are his only close relatives. He used to tell me about them when we were in the hospital, said they were delightful but eccentric, fossil addicts or some such thing. Live in Lyme Regis, you know, prime place to hunt fossils apparently. I told him I had an eccentric sister too, wrote novels!' Mortimer grinned at her provokingly and Hester marveled at his suddenly youthful appearance.

Ignoring his last remark, she nibbled a piece of toast and continued to probe, 'And is Major Davenport coming to London? Of course, I recall you mentioned him frequently in your letters and he was kind enough to send me a packet from you when he returned to England. I would so like to meet him again. We did meet many years ago, you recall, when you were both training in Kent.'

'So you did, but I'm afraid not, at least not at once. He wants me to visit him in Dorset.'

'Ah, I see,' said Hester, and indeed she did. The

reason for her brother's good humour had occurred to her in a flash of revelation. Stephanie de Beauclerc, once Lord Montfort's ward and still his cousin, had married Sir Lawrence Tremaine and settled in Bridport, some eight or nine miles from Lyme Regis. In the summer of 1804, Mortimer had been captivated by the vivacious Stephanie, with her dark curls, beautiful, heart-shaped face, and soft French accent. They were both very young and shared a passion for horses. On Mortimer's side the affection had gone deep, but the young lady was uncertain and they had parted, he to join Sir John Moore's regiment and she to marry, quite unexpectedly, in the month of The Battle of Trafalgar in October 1805, soon after her first London season. They had not met since her wedding.

Deep in thought, Hester was roused by a voice asking impatiently, 'What do you see? You're sitting there like a broody hen, failing to lay an egg!'

She tried to maintain a dignified mien, but failed and chuckled instead. 'Do not tease me. Forgive my suspicions, but I have a concern for you. Tell me, dearest, are you hoping to see Stephanie?'

To her relief, for the first time since his return, Mortimer did not attempt to hide behind a barrier of reserve when asked a question of a personal nature. He met her eyes across the table and answered honestly, 'I do not know. Yes, perhaps. I cannot forget her until I have seen her again and assured myself that she is happy in her present situation. But I have another reason also. I would like to see Jack and I need some activity. One cannot enjoy a good gallop in Hyde Park. Now that Hugo is home I need not fear to desert you. Do not look so distressed. I promise I will do nothing foolish. It is just that it is hard sometimes, being with you and Hugo ... it is like being outside a window, looking in on happiness which I cannot share.'

He stopped and stood up abruptly. After a moment

he came round the table to sit beside Hester, saying earnestly, 'You must not pity me, or think that I grudge you one ounce of contentment.'

'Of course not. You must rid your system of these distempered freaks and London is not the place to clear the head. I admit to some misgivings, but I do understand. When will you leave us?'

'Tomorrow, if that will suit you. I may perhaps return next month, when Wellington is in town, but I will send word. Will you and Hugo be going down to Huntsgrove at all in July?'

Hester shook her head. 'No, I think not. We have too many engagements here, but the boys will go and we may join them later in the season. Write to me here, and take care. Now, go away and see to your affairs. I know you are longing to be off.'

Mortimer bent to kiss her and she ruffled his thick, curly brown hair affectionately. 'Best of sisters!' he exclaimed lightly. The next moment he was gone, treading briskly and calling for his valet and ink and paper as he went.

II

There Was a Fair Maid Dwelling

It was a fine morning in late June. The sea breeze gently lifted the dark hair of a young lady who stood on the shoreline of Monmouth Beach, watching some tardy fishing boats regain the shelter of the Cobb Harbour after their night's work. Her bonnet had slipped back on her shoulders and she shaded her eyes from the bright sunlight with her hand. She stood lost in thought for some minutes, but was recalled abruptly to awareness of her surroundings by the sound of sharp yelps coming from behind.

'Oh no, Mincemeat. Not again. Stop it, sir, this instant!' she cried, running nimbly over the shingle to where a small, but handsome pug dog was planted squarely and aggressively in the way of a surprised black Labrador. Quickly she bent down and slipped on Mincemeat's leash, just as the owner of the Labrador arrived on the scene.

Panting a little from her exertions, she exclaimed, 'I'm so sorry. I didn't hear you coming, Mr. Gresham. I thought we had the beach to ourselves. I fear that Mincemeat always feels called upon to live up to the promise of his name when he encounters dogs larger than himself.'

'Which must be most of the canine population, Miss Anne,' responded the gentleman, smiling good-naturedly, as he raised his tall beaver hat. He was a fine-looking man of middle years and athletic build and his eyes rested appreciatively on Anne's trim figure, flushed cheeks, and sparkling, long-lashed brown eyes. Mincemeat growled menacingly and tugged at his leash. Recognizing defeat, Mr. Gresham requested Anne to convey his compliments to her cousins, the Misses Prawne and expressed the hope that he might see her soon at the Assembly Rooms, unaccompanied by her fierce protector. Anne inclined her head graciously, but gave vent to a slight shiver as she retraced her steps towards the Cobb in the wake of the pug. Mr. Gresham was a little too confident of himself and his attraction and she had the feeling that he looked right through her with his clear blue eyes to the trembling soul beneath.

'He is the sort of man who would use his telescope to spy on the bathing machines!' she muttered indignantly to Mincemeat, as they scrambled up the steep slope and rejoined The Walk. Here she resettled her bonnet securely upon her head, passed the Assembly Rooms with a disdainful snuff, and soon afterwards turned inland. The pug showed a distressing desire to linger by the ancient public water channel, but Anne towed him firmly up Broad Street to a tall, narrow house about halfway up the incline on the right-hand side. They entered upon a scene of animated conversation. Two elderly ladies were seated one on either side of the fireplace in the small, crowded parlour, listening intently to a young man, stationed by the window, who was reading aloud portions of a letter. He broke off as Anne came in and Mincemeat rushed to a fringed cushion, where he curled up with snuffling grunts of contentment.

'Anne, my dear, come and be seated. Jack has just had such an interesting communication from his friend, Sir Mortimer Vane.' Miss Ippolita Prawne, the elder of the two ladies, patted the seat beside her invitingly. She was a tall, thin, angular woman with bright dark eyes, but no other pretensions to beauty. Obediently Anne crossed the room and seated herself, having first taken the precaution of removing a wooden box containing an assortment of jagged rocklike objects, which she knew to be fossils. The other lady smiled at Anne sympathetically, revealing crooked teeth. Anne smiled back. She was very fond of Miss Letitia, who was shorter, rounder, softer, and more practical than her sister. They waited expectantly. The young man by the window cleared his throat and continued to read aloud from his letter:

' ... and the long and the short of it is, my dear fellow, that I should be infinitely obliged if you could put me up for a week or two. Your kind invitation came at exactly the right moment. I shall drive myself and will arrive in Lyme in the late afternoon on July 1st. I can't tell you how good it will be to see you again and I look forward to making the acquaintance of your aunts and Miss Milton. In haste, Yours Ever, Tim Vane.'

'A very proper letter. I can quite see how he would long to escape from the dissipations of the London season and it will be good for you to have some masculine company now that you can get about again, with your leg so much improved,' observed Miss Ippolita decidedly.

Jack Davenport winced, disliking any reference to his lameness, and Miss Letitia hurriedly intervened, saying, 'Of course, it will be splendid for you. Always such a pleasure to renew old friendships. But, Jack dear, is he quite aware how limited our accommodations are? He must be used to such fine surroundings while staying with Lady Montfort in Portman Square. Did you explain to him ...?'

'Dear Aunt Letty, don't be in such a fuss. When we were in Spain we lodged as often as not in barns or peasants' hovels, or under the open sky. Mortimer has been a soldier since 1804 and a featherbed is a luxury to him, I do assure you.'

Miss Letitia's soft, pale blue eyes filled with tears, as she dimly visualized the hardships of a soldier's way of life. However, they cleared in a moment and she dimpled delightfully, exclaiming, 'Well, we must do what we can to make him comfortable. I do so like to have young people about me. It helps to counterbalance Ippolita's fossils.'

Anne and Jack exchanged a quick smile, as Miss Ippolita gave vent to an unladylike snort. Her fine eyes flashed as she said reprovingly to her sister, 'Fossilists know how to put life in perspective, Letitia. They are not subject to the whims of fashion. Palaeontology is a subject which women can study on equal terms with men, and we are indeed fortunate to live in Lyme, where fresh evidence is provided almost daily for our scientific circle, due to the instablility of the ground on which our town is built. The Philpot sisters have discovered a number of new species, and it is my ambition to unearth a holotype of my own.'

'You lack the patience, Ippolita,' retorted her sister tartly. 'Why, the child Mary Anning spends more time searching and collecting in a day than you do in a month.'

'So she does. She is but sixteen years of age, nimble on her feet, and out in all weather. She has uncanny instincts, amounting almost to genius. You recall her discovery of the first complete ichthyosaur in '11? Of course her brother did the digging, but 'twas Mary who selected the location.' The elder Miss Prawne was nothing if not fair-minded and was always ready to give credit where due. She delighted in scientific inquiry, but her sister did not share her passion and their squabbles on the subject took place almost daily. Anne and Jack were used to their disagreements, which they knew were

minor tempests, giving spice to their generally tranquil
lives. They waited quietly for this storm to blow over.
Jack took up the newspaper and, as he did so, a letter
fluttered to the floor. He retrieved it, glanced at the
inscription, and crossed the room at once to hand it to
Anne.

Miss Letty noticed the movement and broke off her
discussion, crying, 'So remiss of me. I quite forgot that a
letter came for you, Anne. Janet brought it from the
posting house with Jack's while you were out. Well, this
will not do. I cannot sit here gossiping all day. I must see
that Sir Mortimer's room is aired and order some fish
for Friday's dinner.' She bustled from the room,
followed by Anne, who slipped upstairs to her own
chamber, to read her correspondence in peace.

Left alone in the sitting room, Jack and Miss Ippolita
glanced speculatively at one another. Her eyes softened
as they rested on her nephew's tall, upright figure. He
was really very like her dead sister, with his fine, straight
fair hair and brilliant blue eyes. He was a kind man,
somewhat lacking in direction since he had been obliged
by his wounds to quit the army. He possessed a
sufficiently comfortable income and was not totally
dependent on his half-pay army pension, but he needed
an interest, a purpose in life. At one time Miss Ippolita
had hoped that Anne might supply this purpose. When
that young lady first came to stay with her distant
cousins, some three months ago, Jack had been instantly
attracted by her dark beauty, her quick sense of
humour, and her keen intelligence. However, although
they lived under the same roof, Jack made little
progress. He knew little about Anne's early life, and
although generally friendly in her disposition, her
manner towards him remained reserved. He sensed
some mystery about her, but being an open, uncompli-
cated person himself, he hesitated to probe the barrier
which kept him at a distance.

Miss Ippolita was the first to break the silence, observing with unwonted gentleness, 'You are fond of Anne, I think.'

It was a statement, not a question, and Jack did not attempt to deny it. He rubbed his chin, as he often did when perplexed. Seating himself in the chair lately vacated by Miss Letty, he faced his aunt squarely. 'She's a puzzle to me, y'know,' he admitted lowering his voice confidentially. 'Do you realize that that was the first letter she has received since she came to Lyme? Surely that is unusual for a young lady. Has she no relatives closer than us? How exactly are we related to her, Aunt Polly?' No one else dared to use this familiarity with Miss Ippolita, but Jack had used it in childhood and she allowed it to pass unremarked.

She pondered a moment before replying, 'Relationships are always difficult to unravel, but I believe we are Anne's nearest kin. Her parents are both dead and she has no brothers or sisters. My father's sister, Aunt Matilda, married Sir Edwin Fairleigh of Fernditch Hall in the county of Somerset. Their son, Charles, was my first cousin, and Anne is his daughter.'

Jack frowned in an effort of concentration. 'Then surely Anne's name should be Fairleigh, not Milton,' he objected, after deep cogitation.

Miss Ippolita nodded calmly. 'Yes, indeed it is. But Anne had her reasons for wishing to keep her real name a secret when she came to Lyme, and Letty and I have respected her wishes. I fear I have betrayed a confidence, but on reflection, I thought you had a right to be told.'

Jack had been a good officer and an astute judge of character among his men. He had also observed a number of females of all conditions, who followed the drum, and was not inexperienced in matters of the heart. He asked shrewdly, 'I do not mean to pry, but why are you telling me this now? I assume that there is some affair of the heart involved. Young ladies of quality do not generally leave their homes and disguise their names without some such reason. I was sick with a fever when she came to Lyme, but now that I think about it I do not recollect that her coming was much talked of before the event.'

His aunt smiled and patted his hand with her own black-mittened one. 'Very perceptive for a mere male, my dear Jack. I see you are not as guileless as you would have us think. Well, you are quite right, of course, or close, in any event. My cousin Charles passed away some six months ago, which is why Letty and Anne and I are all garbed in these miserable mourning clothes. We did not think it necessary for you to wear black, as he was quite a remote connection to you. Poor Charles was a rather unworldly, scholarly man. In his later years he lived much in seclusion at Fernditch Hall, which I understand is situated in a remote part of the county. However, he did emerge occasionally to visit Bath, where Anne attended a young ladies' seminary. I believe they were much attached, as his wife died when Anne was a small child. It seems that a few years ago, on one such visit, Cousin Charles made the acquaintance of a Bristol trader named Simon Pontefract. They met in a bookshop, discovered they were staying at the same hotel, continued their philosophical conversation over dinner, and developed a mutual liking and respect, which had ripened into friendship over the years. When Charles knew that his end was near, he made a will in which he appointed Mr. Pontefract to be Anne's guardian until she came of age.'

'When will that be?' interrupted Jack, who had been following this narrative with close attention.

'Quite soon. This coming December on Christmas Day. But pray let me continue, or I shall lose the thread. Anne is heiress to considerable wealth and will come into possession of her fortune on attaining her majority.

Now, Mr. Pontefract is quite a young man, certainly not above forty, and he is determined to wed Anne, by force, if necessary. No, hush, let me finish and then you may ask questions.'

Jack had half-risen from his chair, but he sank back and waited impatiently as Miss Ippolita drew a deep breath and smoothed her skirt meditatively.

She resumed slowly. 'From what Anne tells me, I gather that Simon Ponetfract is both resourceful and unscrupulous. He won Charles's confidence quite easily and took advantage of the dying man's wish to protect his daughter from fortune hunters. He obtained my cousin's consent to the marriage, in writing, only hours before his death. Anne's wishes were barely consulted, but it seems she was torn between the desire to obey her father and her natural inclination to wait until a less emotional time before making such a commitment. Filial duty prevailed and she agreed to the match. In my opinion Charles was mistaken in his action, but he thought that Pontefract was a rich man, who was motivated by affection. It is true that he was a wealthy man, for I have made discreet inquiries since Anne came to us. It is also true that the man is an adventurer who made his money in the slave trade, and since the law was passed in 1807 abolishing the slave trade, and the shipping and sale of slaves, he has suffered a steady diminution of income and may now be deeply in debt, but this is a matter for conjecture. In any event, it is clear that a young heiress of good birth would be a most desirable acquisition is his present strained circumstances.'

Jack nodded grimly. 'But surely the man would not seek to force his attention on Anne while she was in deep mourning for her father?' he objected, scowling at the prospect.

Miss Ippolita shook her head. 'Not at first. He was in a a privileged position as her legal guardian and sought to

win her confidence by subtle means. Anne was alone at
Fernditch, apart from the servants, and was obliged to
turn to him for advice in the management of the estate.
She was alerted to the true state of affairs by the family
lawyer, an elderly man that she had known and trusted
all her life. It seems that Pontefract was issuing orders as
if he were already master of the Hall. When Anne taxed
him with this, Pontefract, perhaps made reckless by his
financial situation, or by the violence of his affections,
sought to press his attentions. Anne was repulsed by his
unseemly ardour and realized that she had made a
serious mistake in consenting to be his wife. This
incident occurred about three months after her father's
death and she at once decided that she must quit her
home and seek refuge. She wrote to Letty and I asking
if she might pay us a visit. We had not seen Charles for
many years and she was convinced that Pontefract was
unaware of our existence.'

Suddenly Jack grinned, exclaiming, 'Good lord, Aunt
Polly, what a melodrama. I vow 'tis better than a play at
Drury Lane. How did our heroine escape the clutches of
this blackguard?'

Miss Ippolita permitted the corners of her mouth to
relax in a slight smile. 'Remember, we have only Anne's
word for all this, and I am aware that young ladies are
prone to exaggeration, but I must confess I am
sympathetic to her desire to escape this marriage. I do
not believe that women should be men's chattels. Nor
should they be stampeded into marriage before they are
ready. Anne's reluctance is perfectly understandable in
the circumstances. If women have the means to control
their own destinies, then by all means they should do so.
I prize my independence above all things.'

'Is that why you never married, dear aunt?' inquired
Jack, wickedly.

'None of your affair, young man,' retorted that lady
sharply. 'I was much influenced in my younger days by

the writings of Mary Wollstonecraft and infinitely lamented her foolishness in marrying that pompous man, Godwin, which led to her early death in childbirth. But she remained a free spirit to the end. However, we are straying from the point. Without waiting for our reply, Anne told her guardian that she must have time to purchase her bridal clothes and to inform her old schoolfriends of her impending nuptials. He agreed that the wedding should not take place with unseemly haste and she persuaded him to escort her to her friend's home in Bristol. He left her there and returned to his own house to transact some business. Anne confided in her close friend, who lent her some money for the coach fare – Pontefract had kept a tight hold on the purse strings, bye the bye – and she took the common stage to come to us, carrying only one small carpetbag. Later, of course, she wrote to her lawyer, who sent funds from her allowance. Is she not an enterprising young lady?'

'Yes, indeed, but also uncommonly reckless. Suppose you had removed to another area, or – died of fossil addiction. What then?' queried Jack, half-laughing, half-disapproving of such rash imprudence.

'Then I gather she intended to go to London and seek out her old teacher, but fortunately such a contingency did not arise.'

Jack persisted. 'Do you think it right to conceal Anne's whereabouts from her legal guardian?'

'Oh, yes. She is very young and inexperienced. She needs time to consider before taking any irrevocable step,' responded Miss Ippolita. Footsteps sounded in the passage. She shook her finger at Jack, whispering hurriedly, 'Not a word of this to Anne, mind. But I thought you should be aware of her situation, if you are seeking to fix your interest with her.'

Jack nodded reassuringly and retired behind the newspaper,as Miss Letty reentered the room, followed by the maid, Janet, bearing a tray of hot chocolate for their mid-morning refreshment.

Meanwhile, in her neat little whitewashed bedchamber under the eaves, Anne sat perched on the edge of a wicker chair, her elbows resting on the wide sill by the open window, with her chin cupped in her hands. The sea gulls swooped and screamed noisily to one another and the sounds of the street drifted up from below. Normally Anne loved to observe the busy throng, particularly on market day, but today she gazed unseeingly at the clock on the old Shambles bell tower, giving full attention to the scene conjured up by her inner eye. At length she stirred, sighed, and picked up the letter which had fallen to the floor. It had been sent from Bristol by her friend, Mary Lovelace, and was dated a week earlier.

Slowly she reread the closely written sheet. Mary's tiny, legible script was blotched in places as if by falling tears, and appeared to have been penned in a mood of great excitement or agitation. The second paragraph contained the heart of the communication.

And so you see, my dearest Anne, that I could not write to you before for fear my letter would be intercepted. Papa and Mama were much angered with me, because I assisted you to run away from under their roof. As you know, Mr. Pontefract is a much-respected citizen in Bristol and my father has frequent business dealings with him. My parents thought that it was a most suitable match and quite fail to understand your reluctance to wed such an eligible gentleman (their words, not mine!). When I attempted to point out the disparity of age and the lack of true affection between you, they pooh-poohed my objections, saying I was a silly romantic schoogirl who had no notion of the real nature of such arrangements. I dread to think what my own fate will be! I have been in such disgrace, because I refused to tell them where you had gone. I said I did not know, but they do not believe me and I have been constantly watched and much confined to the house since you left us. Pray do not think I repine, I would do ANYTHING to help you, but I have been so unhappy. Mr. Pontefract calls upon us constantly to see if there is any news of you and he is very cunning and sharp in his questions to me, while seeking to play on my sympathies for him as a lovelorn suitor.

Oh, Anne, he was here again yesterday. He asked to speak to me privately and when we were alone (with the door ajar and Mama in the morning room, of course) he pleaded with me, saying that he was wretched thinking what a plight you could be in and begging me to tell him anything I knew of your whereabouts, just to set his mind at rest. He was very convincing, he is a good actor. When I told Mama that he had practically seduced you she dismissed the notion, saying that you were hysterical and did not appreciate your true protector. She added that a young lady must expect and accept some display of physical ardour from her betrothed. Well, yesterday, he seemed quite desperate and spoke wildly of going in search of you. He hinted that he had an inkling where you were hiding and took his leave, saying that he would write from London when he had some news of a definite nature. I assure you I believe he was trying to trap me, so that in an unwary moment I would reveal your whereabouts – for I have recently read of just such an instance in a new novel by Hester Vane – but I kept quiet and merely wished him a pleasant journey, which I was obliged to do in common civility. After Mr. P. left us I had a long talk with Mama, and she said that she thought my punishment had gone on long enough and that I might now be allowed some more freedom. Accordingly, I am to take tea with Clarissa Campbell tomorrow and will be accompanied only by my maid. If the day is fine, we can walk and I will do my utmost to find an opportunity to send this letter to you. Oh, how I long to hear from you, but I know we agreed that you would not write until you were quite safe, and indeed that was a prudent decision. I wish I knew if your relatives were kind to you ... I must stop, my bed candles are almost burned out. Believe me, dear Anne, your true and loving friend in affliction, Mary L.

Anne relaxed and smiled, thinking of Mary, with her mop of golden curls and round, innocent blue eyes. Then she tensed, wondering if Mary had been trapped after all. She examined the envelope to see if it had been tampered with, but all appeared to be in order and it was addressed to Miss Milton, the name they had chosen because he was Anne's favourite poet. Perhaps Simon Pontefract had gone to London, following some false trail. A vision of his dark, saturnine visage and lean, powerful form swam before her and she jumped up, resolutely declining to dwell further on such a disagreeable topic. Brooding could serve no useful purpose, she decided as she tidied herself for luncheon. She needed some distraction; she had been too much confined, but now that her period of deep mourning was coming to an end, and Jack's friend was about to pay them a visit, it was time to reenter society, albeit the limited one which Lyme afforded.

She was in cheerful spirits throughout the light noontime meal. Her cousins regarded her with some surprise, for she had been generally very subdued in her demeanour since her arrival and they had not suspected such a lighthearted and playful aspect to her character.

'Your letter afforded you some pleasure, I think?' suggested Miss Ippolita, artfully.

Anne's expressive face clouded briefly,but then she responded warmly, 'Why, yes, it was from my old schoolfriend, Mary Lovelace. She sent news of our mutual acquaintance in Bristol.'

Jack set down his pudding spoon with care. He regarded Anne's animated countenance with curiosity, observing, 'You must miss your friends and old haunts, cousin. Do you find Lyme very tame and provincial in comparison?'

Anne shook her head vigorously. 'No, of course not. You seek to provoke me, sir. I think Lyme a most delightful place, large enough to provide some society, but not busy and crowded like a city. Its situation by the sea is very refreshing. I am sure the kind hospitality which I have received here and the sweet air of Lyme have done much to lift the oppressively low feelings which I suffered when I came, so soon after my father died.'

Tactfully, Miss Letitia intervened. 'It is our pleasure to have you with us.'

Impulsively Anne bent over to kiss her cousin's soft, pink, cheek. There was silence for a moment and then Jack looked round the table and inquired, 'Can I execute any commissions for you, this afternoon, ladies? The wind is fair and I feel the need for some exercise after that excellent lunch. Mortimer will think I am sadly overweight and out of condition after so much soft living.'

'I have some volumes to return to the lending library, if you will be so good. But do not tire yourself on my account.'

'Don't fret, Letitia. Jack does not wish to be coddled. You may have your nap in peace, for I am attending a meeting of the fossilist circle. We are to hear a most interesting lecture on dinosaur footprints. Would you care to come, Anne?'

'If you would excuse me I also would like to go to the

library. I want to see if they have a new book by Hester Vane.'

'Gothic taradiddle!' scoffed Miss Ippolita.

'But written by Mortimer's sister!' protested Jack, laughing.

'Hester Vane is Sir Mortimer's sister?' asked Anne, her eyes sparkling with enthusiasm. 'Did you know that, cousin? Does he then have two sisters?'

'Not so far as I am aware. Lady Montfort was Hester Vane before she married and still writes under that name,' replied Jack.

'How intriguing. Mary and I read all her novels while we were at the seminary.' Twas she who told me of the new book, in her letter this morning.'

Miss Ippolita raised her fine eyebrows and remarked severely, 'In my opinion young ladies should read improving books, not be permitted to stuff their heads with such nonsense. I would not have thought it of Lady Montfort.'

'You make it sound like a crime, sister. I confess your attitude puzzles me. It is not in keeping with your general principles concerning women using their heaven-sent gifts for the benefit of mankind. I hope you will find one of Miss Vane's, I mean Lady Montfort's, books for me, Anne, if you please,' said Miss Letitia, boldly.

During this interchange, Anne and Jack refrained from meeting one another's eyes for fear of giving vent to unseemly mirth. Miss Ippolita drew breath for a sharp retort, but Jack said hastily, 'Let us go together then, Anne. Shall we take Mincemeat with us?'

'No, he dawdles so. He can come with me to the meeting. He always enjoys sniffing among the exhibits,' interposed Miss Ippolita. This being settled, Anne ran upstairs to fetch her bonnet and a few moments later she and Jack were on their way to the Marine Circulating Library.

III

Reunion of Two Friends

'You must have found it very hard to be confined so long,' remarked Anne, suiting her naturally brisk pace to Jack's more halting one.

'It irked me very much at first,' he admitted. 'But of late I have grown more accustomed and I would like to thank you, Anne. You have been very patient and kind in seeking to provide distractions for me, reading to me, playing at cards, singing in the evenings. It has been a relief to my aunts, for I was truly a burden and a very troublesome invalid for many months.'

'No thanks are necessary. I am glad if I have been of some small service, for you have all been very good to me. In seeking to divert you, I have amused myself as well.' She smiled sunnily, her cheeks glowing in the fresh breeze. She tripped along beside him, her head reaching no higher than his shoulder, and Jack caught his breath, fearing to trample on the delicate flowering of intimacy between them. They walked the remainder of the way to the library in companionable silence and Jack said he would wait while Anne exchanged her books. He leaned against the low wall, sniffing the salt sea air and easing the weight on his right leg, which still pained him more than he cared to admit. He closed his eyes, hearing again the thunder of besieging cannon and the whistle of musket balls as they flew thick and fast all about him; then the sharp pain in his leg as one of the balls found its mark. He struggled on in the darkness until he stumbled and fell, crushed by the pressure of his own men following up behind him. He knew again the sensation of being trodden to death by the ceaseless onrush before he sank into merciful unconsciousness.

A light tap on his arm roused Jack from his reverie. He was shivering and very pale. Anne viewed him with alarm.

'Jack, what is it? Are you ill? Look, there is a bench yonder. Come and sit down a moment and I will see if I can procure some water to restore you.'

He gazed at her blankly for a few seconds and she shook him gently, watching his face intently. Gradually his eyes took focus and became keen again. He straightened and allowed Anne to lead him to a wooden seat, which was set in a little hollow curve of the wall, surrounded by hardy shrubs.

They sank down in the comparative privacy thus afforded and when Anne would have risen again to go in search of water, Jack prevented her by catching her hand and drawing her back to sit beside him, saying, 'I am almost recovered. Let us just sit here quietly a little. I am sorry to have given you such a fright, but I was dreaming of the assault on Ciudad Rodrigo and it was most extraordinarily vivid. Tell me, did you get any interesting books? You were not long, I think. I hope you did not hurry on my account.'

Despite her concern, Anne rallied. 'Well no, not on your account, sir! I thought I had left you quite contentedly sunning yourself. It was that odious Mr. Gresham who speeded my departure. He was ogling me with his eyeglass. I cannot understand how such an unpleasant man can have such a nice dog. I met them on the beach this morning. However, I ignored him and was fortunate enough to find the volume I was seeking on the newly returned shelf. See, here it is. *The Secret of*

Moon Manor by Hester Vane.' She held it out for him to see, adding, 'I was not aware until you mentioned it that the authoress was Sir Mortimer's sister. I never thought to connect the names. Do you know her? How I wish I could meet her. I cannot imagine what she must be like.' She chattered on, pleased to see that the young man's pallor had receded and he soon appeared his normal self. At length she paused for breath and Jack leaned forward to take the book from her. He glanced through it, examining a paragraph here and there closely.

Finally, he looked up with a grin. 'Not my cup of tea, I'm afraid, but I'm sure she writes very well. She is immensely popular, I know, and Mortimer is always singing her praises. There is much affection between them and they have a similar sense of humour. I have met her several times in Tim's company and I admire her enormously. She is an elegant, unaffected lady, completely devoted to her husband and their two sons, but with a mind of her own. She is everything one could hope for in a wife, though I confess I fail to understand why she writes novels. She leads a busy social life and is not at all a bluestocking ...' Jack shook his head and Anne could not help laughing at his puzzled expression.

'But is she beautiful?' she wanted to know.

'Not in a conventional sense. She is several years older than Mortimer and has a sort of radiance which one only sees among happily married people. But don't ask me to describe her. I am not a novelist. Charm is a very elusive commodity.'

'But I think you have done very well,' exclaimed Anne, amused. 'I am looking forward to meeting her brother. It will be a great pleasure for you to see your friend again, I'm sure. You must be longing for some masculine companionship after being surrounded by females in your aunts' household.'

He nodded ruefully. 'Y'see Anne, 'tis a matter of feast or famine. In the army one can go months without laying eyes on a respectable female with whom one can associate, apart from other officers' wives, and there are few enough of those who survive the hardships of campaigning without falling sick or losing their femininity with the rough life.'

Anne frowned thoughtfully.

'I must admit I envy them their freedom,' she said. 'And their experiences in a way. The companionship. I have had so few opportunities to travel and have frequently felt much alone and isolated.'

Jack half-turned and surveyed Anne's profile meditatively. He could see the tendrils of dark curls brushing her cheek, the wayward tip-tilted little nose, and the fringe of long, dark lashes. Gently he reached out and touched her chin, obliging her to face him fully.

He said, 'I had thought you would have many friends in Bristol, which is a very flourishing city. How could such an attractive young lady be lonely?'

Anne dropped her eyes beneath his searching gaze. Her fingers plucked nervously at the ribbons of her bonnet. She replied evasively, 'I grew up in the country in quite a remote spot. I attended school in Bath and some friends lived in Bristol, that is all. But my history is very uninteresting. Pray tell me, how came you to meet Sir Mortimer?'

Jack released her and stared out to sea. 'You do not mean to trust me, do you, Anne?' He shrugged bitterly. 'I had hoped you might come to regard me in the light of a friend.'

Impulsively, Anne stretched out her hand, crying, 'Oh, Jack, don't be so foolish. You are like a dear brother to me, but I do not mean to burden you with my small cares, when you have your own problems. And you are very restless to be off, are you not?'

'Anne, you are uncommonly acute. How did you guess?'

'It would be unnatural if it were otherwise for an active

man. What do you hope to do?'

Jack sighed deeply. 'Ah, that's the rub! I'm not sure. All my old comrades have dispersed now that Napoleon is safe on Elba. I'm hoping that Mortimer may be able to suggest something.'

By mutual consent, they rose and began to stroll slowly back to Broad Street. Anne tucked her hand confidingly in Jack's arm.

'You have great faith in Sir Mortimer Vane, I think. Have you been friends for long?' she inquired, as they steered their way through the throng of afternoon promenaders taking their constitutionals on The Walk.

'Tim and I have known one another since we met at Shorncliffe Camp, back in 1804. We were both green lads, full of enthusiasm. We trained under Major General John Moore, who was an inspiration to us all. He believed in disciplined teamwork combined with individual initiative, and he encouraged his officers to set an example to their men. We became the élite of the army. Mortimer and I stayed together through the retreat to Corunna and somehow we both survived that terrible winter campaign. Mortimer was outstanding in his ability to rally the men and must have saved many lives, for he went back and forth rounding up strays, always ready with a jest or word of cheer when it was as much as most of us could do simply to stay on our feet and keep moving. The hardships which the soldiers suffered are almost indescribable. It was January and the weather varied between snow and heavy rain. Food and shelter were practically nonexistent, our packs were dead weights, and many of us were obliged to go barefoot over the rough ground with the French close on our heels. Those who dropped out had little chance of survival.' Jack sighed.

'It must have been dreadful to lose so many of your comrades,' said Anne, softly.

'It was heartbreaking, although we did not feel it so much at the time. And of course we were all disheartened by the death of Sir John. It pains me even now to dwell on it. But there are compensations – one comes to know men pretty well in such circumstances and Tim Vane is one of the best. A great fellow to have beside you in a scrape. After we returned to England I lost track of him for a time. He became one of Wellington's aides and I remained with the Regiment. We met again under the walls of Ciudad Rodrigo and he saved my life that night. He was close by and saw me fall and I was told he stood over me with drawn sword until the first wave of our men had passed over. Then he summoned help to carry me to safety before going on to join in the assault. He visited me in the hospital and later, when I was well enough to travel, he arranged my passage home.'

'And Sir Mortimer survived unscathed?' queried Anne, curiously.

Jack shook his head. 'Not so. He was wounded at Salamanca – caught a spent ball in the hip. Later his face was badly slashed by a sword cut, but he stayed on in Spain and only returned a month or two ago. If only ...' he paused, biting his lip in frustration.

Anne blinked, feeling that such heroism was beyond her comprehension. After an interval, she said lightly, 'You were going to say, if only I could have stayed and perhaps died in Spain! It seems that England is fortunate indeed to have dedicated soldiers like you and Sir Mortimer, but I confess in your place I would feel I had done my duty and would be ready to take pleasure in the no doubt more trivial pursuits of peacetime.'

Suddenly Jack grinned, catching her mood. He gave her hand a small squeeze as it rested on his arm. 'You are very right to chide me. Why do we talk of such somber matters on such a bright day? In truth the world has seemed a pleasanter place of late – since a certain young lady came to stay in Lyme,' ventured Jack, greatly daring.

Immediately he sensed Anne's withdrawal. She quickened her step and pulled her hand away, exclaiming, 'Why, it must be getting late. Look how the shadows are lengthening. Mrs. Peabody is closing her shutters already. Pray let us make haste, for I promised to help Cousin Letty bathe Mincemeat. He is so naughty in the tub and splashes everywhere if someone does not hold him firmly. He was rolling in the sand this morning.'

Jack limped along in her wake, wondering ruefully if he would ever understand the workings of the female mind; no further words were exchanged as they traversed Broad Street and covered the remaining few yards to their destination.

In the next few days, as the household went about its business and prepared for Mortimer's arrival, Anne avoided Jack's company as much as possible and took care never to be alone with him. While she busied herself about the house or sat in her room with an open book on her lap, Anne brooded long on the nature of her feelings for her military cousin. Her intuition told her that he needed very little encouragement to declare himself; he was kind, quite handsome, and in every way conducted himself as a gentleman should. She did not fear him, as she had feared Simon Pontefract, but neither did he arouse in her any sentiments warmer than those she would cherish for a good friend. Anne was an avid reader of novels and, although she had never been in love, she knew that it was customary to feel some thrilling spark of excitement or even passion when in the presence of the beloved; her favourite authoresses were quite clear, indeed eloquent, on the subject. With Jack she would be comfortable and safe. Common sense suggested that a match between them would be an ideal solution to her difficulties. Still she hesitated, unwilling to take advantage of his affection and doubtful of her own. This was the uneasy state of affairs which existed when Sir Mortimer Vane arrived in Lyme on a warm evening in early July.

He came on foot, having left his groom and curricle at the old Three Cups Hotel. Jack received him warmly and the aunts were not far behind in seeking to make their visitor welcome. Soon Mortimer was presented to Anne. She curtsied, keeping her eyes demurely lowered.

'Your servant, Miss Milton.' The formal salutation held a hint of ineffable boredom. Anne lifted her head indignantly and looked the newcomer fully in the face. His back was to the room, shielding her from the rest of the company, and her expressive eyes widened in shock as she observed the livid scar which marred his otherwise handsome and regular features. He watched her coolly, his lips curling in a satirical smile. Involuntarily Anne stepped back, blushing hotly. Mortimer turned away and she sank into her seat, overcome with mortification. How could she have behaved so foolishly! She seized her embroidery and stitched at random, glad of the excuse to keep her head bent, while she struggled to regain her composure. Gradually she became aware of the conversation going on around her.

'The town seemed to be full of Russian sailors,' Mortimer was saying, 'And it was with some difficulty that I found someone who could speak English to give me directions.'

'Oh, yes, they'll be from the timber ship which I saw anchored in the Cobb this afternoon,' responded Jack.

Miss Ippolita frowned. 'They're a very rowdy set of men. I hope they do not mean to stay long in port.'

'They seem very good-natured. One of them disentangled Mincemeat for me; his leash was caught in the railing. I believe they only come ashore to play skittles at Mill Green,' Miss Letty protested.

'Nonsense, sister. They come ashore to drink them- selves silly at The Dolphin,' retorted the elder lady robustly. 'I think, Anne, it would be wiser if you did not walk alone until the ship has departed for the Baltic.'

Anne nodded obediently, silently chafing at the restriction thus imposed on her liberty. Jack said quickly, 'Don't fret, Anne. We will be happy to escort you, eh, Tim?'

Before Sir Mortimer could reply, Anne exclaimed, 'You are very kind, but I'm sure there will not be the least necessity for you to be discommoded. Janet can accom- pany me. You will wish to explore the neighbourhood with Sir Mortimer.'

Feeling ungracious and vexed with herself after this speech, Anne resolutely applied herself to her needlework. She felt Sir Mortimer's eyes resting on her and was convinced that he was amused by her discom- fort. Miss Letitia provided a welcome diversion, pressing more tea and cakes on their guest.

He held up his hand, laughing, 'I vow, I'm stuffed like an owl, ma'am. I believe I mentioned that I had already dined with the Tremaines at their home near Bridport and that is only a little more than an hour's drive from here.'

'An hour's drive. You must have made very good speed, sir,' commented Miss Ippolita. 'The Tremaines are a very well-known family hereabouts. Are they connections of yours?'

Mortimer swung round in his chair and recrossed his legs, still encased in military long boots, which showed to advantage his lean, muscular thighs. He was evidently a man of taste, thought Anne, sitting quietly observant in her corner. He was dressed with neatness and propriety, but he wore his clothes with an air and his thick, curly brown hair was a shade longer and more unruly than was common among the military.

He answered Miss Ippolita easily, 'Not directly, Miss Prawne. Lady Tremaine is related to my brother-in-law, Lord Montfort. She was Hugo's ward before her marriage to Sir Lawrence. I used to know her quite well, but had not seen her since her removal to the country. As I was passing it seemed a good opportunity to pay my respects.' He spoke casually, but Anne saw his fists clench until the knuckles whitened, as they rested on the seat beside him. She peeped at him curiously. The candles shone brightly on his scarred face, but his expression remained impassive. Jack's chair creaked; he was gazing intently at his friend. The two elder ladies seemed unaware of any tension in the room.

'How pleasant for you to have friends in the county,' remarked Miss Letty. 'I believe Sir Lawrence sometimes visits Lyme on business. I have seen him at the Custom House. Lady Tremaine accompanies him occasionally. She patronizes our local milliner and I heard she once attended a Friday evening Assembly, but we have not been ourselves for some time. We used to enjoy a game of cards, but since Jack's illness we have played mostly at home. And dear Anne has been in mourning for her father. However, your arrival is most opportune, Sir Mortimer. It is time we began to go into society again; our young people have been out of circulation long enough.'

Miss Ippolita nodded her head firmly in agreement. She added, 'But you must take care, Sir Mortimer, and not drive too fast about our country lanes. There will be deep ruts after the recent rains.'

The face of the gentleman thus admonished was transfigured by a sudden irradiating smile. 'If you are going to scold me, I beg you will call me Mortimer. I promise faithfully that I will not overturn my curricle while you are in it. In truth, I have too much regard for my horses to drive recklessly. A speed of six to seven miles an hour is quite usual these days, I assure you, Miss Ippolita. My sister, Hester, rode with me without a qualm last month, when I took her and my nephews on an expedition to Richmond Park. Do permit me to take you fossil-hunting. I understand that this is one of the best regions in the country for this pursuit and Jack has often told me how knowledgeable you are in the science.'

Flattered, Miss Ippolita allowed herself to be drawn into an account of the different specimens to be found in the vicinity. Anne admired his adroitness in deftly changing the subject. It was clear to her that Sir Mortimer did not wish to discuss the Tremaines. His reasons for such reticence were more obscure.

In the days that followed, Anne sensed an attitude, not exactly of hostility, but of disdain towards herself, on the part of Jack's friend. Mortimer was charming to the two older ladies and was soon a firm favourite with them. However, in Anne's company he was exceedingly reserved and seldom addressed her directly. He and Jack were out a great deal, walking and riding. In the evening the two gentlemen played cards with their hostesses, while Anne played the pianoforte or sang for them. She frequently retired early with her book and listened to the sounds of animated conversation drifting up through the open windows. She began to feel lonely and ignored, despite the fact that her cousins made repeated attempts to include her in their activities. She made valiant efforts to overcome her ill humour; never before had she indulged in such a fit of self-pity, not even when her father died and Simon Pontefract had been his most importunate self. She did not understand herself or her reactions; she only knew that in Sir Mortimer Vane's company she felt like an awkward, tongue-tied schoolgirl. Jack had been her companion and now she missed him. While she acknowledged his friend's superior claims, she much resented Mortimer's haughty manner.

Perhaps Jack had confided in his old comrade, she

pondered miserably, as she sat alone at the breakfast table about a week after the visitor's arrival. Perhaps he disliked her because she did not return Jack's regard. But no, men did not think like that; they did not gossip on personal matters. Their talk was all of horses, politics, and shared campaign experiences. Even Mincemeat deserted her for masculine company. Anne sighed fretfully as she sipped her tea and bit her tongue on a hard piece of toast. No doubt Sir Mortimer had many qualities and on Jack's account she knew him to be exceedingly brave, but try as she would, she could not like him. In her limited circle, Anne had met few, if any, people who either avoided her or accorded her the barest civility which proximity and good manners required. She had been willing to extend the hand of friendship to Sir Mortimer for Jack's sake and felt keenly the rebuff which his coolness implied. She tapped her foot meditatively. No one else seemed aware of his hostility. How should she deal with it? Abstractedly, she reached for her teacup and knocked it over, splashing some on her favourite lilac-sprigged morning gown.

The object of her reflections chose this inconvenient moment to appear in the doorway. He took in the situation at a glance, approached the table, and gravely proffered her a clean napkin. Anne felt her toes curl in vexation; she ceased to feel like a rational human being in his presence. Hastily she mopped the stain, with a muttered word of thanks for his assistance.

Sir Mortimer tactfully turned away and gave his attention to the dishes laid out on the sideboard. Having made his selection, he seated himself across the table and observed, 'My sister is forever spilling things. She always pleads in excuse that she has reached a difficult stage in her plot and her mind was distracted. Perhaps you are a writer, too, Miss Milton?'

Anne slowly placed the crumpled napkin by her plate.

She knew she was being teased; she lifted her chin defiantly and responded gamely, 'You jest, I think, sir. I fear I have no such excuse, but I greatly admire Lady Montfort's novels. I was reading one last night.'

'Indeed!' Sir Mortimer's eyebrow lifted sardonically.

To her annoyance, Anne felt her cheeks redden. She asked distantly, 'Do you disapprove of novels, Sir Mortimer?'

Realizing that he had transgressed, Mortimer startled Anne by giving a hoot of laughter. 'Good lord, no, whatever gave you that impression? Can't say I care for the Gothic variety that m'sister writes, but that's neither here nor there. I beg your pardon, Miss Milton. I have offended you and such was not my intent. Hester will be happy to know that you find her books entertaining. I'll tell her next time I write. What other authors do you like? Is there a good bookshop in Lyme?'

Mortimer exerted himself to draw Anne out of her shell and he succeeded so well that they both looked up in surprise when Jack came in some half an hour later to see what was delaying his friend.

IV

The Shopping Expedition

After their breakfast-time conversation, Anne became more at ease in Sir Mortimer's company and enjoyed being included in the gentlemen's various activities and expeditions, whenever their nature made this possible. Jack was a keen angler and several times he and Mortimer fished, while Anne sketched or read. Once she took a turn with the rod, but this was not a success as she nearly overbalanced in her eagerness and dropped the line, letting her quarry escape.

One day they made up a carriage party to picnic at a local beauty spot, accompanied by Jack's aunts and the indefatigable Mincemeat, who was allowed to scamper about freely when they reached their destination. He soon became wedged in a large rabbit hole from which he was extricated with difficulty by the combined efforts of Mortimer and Jack. On the return journey, Jack surrendered his place in the curricle to Anne, for his leg was troubling him and there was more space in the hired chaise.

Anne found it very exhilarating tooling along the country lanes beside Mortimer, with his groom up behind. Above the hedgerows she could see a vista of soft green countryside, stretching away in the distance to the blue line of the sea. She was unused to light, sporting vehicles, but Mortimer held his spirited horses to a gentle, steady pace with a firm hand. Soon Anne ceased to worry about the precariousness of her

position. She relaxed her tight grip on the seat and
closed her eyes, feeling the warm breeze tug at her
bonnet as it rushed by.

'I used to dream about days like this in Spain,'
observed her companion.

Anne's eyes flew open. She nodded sympathetically. 'I
can imagine that you would. It must have been very
different, hot and dusty, with the glare of white
buildings and the rocky, parched countryside. It must
be so distracting to be always with people. I expect there
is very little privacy and much noise with an army on the
move.'

Mortimer glanced down at Anne sharply. 'You are
very perceptive, Miss Milton,' he commented, dryly. 'Of
course, it also rained a great deal and then the dust
turned to mud.'

Sensing sarcasm in his tone, Anne fixed her gaze on a
distant church spire and regarded it unwaveringly for
several minutes. At length she remarked quietly, 'It
pleases you to mock me, sir, when I was merely trying to
enter into your sentiments on returning to England. It
would be kinder of you to make allowance for my
inexperience.'

Disconcerted by this reproof, Mortimer again glanced
sideways at the young lady, watching her through
narrowed lids. She was seated very erect, dignity in
every line of her slim figure. While his attention was
momentarily distracted from the road, the vehicle gave
a sudden lurch and Anne fell forward. He stretched out
a quick hand to steady her, bringing the horses to a
standstill. In the distance they could hear the rattle of
harness as the other carriage, bearing Jack and his
aunts, followed at a sedate trot. The groom, roused
from his doze, jumped down on a quick command from
his master and ran to check the horses. They waited
silently, listening to the baaing of sheep in a field close at
hand. Fortunately the horses were unhurt and they

proceeded slowly down the hill towards Lyme. Shaken, Anne edged farther away from Mortimer on the narrow seat. She could still feel the hard clasp on her wrist and all her earlier nervousness in his presence came flooding back. He looked very stern. Anne shivered, at a loss to explain the force of her reactions to so small an incident.

'I think it may rain tomorrow. The sky looks very black on the horizon,' she ventured.

'If you feel chilled there is a rug under the seat. I must apologize for giving you such a fright. I am not usually careless with my horses,' replied Sir Mortimer, adding irritably, 'Take heed, Miss Milton. If you move any farther away, you will indeed take a tumble into the road. I am aware that my appearance is repulsive to you. I should not presume on our proximity to catch you again.'

This remark not unnaturally deprived Anne of speech. Mortimer touched the beasts lightly with his whip and they sped along, obliging Anne to cling miserably to her seat until they reached Broad Street, where the groom assisted her to jump down. Mortimer saluted her, touching his whip to his scarred cheek with sinister effect. Anne fled to her room, a prey to conflicting emotions, and retired to bed, pleading a severe headache.

Anne's weather prediction was fully justified the next morning. It was raining heavily when she awoke and a strong wind was blowing in from the southwest. She spent a dismal hour or two helping Janet in the kitchen and emerged looking so pale that Miss Letitia insisted she should go out for a breath of air now that the storm appeared to have abated. It had been settled among them at the picnic yesterday that they would attend the Friday evening Assembly. This was to be the first large social gathering which Anne had gone to since her father's death and in the congenial atmosphere of the picnic she had allowed herself to be persuaded that it was time for her to make her reappearance in society. Now Miss Letitia was suggesting that they should visit the linen draper to choose some ribbons and laces to refurbish Anne's evening gown. Although her eager anticipation of the event had been quite destroyed on the drive home, Anne reluctantly agreed to accompany her cousin. When she returned to the drawing room, clad in her heavy, waterproof country cape and boots, she found that Sir Mortimer had volunteered to go with them.

'Gentlemen do not generally like to go on shopping expeditions,' chattered Miss Letitia gaily, as they splashed their way through the puddles.

He responded cheerfully. 'You forget I have a sister, ma'am. I have been well-trained. And I find I am in need of some fresh neckcloths. I miss my valet to starch them for me.'

'The prevailing fashion for very high, wide neckcloths seems most uncomfortable to me. So time-consuming, too! I believe some gentlemen spend hours in their chamber before they achieve the perfect knots and folds dictated by the latest mode. Jack has no patience with such intricacies, he favours a plain military stock.'

Sir Mortimer grinned. 'Jack is a wonderfully good fellow, but no one could ever accuse him of being a dandy. I wish I could persuade him to patronize my tailor.'

Laughing in agreement, Miss Letitia tucked her small hand in his arm. Gallantly, he protected her from the mud thrown up by passing carts and carriages, while Anne trailed despondently in their wake. They rounded a windy corner and sought shelter in the relative protection of the main shopping thoroughfare.

'What do you say, Miss Milton,' inquired Mortimer, as Anne caught up with her companions on the wider pavement, 'Don't you think that a high cravat can hide a multitude of sins?'

'Like a weak chin, for example?' she suggested, lifting her own small, determined one and facing him squarely. Mortimer regarded her quizzically. She went on, 'I agree with you, Cousin Letty, it is a silly mode. Sir Mortimer may think our taste provincial, but I confess I admire Jack's style of dress. It is neat and sensible,' she finished loftily.

Miss Letitia looked from one to the other in amusement. 'Why are you two forever at loggerheads? But you young people are good for Jack. He grew up in a hard school and is too serious for his age. You must see if you can give him a little town bronze, dear sir. He will listen to you.'

Mortimer shook his head. 'My friend is indeed fortunate to have such a fair champion to defend him. I would not change a hair of his head.' He might have said more, but to Anne's relief they were accosted by the ubiquitous Mr. Gresham.

'Miss Letitia, Miss Anne, you are rays of sunshine on this dull day,' he pronounced effusively. Anne sniffed, acutely aware of her muddy boots and shiny red nose, but Miss Letty dimpled and made haste to present her guest. The gentlemen bowed and it was instantly clear to Anne that they had conceived a mutual dislike for one another. Mr. Gresham stepped back and lifted his monocle. Involuntarily Anne moved closer to Mortimer, not wishing to endure the full glare of the enlarged blue orb.

'I hope we shall have the pleasure of seeing you at our little Assembly on Friday, Sir Mortimer,' said Mr. Gresham, lazily swinging his glass between two plump, beringed fingers.

'Oh, yes, we all mean to attend,' interrupted Miss Letty, smiling happily. 'It will be Anne's first visit, too, you know.'

'Then may I have the honour of standing up with you for the first set, Miss Anne, on this special occasion?' asked Mr. Gresham, with commendable promptness.

Beside her Mortimer stiffened and she thought he was going to object, but he remained obstinately silent. She was obliged to reply, politely, 'Thank you, sir, but I am already engaged to my cousin, Jack. Perhaps later in the evening.'

'We must not keep you ladies standing in this chill wind,' intervened Sir Mortimer, at last.

They walked on and he asked curiously, 'Are you really engaged to Jack for the opening dance?'

Anne gave a small giggle. 'I hope so, Sir Mortimer. Oh, dear, I forgot about his leg. Well, if he does not feel equal to it, I can sit beside him and watch.'

They reached the linen draper's. Miss Letty went through, as Mortimer held the door courteously ajar for the ladies. Anne was about to follow, when he muttered in her ear, 'Demmed impertinence. Why do you allow such familiarity? Or perhaps I err. Does Mr. Gresham claim sufficient acquaintance with you to make use of your given name?'

She bit her lip, but replied composedly, 'He is an old acquaintance of my cousins and his age gives him certain privileges; his dog and Mincemeat are arch enemies,' she finished inconsequentially, and swept ahead to join Miss Letitia at the counter. The small exchange had unaccountably raised her spirits and Anne took a lively interest in the choice of some pretty jonquil silk ribbons. She also indulged in an exquisitely soft Indian shawl. Miss Letty was an indecisive shopper and took some time to make her purchases. Sir Mortimer wandered back to the door in search of fresh air, for the atmosphere was damp and very stuffy. Idly he looked across the street to the coaching house opposite. A handsome carriage had just drawn up and his attention was caught first by the horses, which were fine beasts, powerful and spirited. The hostler ran to their heads, while the coachman let down the steps on the side farthest away from Mortimer and assisted his passenger to alight.

A moment later an umbrella appeared, with a diminutive lady beneath it. The watcher across the street heard a well-remembered voice saying, 'Thank you, Benjamin. Please see to the horses and get some refreshment yourself. I shall return in an hour.'

The lady waited until the carriage had pulled under the archway into the stable yard. It was drizzling again and she lifted her skirts daintily as she hopped over the cobbles, vainly trying to avoid the puddles.

'Oh, la la! Quel temps!' Exclaiming volubly in French, she scampered up the steps and entered the draper's shop through the door which Mortimer held open for her. She paused to close her umbrella, then turned to thank the gentleman who had assisted her.

'Mortimer!' she squeaked, 'how nice to see you again so soon. But I did not expect to find you shopping. On such a day I thought you would be playing at billiards, or sleeping behind the newspaper. See, my feet are quite wet through.' She lifted one for his inspection, elegantly shod in a silk half-boot.

The lady's entrance had aroused a good deal of attention in the crowded emporium. Aware of this, Sir Mortimer bowed formally and said, 'Good afternoon, my lady. The weather is indeed inclement. Allow me to present you to my companions. Perhaps they can suggest some solution for your wet feet. Let me place your umbrella in the stand.' Carefully he performed this small service, then led her to the counter, where Anne and Miss Letty were standing, awaiting his pleasure and watching curiously.

'Oh, 'tis of no consequence. They will soon dry. One gets accustomed, living in the country,' the lady replied cheerfully, as they approached.

'Stephanie, this is one of my kind hostesses, Miss Letitia Prawne. Miss Letty, permit me, Lady Tremaine of Battlecombe Hall.' The ladies curtsied. 'And this is Miss Anne Milton, cousin to Miss Letitia.' Anne made

her acknowledgement, noting with amusement that
Lady Tremaine certainly made few concessions to
country life in her attire. Though small in stature and
perhaps a trifle plump to Anne's critical eye, she was
dressed in the latest mode. She wore a spencerette of
deep blue velvet, edged with lace, and an enormous
bonnet, trimmed with cornflowers, which framed to
perfection her beautiful heart-shaped face and soft,
dark curls. Her flawless complexion owed little to
artificial aids, Anne admitted to herself enviously, as she
stood quietly while the two older ladies conversed.

'But of course, I am a leetle acquainted with Miss
Prawne, Mortimer. Our provincial society is so small
that one cannot help knowing everyone, at least by
sight. However, I have not seen you at an Assembly for
some time, Miss Prawne. I hope you have not been
indisposed.' Lady Tremaine spoke with a slight, but
attractive French accent. Miss Letty was captivated.

'Oh, no, your ladyship. Not at all. We have been in
mourning for our cousin, Anne's father, but we intend
to go on Friday. Shall we have the pleasure of seeing
you there? Of course, it is quite a long drive from
Bridport, but so pleasant for Mortimer to have the
opportunity to see family connections,' she beamed.
That gentleman stood impassively by, displaying no
apparent pleasure in the prospect.

No whit disturbed by his lack of enthusiasm, Lady
Tremaine rallied him gaily, 'We must make the most of
you, sir, now that you are in the neighbourhood. You
have neglected us shabbily this many a year. Why, I was
no older than Miss Milton when last you paid me a visit.
And now I am an old married lady with two little ones in
the nursery.' She pouted adorably and fluttered her
eyelashes provokingly. Anne wondered how she
managed to do both at the same time. Sir Mortimer
remained obstinately silent and she went on, 'I shall try
to persuade Sir Lawrence to bring me to Lyme on

Friday, but it is always so impossible to converse at an Assembly. We must have a dinner party and you shall all come, including your sister, Miss Prawne, the lady who is so fond of fossils, is she not, and Major Davenport, Mortimer's friend, of whom I heard so much when you called on us the other day on your way here. Perhaps next Tuesday. I shall invite the Oliphants to meet you. Miss Oliphant is a notable horsewoman and you will be able to talk to her, mon cher Mortimer. You see, I have not forgotten your passion for horses. Do you like to ride, Miss Milton? But, forgive me, I go too fast. Perhaps Tuesday is not a date convenient for you, Miss Letitia?'

Somewhat overwhelmed, Miss Letty hesitated, 'You are very kind, Lady Tremaine. I must consult my sister, but I do not believe we are engaged. May we send a message tomorrow?'

Here Mortimer judged it was time to intervene. He said stiffly, 'I fear I may not be able to accept your invitation, Stephanie. I must return to Town soon; I have trespassed on Miss Letty and Miss Ippolita's hospitality quite long enough and I promised Hester I would be back to escort her to the celebrations in honour of the Duke.'

'Nonsense, my dear. I received a letter from Hester only yesterday, announcing her intention of going into the country for a few days. She said the crowds were very fatiguing and mon cousin, Hugo, insisted that they visit Huntsgrove to recuperate. I think you may find yourself de trop; I understand they have been separated for quite some time and they will be glad to be alone. Am I not right?' she asked frankly.

Miss Letitia looked from one to the other and added her own entreaty, 'Do stay a little longer, Sir Mortimer. We have been so lively since he came, Lady Tremaine, picnics and drives. And Jack will miss you sorely. We all enjoy your company and I assure you, you are no trouble, quite the contrary.'

Mortimer flushed slightly and bowed to Miss Letitia. 'Thank you, ma'am. It would be churlish to refuse. I will be happy to remain in Lyme for the present.'

'Bon. It is settled. You were not always so reluctant to attend my parties, Mortimer,' Lady Tremaine smiled at him reproachfully.

He gazed at her wistfully for a moment, quite forgetting his companions. Then his jaw hardened, the disfiguring mark standing out in vivid relief. Anne felt as if her presence was an intrusion. She said hastily to her cousin, 'Have you finished your purchases, Cousin Letty? Or did you wish to examine some ribbons? They have some pretty ones over there. Lady Tremaine will get chilled if we keep her standing too long.'

Not daring to look at Sir Mortimer, Anne moved away, pulling Miss Letty with her. The other two remained where they were, and when Anne glanced back, while Miss Letty fingered the ribbons, she saw their two heads close together, seemingly oblivious to their surroundings.

Anne kept her cousin engaged as long as possible, until, at length, they were joined by Lady Tremaine, who took great interest in their selections and offered good advice on the exact shade of pink to match Miss Letty's evening slippers. Sir Mortimer stood apart, scowling ferociously and his dark mood persisted when they rejoined him, laden with numerous little packets and boxes.

They parted from Lady Tremaine at her carriage, Miss Letty promising faithfully to send word on the morrow regarding the proposed dinner party. Mortimer escorted the ladies to Broad Street and Miss Letty maintained an easy flow of innocuous chatter as they went. Sir Mortimer responded in monosyllables when necessary. At length, she said casually, 'It was very gracious of Lady Tremaine to invite us to visit her; but it was in compliment to you, of course, Mortimer. Our acquaintance with the family is very slight. I had not remarked upon it before, but she speaks with a pretty foreign intonation.'

An unexpectedly boyish grin lightened his sombre countenance. 'Her accent is variable, ma'am. It becomes more pronounced when she is excited or animated. Stephanie has lived for many years in England, but she spent her childhood and youth in Luxembourg. She was a de Beauclerc before her marriage and fled to England to escape the French occupation and the possibility of a dynastic alliance.'

'I see. It must have been very hard for her to be wrenched away from her family and familiar surroundings. Our English culture and habits are so very different, I believe, from those prevailing on the Continent.'

Sir Mortimer lifted his eyebrows at this sweeping statement, but replied politely, 'So far as I can recollect, Stephanie did not experience any particular difficulty in adjusting to our ways. Her parents were dead, so her ties to Luxembourg were quite tenuous. Hugo and his mother, Lady Elizabeth, were her nearest kin and they made her very welcome at Huntsgrove.'

'Huntsgrove Priory is quite close to your own family estate, is it not?' asked Miss Letty.

'Yes, indeed. The Priory and Shawcross Manor are both located in the downs of Sussex, just a few miles apart.'

Miss Letty nodded. 'It is very pretty countryside. I visited Brighton once some twenty years ago. I liked it, but Ippolita thought the society too raffish, so now we usually go to Bath or Weymouth for a change of scene.'

They had reached the foot of Broad Street when suddenly Mortimer stopped and clutched his throat with a comical expression of dismay.

'Ladies, will you excuse me, I have forgotten to buy neckcloths. Since the rain has stopped, I think I will go back for them.'

He turned and strode rapidly away, still carrying several of their packages under his arm.

Miss Letitia watched him go and shook her head in puzzlement. 'How very odd, so abrupt. Did I say something wrong, do you think? Perhaps he did not like so many questions.'

Anne regarded the older lady with affection as they trudged wearily up the hill. She had been listening with silent interest to the conversation and she wondered, not for the first time, if Miss Letty's powers of understanding were more acute than was generally supposed. She replied reassuringly, 'I am sure you said nothing wrong. I believe Sir Mortimer was just a trifle preoccupied and that is why he forgot his neckwear in the first place.'

Her cousin sighed. 'I confess I'm longing for a cup of tea. I hope Janet has put the kettle on. Walking in pattens is very fatiguing.' Miss Letty still followed the old country custom of wearing heavy wooden overshoes raised off the ground by metal rings.

They were relieved to find Miss Ippolita presiding at the tea table when they entered the drawing room a few minutes later. She had had a stimulating afternoon preparing a short talk which she was going to give to her scientific circle and it was some time before she could be persuaded to give her attention to another subject.

Eventually, fortified by two cups of China tea, Miss Letty could wait no longer. 'We met Lady Stephanie Tremaine in the linen draper's, sister, and had quite a long conversation. She was wearing a very fetching bonnet, was it not, Anne – trimmed with flowers, delphiniums or some such.'

'Cornflowers, and yes, it was very modish. It is strange how such a small lady could wear such a large bonnet and not appear ridiculous.'

'She has style. It is unexpected because one hears that she is an intrepid horsewoman and frequently rides to hounds. Often that kind of female is somewhat rough and coarse in her ways,' commented Miss Ippolita.

Miss Letitia frowned worriedly. 'Do you think she belongs to a rather fast set, Ippolita? You see, we have been invited to dinner next week at Battlecombe Hall and I would not want to take Anne into such circles. Perhaps Jack and Sir Mortimer should go alone. But she was very pressing in her invitation and it would not do to be uncivil. Oh, dear, what do you say, sister?'

Thoughtfully, the lady thus appealed to set her cup on the tray. 'The Tremaines are an old and perfectly respectable county family. I do not have any doubts on that head and if Sir Mortimer vouches for them, I trust his judgement. It would be interesting to visit the Hall, but it is a long way to travel and we must not leave too late. Did Lady Tremaine mention if anyone else would be present?'

'Now you make me think of it, she did say she would ask the Oliphants.'

'Then what are you fussing about, Letty? You are making a mountain out of a molehill. Sir Jasper Oliphant is a valued member of our scientific circle and complimented me only last week on my grasp of the basic principles of anatomy. Such knowledge is necessary, you understand, when examining holotypes.'

'Holotypes?' repeated Miss Letitia, all at sea.

'A holotype is the individual specimen on which a new species is first described,' explained Anne, laughing. 'One of the Miss Philpots was good enough to take pity on my ignorance when I attended a meeting with Cousin Ippolita.'

'Common knowledge, my dear Anne,' observed her cousin, with a condescending smile. Amid the general merriment which followed, Miss Letty exclaimed, 'Then it is settled. We are to go. I will just wait and confirm it with Jack and will write to Lady Tremaine after dinner. I am so pleased I bought some extra lace. Anne, where is your Indian shawl? Do show Ippolita your purchases. Such pretty ribbons we found, and so very inexpensive, as they were remnants.'

The ladies sat happily examining their new acqui-sitions and anticipating the coming festivities long after the tea tray was removed, and when Jack returned and consented to accompany them to the party at Battlecombe Hall, their satisfaction was complete.

V

Local Society

It was a little after eight on Friday evening when the
Prawne ladies and their guests entered the Assembly
ballroom. A lively country dance was in progress and
they threaded their way through the company gathered
to watch around the perimeter of the floor. A fair
smattering of local society was already present and they
were obliged to halt several times to exchange greetings
with friends and neighbours. At length they gained the
far side of the room, where seats had been provided for
the comfort of the chaperones and their charges, when
not otherwise engaged. The Misses Prawne were quickly
settled among ladies of their acquaintance, on chairs
free from draft, but affording an excellent view of the
proceedings. The young people stood a little to one
side, waiting for the set to finish.

Anne tapped her foot softly in time to the music. She
felt happy tonight. She was pleasantly aware that she
was looking her best in a trained gown of delicately
sprigged India muslin, over a bodice of blue satin. She
had grown her hair since she came to Lyme and Janet
had teased her curls forward, so that tendrils rested on
her forehead and cheeks. Thank heaven she had no
visible spots or blemishes, and she only hoped the small
wreath of flowers twisted through her curls would
remain securely in place when she danced. At this
thought, Anne experienced a moment's apprehension.
The ignominious possibility of being without a partner

for the entire evening suddenly occurred to her. Jack could not dance much; Sir Mortimer was standing aloof, with a haughty expression closely akin to disdain on his stern features. He was undeniably elegant in a coat of dark blue, with an embroidered silk waistcoat, impeccable oyster-coloured breeches and stockings and buckled shoes. He was watching the door intently. Following his gaze, Anne saw Mr. Gresham enter and hastily turned to address some random remark to Jack. When she dared to look again, she observed with relief that Mr. Gresham had been detained by the Master of Ceremonies, who had obliged him to lead out a plain, but much befrilled damsel in the next set.

As the couples moved to take their places, Anne's eye was caught by a movement near the door. She saw that Lady Tremaine had arrived, accompanied by a short, square, ruddy-faced man with sandy-coloured hair waving thickly over his head. He was correctly, but not fashionably, attired in shades of brown and buff. Anne rather liked his open, cheerful countenance; one could hear his hearty laugh across the room.

Beside her, Sir Mortimer stiffened at the sound, but it was soon drowned in the hum of conversation and the opening bars of music. He swung round abruptly on his heel. 'May I have the pleasure of this dance, Miss Milton?'

Jack nodded approvingly, as Anne placed her hand on Sir Mortimer's arm and allowed him to lead her forward. They trod the opening measure sedately, separated frequently by the movements of the dance. Anne had been well-taught; she performed her part lightly and gracefully. Her partner did not step on her toes, but his air was evidently abstracted. Piqued, Anne decided to tease him a little. 'I suppose you need all your attention for the steps, sir? I presume you had few opportunities to practice in Spain.'

Anne felt his grip tighten as he swung her round. He

said coolly, 'Not so, Miss Milton. Wellington likes gaiety and we had many impromptu balls when the army was encamped.'

Anne was obliged to turn away. When they came together again, she said quickly, 'It was not my wish to probe into your reasons for being absentminded, Sir Mortimer. My remark was prompted entirely by selfishness – I was simply concerned that I would get no more partners if my first one is so obviously bored in my company.'

Mortimer flushed deeply under his tan and Anne regretted her sharp tongue. There was no chance to make amends, for the set ended and she was returned to her chaperones in a state of considerable confusion. She felt that her reproof had been just, but she had not expected her partner to be so vexed. Jack had disappeared and Sir Mortimer excused himself curtly. What a provoking man he was, thought Anne, as she watched him approach the Tremaines and bow before Lady Stephanie. His reactions were so unpredictable, his behaviour towards her so ambivalent, that she was constantly on tenterhooks in his company. From the first they had shown a marked tendency to rub one another the wrong way. Odious creature! She would think no more of him. She tossed her head and bestowed a dazzling smile on Mr. Gresham, who seized his opportunity and begged her for a dance.

Mr. Gresham proved to be a very creditable dancer, well able to perform intricate maneuvers and converse amiably at the same time. He paid her several neat compliments, which were a balm to soothe her wounded spirits, and she found him very knowledgeable on the subject of dogs. She learned with interest that pugs had first been introduced into England by King William and Queen Mary. When the dance ended she sensed that Sir Mortimer was watching her disapprovingly. Immediately, she requested Mr. Gresham to procure her a glass of lemonade. She sipped it slowly, while he hovered attentively at her elbow, and it was some time before she rejoined her own party.

When she did so, she found that Sir Mortimer had also returned, accompanied by the Tremaines. Introductions followed and they all chatted agreeably until the musicians struck up a waltz. Sir Lawrence, sanctioned by a quick smile from his wife, begged Anne for the favour. She hesitated, but Miss Ippolita nodded her encouragement, so Anne stepped forward in some trepidation.

'I have never danced the waltz in public before,' she confided to Sir Lawrence, stiffening as she felt his arm encircle her waist. Over his shoulder she could see Sir Mortimer leading Lady Stephanie onto the floor.

'Just relax, Miss Milton. It is really much easier than a country dance.' Sir Lawrence smiled at her reassuringly. He was not a tall man and their eyes were almost on a level. Anne smiled back warmly. She knew she was going to like Sir Lawrence. She soon found that he was far from being a typical country squire, preoccupied with horses and methods of crop rotation. His eyes were uncommonly shrewd, his flow of small talk smooth and his manners impeccable. Anne began to understand the attraction he had for his lively, vivacious wife. He was a good listener and knew how to ask the right questions. Unobtrusively, he drew Anne out and encouraged her to speak of her early life. She responded animatedly, until she remembered – belatedly – that she must guard her tongue.

Sir Lawrence was evidently a gentleman of importance in the neighbourhood. After he had danced with her she had a constant flow of partners, which she was not vain enough to attribute to her charms alone. She was grateful to Sir Lawrence for giving her the seal of approval. She noticed that he conferred the same honour on several other young ladies besides herself and she liked him the better for his good nature – in marked contrast to certain other gentlemen!

At length, hot and flushed after a particularly energetic dance, Anne asked Jack if he would accompany her out to the terrace, overlooking the sea, for some fresh air. He assented willingly, but insisted on draping her shawl carefully about her shoulders before they ventured outside. Jack limped beside her to the stone wall. It was very dark after the warmth and light of the crowded ballroom. Anne shivered involuntarily and Jack moved protectively to shield her from the cool breeze. It was high tide and they could hear the waves lapping close at hand. Anne peered through the gloom, but could see very little in the faint light of the sickle moon. They were beyond the arc of light thrown from the ballroom and stood silently side by side, surveying the scene. They were disturbed by the opening of the door. Sounds of laughter and music flooded through. When Anne turned, the noise faded and she could just make out another couple standing on the step, gazing at the dark prospect. The looming figures were familiar. Anne did not need to hear their voices, which carried clearly in the stillness, to recognize Sir Mortimer and Stephanie Tremaine. They were absorbed in one another and seemed unaware of any other presence on the terrace.

'But I am so happy with my dear Larry,' exclaimed Lady Tremaine. 'You must not tease me so, for I am a respectable married lady.'

Sir Mortimer groaned, 'You should have waited for me, Stephanie. Surely you knew that I was your devoted slave.'

He attempted to seize her hands, but she pushed him away, saying gently, 'My dear, we should not suit. We are too much alike, you and I. Always our personalities would clash and we would be very miserable.'

Before they could say more, the door opened again

and Sir Lawrence appeared between them. He addressed his wife in tones of unwonted grimness, telling her that it was time to leave, as they had a long drive ahead of them. Stephanie sounded rather flustered as she said good night to Sir Mortimer and reentered the ballroom followed by Sir Lawrence. The rejected lover lingered a few moments, his face in shadow, then he too disappeared inside and all was quiet once more. Anne stirred; Jack laid his hand on her arm. He said softly, 'Wait a little. It will be better if he does not see us come in yet.'

Anne acquiesced, standing rigid, with her back to the wall. After some minutes she whispered, 'Oh, Jack, do you think Sir Lawrence heard?'

'Possibly, or suspects. Mortimer was headlong in love with Lady Stephanie ten years or more ago and has never looked seriously at another woman since. But she has the right of it – they would not have suited. Hope Sir Lawrence has not misunderstood the situation. He probably has a quick temper with that thatch of red hair. You will help us out at the dinner party on Tuesday, won't you, Anne? It may be an awkward occasion, but it cannot well be put off, for it was all settled with my aunts this evening. The other guests have already been invited. I may be wrong, but I feel the situation's a trifle sticky – Mortimer is at a loose end and we need to give his thoughts a new direction.'

'Lady Stephanie has done nothing to deserve reproach. I hope she will be able to convince Sir Lawrence. I believe there is sincere affection between them.' Anne sighed. 'It is so unfair, this tangle of love, especially when it is one-sided. One feels true sentiments should be reciprocated mutually.'

Jack shook his head sadly. 'Life is unequal.' He shrugged. 'Probably the best thing Tim and I could do would be to go to America and start afresh.' He glanced down tenderly at his companion. He wished fervently

that he could ask Anne to marry him and go with him to
the New World, but he checked the impulse, reminding
himself that he had little to offer and would have his
own way to make. Anne's fortune was a further obstacle
and he was tolerably certain that she did not return his
regard. Major Davenport held his tongue.

Anne was somewhat alarmed by Jack's wild talk, but
she did not take it too seriously. They moved slowly
across the terrace, feeling a wave of warm air fan their
faces as they stepped over the threshold into the
ballroom. Jack remarked casually what a successful
crush it had been, on rejoining his aunts and Sir
Mortimer. That gentleman's eyes were fixed on some
remote point and he gave no sign of having observed
their prolonged absence. Soon after, the crowd began to
thin; wraps were sought, the carriages called for, and
Anne and her party returned to Broad Street, the ladies
chattering happily of the evening's entertainment, while
the gentlemen followed, rather silent and preoccupied.

Anne saw little of the young men for the next two or
three days. Jack and his friend went fishing or riding,
departing very early in the morning and returning long
after sundown. The ladies were left to their own
devices. Anne spent her time walking, reading, and
sewing. With Miss Letty's assistance, she fashioned a
new dark green velvet riding dress, with bugle trimming
to ornament the front and cuffs. She also brushed her
old black beaver hat, which was further refurbished
with the addition of new tassels and a curly green
ostrich feather. This costume accentuated her slim waist
and was pronounced very becoming by her cousins and
Janet, much to Anne's satisfaction. She longed to wear
this new outfit to the Tremaines, but was sensible
enough to realize that, despite the long journey, a
dinner party was hardly an appropriate occasion to
appear in full riding habit. Instead, she chose a
little-worn gown of palest pink silk, with long sleeves

decorated with lace cuffs and collar in a Cavalier style.
To this she added the simple ornament of a gold locket
on a black velvet ribbon. She tripped downstairs on
Tuesday afternoon, in her black velvet slippers, her
evening cloak trailing over her arm, and all eyes turned
to her admiringly when she appeared in the drawing
room. Even Sir Mortimer was obliged to admit to
himself that she was really a very taking little thing!

Miss Letty bustled forward to adjust her locket a trifle
and pat her cheek, saying, 'Very pretty, child. Are you
quite ready? Then we must be off. We don't want to be
late.' The younger Miss Prawne was quite excited. She
still cherished the notion that when dining at
Battlecombe Hall they would be moving in a fast set of
the "Haut Ton", sanctioned now by her sister's
acceptance of the invitation. This feeling of wickedness
added a delicious spice to the event.

They drove to Bridport in a hired carriage. The
weather was fine and the gentlemen elected to ride in
order to avoid a crush in the clumsy conveyance.
Although six-thirty was the fashionable hour to dine,
Lady Tremaine had arranged that they should come
about four-thirty, for dinner at five, in deference to her
guests, who wished to be well on their way homeward
before nightfall. The journey was accomplished without
incident and all three ladies leaned forward eagerly
when the carriage swung through the lodge gates and
entered the long, meandering park drive, which was the
main approach to the Hall.

'A very pleasing prospect,' pronounced Miss Ippolita,
leaning back against the cushioned squabs and
straightening her bonnet.

'Does it remind you of Fernditch, Anne?' asked Miss
Letty.

'A little, but this is much grander and better tended.
There are some fine old trees at Fernditch, but the

gardens are overgrown and the park walls were badly in
need of repair when I left,' Anne smiled wistfully.

Miss Letty reproached herself. 'How thoughtless of
me to speak of it. Do forgive me.' She glanced through
the window. 'Ah, here we are. You descend first,
Ippolita. Look, Sir Lawrence and Lady Tremaine are on
the steps to meet us.'

They were welcomed warmly and ushered into a
salon of handsome proportions, decorated in the
classical style. Here they found two other guests, Sir
Jasper Oliphant and his sister, Meg.

'No one calls me Margaret,' confided Miss Oliphant to
Anne, patting the seat beside her invitingly. 'I grew so
tall when I was eleven that my brother used to tease me
and call me long Meg. John and Sarah think I am a
regular beanpole, do you not, my dears?'

The Tremaine children giggled. They had been
allowed to join the grownups for a little while before
nursery tea and had attached themselves to Miss
Oliphant, who was a great favourite with them. John,
the elder, was seated on a footstool at her feet. He was a
handsome child, about six years old, with an engaging
smile and a mop of dark, curly hair. His little sister
favoured her papa in looks. She still retained a babyish
roundness of face and figure and her nose was
plentifully sprinkled with freckles.

Anne was laughing, too, as she sat down beside Miss
Oliphant on the sofa. She could not help herself, they
were such an attractive trio. She was soon drawn into an
earnest discussion on the rival merits of puppies and
kittens as pets. Little Sarah leaned against her knee,
listening with rapt attention while Anne described her
own dog, a King Charles spaniel called Mischief because
he got into so many scrapes. Then Miss Oliphant
countered with a tale of a kitten who loved to play with
the sponge in the bathtub and was nearly drowned by
an unwary nursemaid. Over Sarah's head, Anne's eyes

met those of Sir Mortimer and she smiled involuntarily. He smiled back and she bent her head quickly, aware of a disturbing, tingling sensation, some current between them. She busied herself, retying one of Sarah's hair ribbons with trembling fingers. When she looked up he had moved to join Lady Tremaine and Sir Jasper by the window. He had no right to exercise such indifferent charm, she thought resentfully, shifting slightly so that he was no longer in her line of vision.

Jack provided a welcome distraction by seizing a footstool and seating himself beside John, at Miss Oliphant's feet.

'Jack Davenport, now I have it!' exclaimed that lady triumphantly. 'I knew I had met you somewhere before. I have been racking my brains since first I saw you. I'm sure you do not remember the occasion.'

'Wrong, Miss Meg, I remember very well. My aunts took me to a Christmas party at your father's house and I locked you in the linen closet during a game of hide-and-seek! But it was quite twenty years ago and I humbly apologize and abjectly beg your forgiveness.' He twisted his face into a comical pleading expression, which sent the little ones off into gales of laughter. Anne laughed too, marveling at the sudden youthfulness of her cousin's countenance.

Miss Oliphant sniffed and said in mock severity, 'Such encounters are not soon forgotten, sir. I had nightmares for weeks. My old nurse used to tell me that a witch lived in that closet, and it did not contain linen, but brooms, Major Davenport!'

'I have been hesitating to approach, fearful of your deserved strictures. Help me, John and Sarah. Beseech your hard-hearted friend to display some Christian charity to this poor sinner.'

'Did you see the witch?' inquired Sarah, round-eyed and anxious.

'Silly, there're no such things as witches,' said her

brother, scornfully. Sarah grew red.

Miss Oliphant hastily intervened. 'No, Sarah darling, of course I did not see anything. Only a few cobwebs and spiders. It was only my imagination. Do you wish me to pardon this gentleman, or shall we make him pay a forfeit?'

'Oh, a forfeit, a forfeit,' cried the children together.

'I'm afraid I can't kneel down, my leg is too stiff, but I would if I could,' said Jack, joking for the first time about his infirmity. Anne listened in amazement, but Miss Oliphant responded promptly and matter-of-factly, 'Well, then, since there's no help for it, your punishment shall be to take me in to dinner!'

The children thought this a very tame punishment and Jack responded gallantly that it would be no punishment at all, but Miss Oliphant threatened to keep him talking so much that he would have no time to eat and would be quite starved at the end of the meal, and everyone agreed that this would be a very satisfactory solution.

Soon after this the children's nurse came to fetch them and they departed reluctantly, having extracted a promise from Miss Oliphant that she would come and tell them a story after dinner, if they were still awake.

'I should not make such promises. They will give poor nurse no peace,' she was saying, when the door opened and Sir Lawrence, who had been absent from the room for several minutes, came in, followed by a lean, dark man, neatly attired in gray and black, with a mustard yellow waistcoat.

Only Mortimer, standing alone in the window embrasure noticed Anne's startled expression and instantly averted face, for all other eyes were fixed on the newcomer. The gentleman bowed with easy confidence to the company. He was a capable-looking man, with good features, but brown eyes set a little too close together and a full-lipped sensual mouth.

Surveying him keenly, Mortimer thought that he had an indefinable air of passions kept on a tight rein, with possibly a streak of cruelty, or at the least of iron determination, in his character.

'Ladies and gentlemen, I would like to present Mr. Simon Pontefract. Mr. Pontefract was passing through Bridport on his way from Bristol to London, and he was kind enough to bring me letters from my brother, who lives in that city. They share an interest in the shipping trade. Stephanie, my dear, Mr. Pontefract will be staying with us tonight. Could you ask Henson to lay an extra plate for dinner.'

Mr. Pontefract advanced and bowed low over Lady Tremaine's hand. He straightened, apologizing gracefully for intruding unexpectedly when she had guests. Her ladyship murmured a polite reply and hastened away to make the necessary arrangements.

Sir Mortimer became further aware of undercurrents in the room as Sir Lawrence escorted the new arrival to each group in turn. He went first to the Misses Prawne and Sir Jasper. The elder lady was at her most dignified. She greeted him civilly, but coolly, and surveyed him with a remarkably hard stare, which Mr. Pontefract blandly returned. Miss Letitia giggled nervously and Sir Jasper glanced at her in surprise.

Mortimer transferred his attention to Jack, who had risen from the footstool and unobtrusively placed himself behind Anne. He was standing very erect, looking every inch the soldier, and his expression of overt hostility was one which had hitherto been reserved for Napoleon's troops and their allies.

Mr. Pontefract followed his host across the width of the large oriental carpet to the other sofa. Watching closely, Sir Mortimer saw his eyes widen in a sudden arrested expression as he approached the young ladies. Impeccably, he bowed before Miss Oliphant, then turned to Anne, who was waiting tensely for her true identity to be revealed. To her surprise Mr. Pontefract held his peace, merely remarking over his shoulder to Sir Lawrence, 'This lady and I are already acquainted. How do you do, Miss Anne?' He took her hand and kissed it. Anne shrank back, pulling her hand away, and he released it, with a twisted smile.

Sir Lawrence noticed nothing amiss. 'Then perhaps you also know Miss Milton's cousin, Major John Davenport?'

Mr. Pontefract swung round quickly. 'No, I have not that pleasure. Your servant, Major Davenport.'

Jack acknowledged the salutation gravely and Mortimer thought it was time to create a diversion. He stepped forward with a friendly smile and made polite inquiries concerning Mr. Pontefract's journey until Stephanie returned and claimed Mr. Pontefract's attention. Dinner was soon announced and under cover of the general movement, Sir Mortimer asked Anne if she felt quite well as she looked a trifle dispirited. To his surprise, she did not seize upon the conventional excuse of a headache, but replied simply that she was indeed discomposed by the unexpected arrival of Simon Pontefract.

Before Mortimer could question her further, Mr. Pontefract reappeared at Anne's side and on the grounds of their old acquaintance, begged the privilege of taking her in to dinner. Mortimer saw Anne shiver and was tempted to intervene, but after a moment of barely perceptible hesitation, she laid her hand on the gentleman's proffered arm. He was left to bring in Miss Letitia, for Jack had moved quickly to Miss Oliphant, ready to take his "punishment" like a man. They followed Sir Lawrence with Miss Prawne, and Lady Tremaine with Sir Jasper, in stately progress down the hall.

VI

Mr. Pontefract Pursues His Quarry

The addition of an extra gentleman had achieved an equal balance between the sexes, Lady Tremaine observed with satisfaction, as she seated herself at the foot of the long, rectangular dining table, with Sir Mortimer on her left and Sir Jasper on her right. From his place at the other end, Sir Lawrence jovially entertained the two Prawne ladies. Miss Ippolita had the chair of honour on his right, with Jack beyond her and Miss Oliphant between Jack and Sir Mortimer. The table arrangement was such that Mortimer could see Anne across the snowy damask cloth, between Sir Jasper and Mr. Pontefract, but he could hear little of their conversation.

The scent of roses filled the air and the cut glass and silver sparkled in the candlelight. There was a pleasant hum of conversation while the servants unobtrusively served the white soup. Sir Jasper was happily engaged in describing a recent hunt to Lady Stephanie. Mortimer reflected cynically that the quality of a man's mind might be judged by the amount of personal narrative in his talk; Sir Jasper's mental horizon was obviously bounded by the locality in which he figured as a prominent landowner and magistrate. Mortimer found himself longing for the sharp wit of his brother-in-law, the comrades of his army days, the keen minds and biting tongues of London – not the gossip of the "beau monde", but the talk of the clubs and the City, where lawyers, bankers, and journalists discussed the latest news from abroad over their dinners. He sipped his soup automatically, without tasting it. Why was it that congenial souls were so few and far between? It had not always been so. He checked himself, aware that he was slipping into a dark humour of brooding melancholy for companions now lost forever. This was not the moment for such self-indulgence and he was almost relieved to be roused from his reverie by a feeling of tension in the air.

Simon Pontefract was holding forth on the American way of life and the necessity for slaves to uphold the infant nation's economy. The streak of ruthlessness which Mortimer's experienced, soldierly eye had already discerned, was clearly apparent now. Evidently Mr. Pontefract was a merchant who had considerable interests in plantations in the American South, notably in Georgia and the Carolinas. His discourse was extremely knowledgeable and Mortimer suspected that he might have been connected with the slave trade, before its abolition several years ago.

'At least the Americans had the good sense to break with our "enlightened" rule before we ruined everything. I would not dismiss the possibility that Parliament might well decide to abolish slavery in the Colonies altogether in the not-too-distant future. There is a deal of sentimental hypocrisy at large in Westminster these days, and the truth of the matter is that slaves are essential to get the work done in hot climates.' Mr. Pontefract glanced round the table, smiling grimly at the shocked silence which his comments had produced. He waited until the soup had been replaced by a fine dish of carp and then continued, 'In my admittedly limited experience, the slaves were generally well-treated. It was not in their owners' interests to do otherwise. Now, I apologize if I have offended anyone's sensibilities. I was forgetting I am in mixed company and such subjects are unsuitable for the table.' He bowed ironically towards Lady Stephanie.

She met his eyes coolly and said slowly, 'You are at liberty to hold any opinion you please, sir. It is a free country and I do not object to the discussion of political topics, if they do not cause discomfort to my guests by their controversial nature.' She turned back to Sir Jasper and smoothly resumed their analysis of the finer points of a new hunter, which she had recently purchased.

Anne was left with no alternative but to converse with Mr. Pontefract on her other side. 'I do not agree with you about slavery, but I think there is some hypocrisy practiced in England,' she said thoughtfully. 'Many of the people who work in this country are virtual slaves. The little boys who sweep the chimneys, for example, and from what I have read in the newspaper it seems to me that the poor people in the northern factories are shamefully exploited.'

Mr. Pontefract looked at her askance. 'Strange reading for a young lady, if I may say so. Factories are the future and you cannot stop the march of progress, you know.'

Across the table Mortimer was straining to hear their conversation. The gentleman's voice was deep and carried resonantly; his last remark caused Anne's head to tilt back sharply, a habit she had, when provoked. Amused, Mortimer could not resist stirring the fire a little. 'You should meet my Aunt Arabella, Miss Milton. For many years she has devoted her energies to the education of the poor, in order, she says, to help them fulfill their potential.'

'Potential for what, sir?' boomed Mr. Pontefract. 'It only leads to revolution if you educate the lower orders.'

Mortimer grinned. Simon Pontefract's eyes glinted in response, but the humour of the situation was lost on Lady Tremaine, who had little experience of men who enjoyed debate for its own sake, whether they believed in their argument or not. Henson the butler, was standing impassively beside Sir Lawrence, as he carved the beef, and the poor hostess feared a revolution on her own doorstep if the Bristol merchant continued long in the same vein. Hastily, she asked him if he had been to Philadelphia, where she had relatives. She was aided in her attempt to divert Mr. Pontefract by Jack, who was genuinely interested in the New World, and by Mortimer, who feared that otherwise a wave of banal trivialities would engulf the company.

Mr. Pontefract, for his part, recognized that he had overstepped the invisible bounds of polite society and smoothly retrieved himself. He craved Anne's pardon for his boorishness in contradicting her and went on to discourse easily and entertainingly of life on the American continent. However, he did not monopolize the conversation, but asked the opinions of others, especially the men. It was evident to Mortimer that he did not expect the ladies to have opinions and, if they did, he had no intention of encouraging them.

Reluctantly, Mortimer felt a twinge of admiration for the man; how he wished Hester could have been there to depress Mr. Pontefract's pretensions on behalf of her sex. He was surprised that the usually forthright Miss Ippolita had remained unwontedly silent throughout. It had hardly been a relaxed, informal occasion, he reflected, as the gentlemen scraped back their chairs and stood to allow the ladies to withdraw in dignified silence.

The drawing room presented a cheerful aspect. It had come on to rain, so a fire had been lit and the curtains pulled to counter the chilly damp night. Lady Stephanie presided at the tea equipage; Anne accepted a cup gratefully and chose a chair a little removed from the fireside circle. She felt the need for a few quiet moments of reflection. She had had no time to

assimilate the unexpected appearance of Simon Pontefract or to anticipate his next move. He had been very
tactful so far, but she knew that he was biding his time
and would soon seek her out. The subject of her medi-
tations was also under discussion among the other ladies.

'Such a forceful man,' Miss Letitia was saying, 'he
makes me quite nervous with his pronounced manner
and strong views.'

Lady Tremaine shuddered delicately. 'Quite obnox-
ious. So bourgeois. I confess I do not understand why
dear Larry tolerates him.'

'He is a man's man,' observed Miss Ippolita dryly. 'I
imagine he is a shrewd and competent businessman and
they respect him. He does not patronize them.'

'He did not appear to hold a very high opinion of
females,' interjected Miss Oliphant, with a smile.

'Typically nouveau riche,' sniffed her ladyship, ratt-
ling her teaspoon ferociously. 'He created, how shall I
say, a hurricane in a puddle. My cozy dinner party was
quite spoiled and I shall not soon forgive him. But I
forget my manners. You are already acquainted with the
gentleman are you not, Miss Milton. Do I misjudge him?'

Uncomfortably aware of her cousins' close attention,
Anne replied evasively that she knew him slightly
because, like Sir Lawrence, her father had had business
dealings with Mr. Pontefract. Before Lady Stephanie
could question her further, Miss Prawne came to her
rescue by requesting another cup of tea. She went on to
praise the excellent white soup and wondered if she
might have the recipe for her cook, as she had detected
an unusual ingredient, which mightily improved the
flavour. Could it be a different kind of nut? She herself
used sweet almonds. The talk became technical and
domestic. Miss Oliphant excused herself to visit the
nursery and Anne drifted over to the pianoforte and
played softly until the gentlemen joined them.

Anne's musical talents were limited. In recognition of

this fact she was about to close the lid when she saw Simon Pontefract approaching, an expression of marked determination on his lean, dark face. Hurriedly she snatched up some music. It happened to be a new collection of Moore's *Irish Melodies* with which she was unfamiliar. She forced herself to concentrate and to her surprise, achieved a tolerable rendering.

Across the room Jack saw her plight. His square jaw jutted aggressively and he tapped Mortimer's arm, nodding in Anne's direction and murmuring in his ear, 'The fellow's too possessive by half. Come along.' He limped over to the piano and was in time to observe Mr. Pontefract's hand brush her cheek, as he leaned forward to turn the page. Anne fumbled and struck a wrong note, but Jack clapped enthusiastically.

'A capital performance, Anne. I'm very fond of a Scottish air.' He spoke loudly, his back to the company, so that only Anne saw the challenging glare directed at Mr. Pontefract over her left shoulder.

With an effort she forced herself to speak lightly, crying, 'Thank you, cousin, but I'm afraid my playing has deceived you. It was an Irish air!'

Casually, Sir Mortimer joined the little group. He placed his cup on the piano and idly leafed through the sheets of music. Triumphantly he pulled out a duet. Smiling down at Anne, he said cheerfully, 'I'm very rusty, but I'm game if you are, Miss Milton. I used to play this piece with my sister when we were children, and very tiresome I thought it.'

In her relief, Anne's face lit up unguardedly in an expression of engaging warmth and charm. With a quick intake of breath, Mortimer seated himself beside her. One, two, three, and they were off, playing with an infectious gaiety, which caused their listeners to overlook their numerous mistakes and clamour for more when they finished. They executed two more airs with increasing confidence and concluded with a flourish, amid delighted applause.

Mortimer grinned at Anne. 'Bravo. I vow I've never played so well before!'

Anne shook her head, laughing. 'Nor I, sir. It must be the excellence of the instrument, for my music master would tell you, I have very little skill.'

'Well done, Miss Fairleigh!' said Mr. Pontrefract, at her elbow. Anne froze. Suavely, he corrected, 'I beg your pardon, I mean Miss Milton. You remind me very much of a young lady of that name.'

They all moved slowly back to the fireside circle. The gentlemen began to discuss military matters and the prospects for a lasting peace. Thankful to be no longer the centre of attention, Anne sank down beside Lady Tremaine, who was watching Sir Mortimer intently.

It had not been a good evening for her ladyship. She had been relegated to matronly status, while the young men buzzed round Miss Milton. Lady Stephanie was not accustomed to being ignored and she had expected that her old admirer would linger by her side. Instead Sir Mortimer had appeared anything but lovelorn. She had intercepted several glances which he had bestowed on Anne and, being a sensible woman, *au fond*, she realized that she could not eat her cake and have it, too. She had given the gentleman his marching orders and it was not to be anticipated that he would continue to dance attendance on her, against her expressed wishes. She must not be selfish, she chided herself. Besides, Sir Lawrence had been very understanding after the incident at the Assembly, but it would not be wise to give him further cause for provocation. She decided to devote her energies to matchmaking; she was very fond of Mortimer and truly wished him to be as happy as she was herself. With commendable zeal, she turned her attention to Anne and began to question her closely concerning her interests and opinions.

At length Miss Oliphant returned from her visit to

John and Sarah and the their doting mama was instantly diverted, leaving Anne temporarily at liberty. Mr. Pontefract seized his chance. He took the vacant chair on her left, without asking her permission, and inquired bluntly, but softly, 'Well Miss Anne, what have you been doing since I last had the pleasure of seeing you? I was not aware that you had any relatives in this part of the world. Why did you never mention them? How close exactly is the connection?'

Anne felt trapped, mesmerized by his bright, sharp eyes. The others were all engrossed in their conversations. In a remote corner of her brain, Anne distantly heard Lady Tremaine saying, 'Oh, yes, we were in London for the Frost Fair. The children enjoyed it tremendously, but I have never been so cold in my life!'

There was a magnetic quality about Simon Pontefract. She could not break away.

'How did you find me?' she whispered.

He shook his head and said in tones of mild reproof, 'Your friends were all concerned about you. Of course, we felt it our duty to intercept Miss Mary's letter to you. I was on my way to London, but Mary's father sent a messenger. I was coming to Lyme tomorrow; our meeting tonight was quite fortuitous. But you haven't answered my question. What are your connections here?'

'They are cousins on my father's side,' replied Anne, wanly. 'Ippolita and Letitia are first cousins to my father and Major Davenport is their nephew.' She wrenched her gaze away, two angry spots of colour in her pale cheeks. 'How dared you interfere with my correspondence? You have no right ...'

She stopped abruptly and Mr. Pontefract grinned sardonically. He leaned forward and took her hand, murmuring, 'My dear, I have every right. I am your legal guardian, remember. And I will soon be your husband.'

Anne could take no more. She leapt up, but was overcome by a sudden wave of dizziness and nausea. She swayed, putting out her hand to steady herself, as someone cried, 'Have a care, she's going to swoon!'

When Anne regained consciousness she was lying on a sofa, in another room, with Miss Oliphant kneeling beside her, holding a bottle of smelling salts to her nose. She pushed them away feebly and struggled to sit up.

'Wait a little,' urged Meg gently, 'you must have been overcome by the heat.'

Anne relaxed against the pillow. 'How did I get here? Where is everybody?' she asked, as the mists dissolved from her brain.

Miss Oliphant sat back on her heels and smiled, pleased to see that Anne was recovering her wits. 'We thought it would be better if you were left in peace for a few minutes. Would you like a little water? You fainted very gracefully, you know. I wish I could do it as well. Fortunately Sir Mortimer sprang forward and caught you before you hit your head on the tea trolley. It was very dramatic, he almost collided with Mr. Pontefract coming from the opposite direction. May I call you Anne?'

Anne nodded. 'Please do.' She smiled shyly at her new friend. 'I feel so foolish to have made such a scene. I've never done such a thing before.'

Lady Stephanie bustled in, followed by Miss Prawne. 'How do you feel now, my dear?' inquired her ladyship kindly, laying her hand on Anne's forehead, 'No fever, I think.'

Miss Prawne regarded Anne with concern. 'Do you feel able to support the ride home, Anne? Lady Tremaine has been so good as to offer you a bed, but she already has Mr. Pontefract staying here.'

Anne did not need this hint to refuse Lady Tremaine's invitation. 'I am sure the fresh air will revive me. Thank you so much, ma'am, but I cannot put you to any further inconvenience. I assure you, I am much better.'

Miss Prawne gave a satisfied nod. 'In that case, I think we should call for our carriage. It is still raining hard. You remain here, Anne, while we fetch our wraps and make our farewells. We will not be long.'

The two older ladies returned to the drawing room with the good news that Miss Milton was almost herself again. Mr. Pontefract approached Miss Ippolita and asked if he might call on the morrow and reassure himself that Miss Anne was indeed well before he continued on his journey. Miss Prawne replied shortly that she did not see the necessity, but he persisted and at length she said rather ungraciously that he might take a glass of wine with them before dinner, if he wished.

The visitors politely thanked the Tremaines for their hospitality and Sir Jasper said they must all meet again soon at his house.

'I will carry Miss Milton,' said Mortimer to Jack, adding bluntly to forestall protests, 'It will not help matters if your knee gives way on the steps.'

He said the same thing to Anne, as he swung her easily off the sofa. In truth she was feeling weak and shaken in reaction to the various stresses of the evening. She was grateful that Sir Mortimer did not linger in the hall, but marched down the slippery steps with Anne clasped firmly in his arms. She tugged at her hood, for the rain was falling fast on her upturned face. Sir Mortimer strode on, easily outstripping Jack and the ladies. Anne felt happy and safe. She wished she could stay forever with her head on his chest and his arms about her. If only he loved her instead of Lady Stephanie. Abruptly she pulled away, appalled at the trend her thoughts had taken. Sir Mortimer tightened his grip. He bent his head, so that his lips brushed her hair and muttered in anything but romantic, loverlike tones, 'Be still, silly wench, or I shall drop you in a puddle!'

This remark had the desired effect and Anne clung to his coat collar like a limpet until she was deposited, half-laughing and half-crying, in a crumpled heap on the seat.

She pretended to sleep during the long ride back to Lyme. After a while two distinct sets of gentle snores indicated that her cousins had followed her example. She opened her eyes and stared at the darkness, thinking hard. One thought kept running through her mind – she must run away again. Simon Pontefract was not a man to be easily thwarted and he was her guardian. She knew that her cousins would do their best to protect her, but she doubted the ability of two elderly ladies and one lame man to be strong and vigilant in her defence at all times. They had been more than kind to her, and she knew they would tell her not to be so absurd, but she had been surrounded by friends in Bristol – to no avail. Her pursuer was cunning, persuasive, and determined and, now that he had found her, Lyme was no longer a sanctuary.

She toyed briefly with the notion of trying to enlist Sir Mortimer's aid, but soon dismissed the idea; she had no claim on him and no right to seek to place such a burden on his shoulders.

Her resolve hardened. The only way to outwit her would-be husband was to disappear until she came of age and inherited her fortune. Then she would be an independent woman of means. Fortunately their betrothal had not been formally announced, but she felt guilty and oppressed when she dwelt on the recollection of her father's express wish. The rain lashed dismally against the windows and Anne was overwhelmed by unhappiness and loneliness. She pulled the carriage rug up to her chin, desperately striving to overcome the enveloping gloom, both within and without. She forced herself to concentrate on her immediate plans.

Everything went smoothly. They reached Broad

Street soon after eleven and Anne retired at once. The others lingered in the drawing room, warming themselves with a hot drink by the fire. Anne heard them beginning an enjoyable postmortem on the dinner party as she ascended the stairs and wished she could have stayed for Cousin Ippolita's pithy assessment of Simon Pontefract. She had had no opportunity to speak privately with her cousins and knew they must be curious about her reaction to his appearance. She blessed them for their tactful silence on the subject during the long evening. No doubt they thought tomorrow would be soon enough.

Once in her room, Anne began swiftly to make her preparations. She changed into a plain, serviceable traveling dress, made a hasty toilette, and seized her old, brown carpetbag, into which she crammed some clothes and other necessities, including a copy of Mary Wollstonecraft's *Vindication of the Rights of Woman* to keep her company on the journey. She smiled slightly as she packed this last item, reflecting ruefully that women had very few rights, when property was involved. When all was ready, she placed her outer garments on the bed with her shoes, and sat down to wait till it was time to leave. She had resolved to take the Dorchester coach, which passed through Lyme at the uncomfortable hour of four in the morning. She counted her money and was distressed to see how her resources had been depleted by the recent shopping expeditions. She would have little to spare after paying her coach fare. It might be necessary to part with some of Mama's jewelry. She glanced round to see if she had forgotten anything. Of course, she must write a note. She chewed her pen thoughtfully. Would it be wise to reveal her destination? Remembering Mary, she decided to be cautious. She wrote a short, affectionate letter, sealed it, and placed it on the pillow. Then she snuffed out the light and waited patiently for the household to retire.

VII

Anne Escapes

She jerked awake just as dawn was breaking and leapt out of her chair in dismay. With feverish haste, she gathered her belongings together and tiptoed downstairs, holding her breath for every little squeak and rustle. Cautiously she unlocked the heavy street door and stepped out into a morning of scudding cloud and buffeting wind. There was no one about, except a few servant girls drawing back shutters and sweeping steps. Anne ran swiftly to the posting house, but found the courtyard deserted with no sign of any waiting passengers or boxes. She could hear the chatter of the hostlers in the stables, mixed with the clink of pails and the stamp of horse's hooves. There did not seem to be any urgency about these sounds and Anne was forced to the unwelcome conclusion that she had missed the coach.

She retreated to the arched entrance to study the notices of fares and destinations posted there. She soon realized that, unlike Bristol, there were relatively few public coach services passing through Lyme and that the next one passing in an easterly direction did not depart until mid-morning. It would be child's play for Simon Pontefract to trace her and overtake a ponderous stagecoach. Besides, she could not hope to linger unremarked in such a public place for several hours. She wished belatedly that she had thought to disguise herself, but there was no time to brood. She walked briskly, following back lanes and alleyways and climbing steadily until she reached the open countryside. When she felt safe from chance observation, she paused in a sheltered hedgerow to rummage in her bag for her old, unbecoming brown cape, which she put on to cover her fashionable pelisse. She scraped her hair up in a severe knot and pulled her bonnet well forward. Then, satisfied that she had made herself as unobtrusive as possible, she trudged on for several miles.

At last Anne reached a cart track, where she sat down to rest on a tree stump. She was beginning to feel very dispirited; her bag was heavy, her feet ached, and she wondered if her departure had not been precipitate. A competent horseman could easily overtake her. As if in answer to her thoughts, she heard the steady clip-clop of horse's hooves. She jumped up nervously and sighed with relief when the animal appeared round a bend, pulling a gig, with a respectable-looking farmer holding the reins.

Anne stepped forward to beg a ride, acutely aware of her disheveled appearance, but too tired to care if she aroused unwanted curiosity. Fortunately, he was a kindly, sociable man, who welcomed the prospect of some company on the road. He surveyed her keenly as she made her request, then nodded cheerfully and leaned forward to help, taking first her bag, which he stowed under the seat, and next her hand to assist her to mount.

The farmer, whose name was Mr. Ham, was an undemanding companion. He evidently took Anne for a governess by her dress and cultivated manners and, beyond a few brief inquiries concerning her destination, he evinced no desire to ask searching questions. Anne relaxed, content to listen while Mr. Ham talked.

He spoke in a rich Devon burr, which reminded her of the country people around her own home. 'I be goin' fur to zee my sister in Dorchester, miss. She were in sarvice with a lawyer's family afore she married. Now 'er 'usband's gone 'n left her fur a pretty widder woman. Bessie has a babe 'n she can't work, so she sent word fur me to come 'n fetch 'er. We was always close, yer see, miss.'

Anne smiled. 'I think Bessie is very lucky to have such a kind brother to come to her aid,' she said encouragingly.

Mr. Ham beamed. He told Anne about his own family, his farm and his livestock in slow, colourful detail. By the time they came to the outskirts of Bridport, about noon, Anne felt as if she were intimately acquainted with every member of Mr. Ham's household, not to mention his neighbours.

They were about to leave the cart track and join the main road from Bridport to Dorchester, when Anne received an unpleasant shock. A couple of hundred yards ahead she saw Simon Pontefract, riding towards them on a brown horse. He was alone and evidently bound for Lyme. Pleading an attack of nausea, she begged the farmer to stop and ran to take refuge in the bushes, which were thick and thorny hereabouts. She remained in hiding for several minutes after the horseman rode by and finally emerged pale and shivering in a most convincing manner. The obliging Mr. Ham again helped her up and sympathetically produced a cup of home-brewed cider to settle her stomach.

After this incident, Mr. Ham became more pressing in his friendly inquiries about Anne's journey. She fobbed him off with a tale of a visit to her sick mother in Dorchester, but she could tell he was suspicious, as he seemed to know the town and families well.

'Would yer mama be related to old Mrs. Sutherland that keeps the milliner's shop?' he inquired. 'I 'eard tell she 'ad a relative that were poorly come to stay.'

'No. She's only recently settled in the district and has

no family apart from myself nearby,' replied Anne
glibly. She now felt tired and queasy in truth and closed
her eyes to discourage further conversation. Mr. Ham
produced a packet of bread and cheese and munched
ruminatively.

They arrived in Dorchester in the late afternoon and
Anne asked to be let down in the marketplace.

'Thank you so much for your kind assistance, Mr.
Ham,' she said, shaking his hand warmly. 'You have
been so good that I would not wish to discommode you
further by taking you out of your way and I know you
are anxious to see your sister. It is only a step to
Mother's lodging.'

Reluctantly the farmer did as he was bid. 'It's been a
real pleasure, miss. If there's aught else I kin do fer 'ee,
jest send word to Peter Ham. I'll be stayin' at Mistress
Freebody's fer a couple o' days yet.'

Anne nodded and waved until he had driven out of
sight, then crossed the square to the coach office. In
order to evade any possible pursuer, she had decided to
continue on her journey to London by way of
Southampton, rather than taking the more direct road
through Salisbury and Winchester. The ticket office was
closed, but a friendly hostler told her that the stage
would pass through at six A.M. sharp, on its way from
the West Country to Southampton. 'Better be 'ere early
loike, miss. We'm expectin' a big crowd termorrer on
account o' the mill.'

Anne smiled her thanks, too weary to question the
man more closely. Feeling very alone and vulnerable,
she retraced her steps past the water trough, where she
paused to rinse her fingers. She straightened her
shoulders, resolutely putting aside a deep longing to be
back among her friends in Lyme. They must be anxious
about her, but she would not think of that now. She
must concentrate on finding a bed for the night.

There were several inns in the immediate vicinity.

Anne tried the nearest, which proved to be small, but quiet and clean. An old woman was dozing over her knitting in the taproom. She started when Anne touched her, but was rather hard of hearing and took some time to understand that the young lady required a room and a modest supper. This obstacle being overcome, Anne retired thankfully to the privacy of her chamber, ate heartily, and slept soundly.

She was roused at five the next morning and, feeling much refreshed, made her way to the coach office in good time to purchase her ticket to Southampton. Somewhat to her dismay, she learned that all the inside seats were taken. It was unusual for a lady to sit outside, but the weather was fine and Anne refused to be deterred. The other passengers eyed her askance as she mounted nimbly to her high perch. Shaking out her skirts, she smiled brightly, wishing them all a "good morning". Her companions were two, older, hard-faced men and a callow youth sporting a dazzling red-and-white checked neckcloth. She soon learned from their conversation that she was fortunate to have obtained a seat at all.

'Well, gentlemen, who do you reckon will win?' inquired the coachman, a broad, burly individual, with a husky voice.

'They were laying ten to one odds against Chris the Cobbler last night,' replied the young man eagerly.

"Course they were, Davy. He's a newcomer. Game, I grant ye, but no science, lad, or nought to compare with The Sledgehammer.' The man beside Anne spoke authoritatively. 'I wager the odds'll be more'n ten to one.'

'Where will the fight take place?' Anne had to raise her voice to be heard above the rumble of the wheels.

'Just beyond Ringwood, miss, in the New Forest,' the driver responded, looking at her fully for the first time. "Tain't no place for a lady. There'll be a big rough crowd, comin' from all directions. Wot's yer destination, miss?'

Anne knew a momentary qualm. Her father had often condemned prizefighting as a brutal sport and she was aware that it was a great social leveler, where all classes mixed freely. However, her fear of Simon Pontefract was greater than her fear of an anonymous crowd, intent upon its own business. She lifted her chin and said firmly, 'I'm going to Southampton. Do you anticipate any serious delay, coachman?'

'I 'opes not, miss, but yer never can tell.'

The stage jolted and the driver was obliged to give his full attention to the ribbons. The man beside Anne leaned towards her and said, confidentially, 'If I was your pa, young lady, I wouldn't want my daughter tangling wiv all them thieves and waggabonds.'

The young man called Davy overheard this remark and grinned at Anne, protesting, 'Pay no heed to Jonas, miss. He should've been called Jeremiah.' He spoke in more refined accents than the older men. Anne guessed that he was some kind of tradesman's apprentice.

'Does the coach road pass close to the scene of this, er, pugilistic display?' she queried thoughtfully.

'Oh, yes, miss, within a mile or two, I'd say,' he answered promptly.

Anne subsided, pulling her cloak about her, for the wind was rising and it was very dusty. The men continued to discuss the "science" of the boxers and she listened, interested despite herself, to their revelations of an unknown world. Young Davy had recently purchased the book *Boxiana* by Pierce Egan. This volume was evidently the last word on the subject, at least so far as the young man was concerned. His companions were inclined to be scornful, but he defended the work robustly, telling them that it was an indispensable adjunct for members of the "Fancy", sporting coves like themselves, with its descriptions of great sparring matches of the past and the lives of the champions. Even his friends were impressed when he read aloud, with great enthusiasm and appropriate gesticulation, Egan's description of the famous match between Tom Cribb and Molyneaux the Black.

Jonas, who had seen this memorable event at firsthand, contributed some reminiscences of his own. They all sighed at the end of this heroic recital, which they knew by heart, but which had lost nothing in the retelling.

'By George, I wish I'd been there!' exclaimed Davy.

'So do I,' echoed Anne, swept away by the vivid tale.

There was a shocked silence. Anne refused to be intimidated. 'I do not think it unfeminine to admire courage,' she said defiantly. The men presented a solid front of disapproval; such trespassing in the traditional field of male prerogative could not be tolerated.

'Ladies know nothing of mills,' gasped Davy, his ears reddening to match his neckcloth.

'It might be better if they did; perhaps they would become more civilized occasions,' retorted Anne, stung.

They were obliged to descend at this point, for the stagecoach had reached the foot of a steep hill and it was necessary to ease the burden for the horses. Anne marched up the slope ahead of the others and had quite recovered her temper by the time she gained the brow. Soon afterwards they stopped at a roadside inn for refreshment, then journeyed steadily through the afternoon. Anne noticed an ever-increasing volume of traffic as the day progressed. Every imaginable conveyance had apparently been pressed into service and the other outside passengers began to be agitated lest they arrive too late for the fight.

'A crown for you, coachman, if we reach Ringwood by four o'clock,' promised Jonas.

They had come to an open stretch of road. The jarvey nodded in agreement, took a quick swig from a bottle previously hidden in his capacious greatcoat pocket, and cracked his whip at the beasts. The vehicle lurched forward, swinging precariously from side to side. Anne clung to the iron rail, expecting every moment to land in the basket, if not the ditch, while Davy added to the danger by bouncing up and down excitedly, urging the driver on.

As they neared the town of Ringwood, the inevitable happened. They met another vehicle approaching at speed. The coachman pulled the horses sharply to one side; they went too far, floundered in a deep rut, and the offside rear wheel spun off. Anne clung to her seat and managed not to fall the considerable distance to the ground, but it was clear the coach could not proceed. General dismay and confusion ensued. The five large inside passengers emerged, grumbling or having the vapours, according to their sex and inclination. The coachman left the passengers to shift for themselves while he inspected his horses, aided by Jonas and Davy. Fortunately the damage was minimal, only one beast having been lamed.

When they were all assembled by the roadside, the coachman announced that someone would have to seek help at the last village which they had passed through, Tricketts Cross. A babble of voices at once arose, some lamenting the inconvenience, others cursing the driver. A general dispute followed, concerning who would go for help and who would remain with the horses and packages, which could not be left unguarded. The three boxing enthusiasts and three insiders unchivalrously decided to continue on foot, having consulted a map and discovered that the venue fixed for the fight was but three miles off. This left Anne, two elderly females in impossible walking shoes, and the driver to cope as best they might.

'Since we have been abandoned by all those sport-mad men, I will return to the village,' volunteered Anne.

The unfortunate driver accepted her suggestion with relief, recognizing that there was little alternative.

'Thank you, miss, but have a care. Best leave your bag here, for you can go faster. Don't want to risk bein' robbed now, for there's all sorts on the road today. And even those as think they're gents don't act like it, nohow, goin' off and leavin' us without so much as a penny tip,' he finished bitterly.

Carrying only her reticule, Anne set off, following the road back the way they had come. The path was thronged with people and it was hard going against the crowd, all heading in the opposite direction. She was tired, hungry, and dusty when she reached Tricketts Cross. Her one thought was to get help for the coach driver and then refresh herself before taking the road again. She paused at the smithy and was obliged to plead hard for aid, for although the stagecoach would normally have priority, there were many more lucrative tasks to be performed with so much unusual activity in the area. However, she prevailed. The smith promised to organize a rescue party within the hour and Anne stepped across the street to the inn, feeling well-pleased with her effort.

This sense of well-being was abruptly dispelled. Two gentlemen stood back to allow Anne to enter the inn. She looked up to thank them, blinking in the shadows after the outdoor sunlight. To her horror she made out first Sir Mortimer Vane and then Mr. Simon Pontefract, both staring at her in disbelief.

VIII

In Which Mr. Pontefract Is Temporarily Vanquished

Aghast, Anne jumped back quickly, poised to flee. Simon Pontefract also moved swiftly, elbowing Mortimer roughly aside and seizing the girl's arm in a vicelike grip. He addressed a watchful crowd of bystanders, declaring loudly, 'This young woman has been cozening her kind benefactresses, the Misses Prawne of Lyme; she is underage and has run away from my protection and guardianship. I hereby assert my right to restore her to safety and I challenge any man to say me nay.' His air of authority and aggressive manner had the desired effect. The group dispersed, shuffling off in twos and threes, muttering among themselves.

Meanwhile, Sir Mortimer had gathered his wits and was inclined to resent Mr. Pontefract's high-handedness. He stepped forward. 'Is it true that this man is your guardian, Miss Milton?' he asked quietly.

Before she could reply, Anne's captor intervened truculently. 'Stand aside, sir. This lady's name is Anne Fairleigh and she is my betrothed.'

Sir Mortimer's eyebrows snapped together and he glanced quickly at Anne. Her stricken expression appeared to confirm Pontefract's words.

The younger gentleman scowled. 'We cannot discuss the matter here in the common taproom,' he said, after a moment.

'There's nothing to discuss,' shot back Mr. Pontefract,

jutting his chin.

Anne wriggled and squirmed in his hold, to no avail. To her anguished eyes it seemed that Sir Mortimer's face expressed nothing but disdain and distaste at being embroiled in such a tawdry incident. He said tonelessly, 'I think you are forgetting one small detail. We traveled in my vehicle. I believe the proper course would be to convey the lady to her relatives in Lyme. I will postpone my journey to London and we can be on our way when the horses are baited.'

Angry and humiliated, Anne received the distinct impression that had he been less of a gentleman, he would have said she was a damnable nuisance and confoundedly in the way. Mr. Pontefract slackened his grasp and Anne wrenched her arm free. They both exclaimed, 'No!' simultaneously.

Sir Mortimer glanced from one irate flushed countenance to the other with a slow smile. He leaned against the lintel and pulled out a pipe, which he proceeded to fill with maddening deliberation. Then he stomped down the tobacco, lit it, and blew a cloud contentedly. These actions were accompanied by a sudden and to Anne, bewildering, change of mood. He said, casually, but firmly, 'I vow I'm deucedly sharp-set. I believe we would all think more clearly after some refreshment. Let me see if I can obtain a private parlour.'

Suiting the action to the word, he swung on his heel and crossed to the bar, taking care to keep his head bent to avoid the low beams. After a moment Anne followed his example and stepped inside, her nose wrinkling as she absorbed the mixed scents of smoke, beer, and unwashed humanity which lingered in the quiet, almost deserted room. She glanced back to the open door, where Simon Pontefract stood gazing blankly at the sunny courtyard as various alternative schemes for action jostled through his mind. Anne's attention was diverted by a slight rustle in the far corner of the room.

At first she thought it was the coals still smouldering from last night's fire, but then she noticed two feet, encased in serviceable riding boots and an elbow protruding over the arm of a high-backed wooden settle which flanked the hearth. She heard a gentle snore and the elbow disappeared.

Meanwhile, Sir Mortimer had finished his talk with the greasy individual behind the bar. He joined Anne, shaking his head ruefully. 'I'm afraid there is no private room available. The fellow says he has given up his own chamber to three, er – ladies, of somewhat doubtful virtue, who are awaiting the return of their male companions from the fight. However, you look weary, Miss Fairleigh, and I have taken the liberty of ordering some bread and cheese and ale. I do not trust the cook in such a place as this.'

He fumbled in his pocket for a clean handkerchief and carefully dusted a chair for Anne, which he then held politely until she was seated. She sunk down, uncomfortably aware of her aching feet and travel-stained appearance. Somewhat unfairly, she blamed Sir Mortimer for reminding her of this deplorable state of affairs; his comment had made her feel doubly fatigued. She jumped up again hurriedly, saying that she must go in search of some soap and water. Mr. Pontefract started from his post by the door as if to detain her, but she stayed him with a gesture, observing with dignity, 'I do not require your assistance, sir, for my toilette. I shall return in a moment, and will leave my pelisse as hostage, if you wish.'

Anne met his keen gaze unwaveringly. The tension in the air was palpable, but then Mr. Pontefract smiled, shrugged, and dismissed her with the pointed remark, 'No need, my dear. A lady's word is her bond, is it not?'

Anne flushed as the full implication of this shaft went home. She turned swiftly and nearly ran into the man bringing their ale. Composing herself, she waited until he had set down the tankards and then requested the necessary facilities. He nodded sullenly and Anne followed in his shuffling footsteps, lifting her skirts fastidiously to avoid the scraps and spills which littered the kitchen floor. The conditions which she encountered did not encourage her to linger; she washed her hands and face at the pump in the yard, dragged a comb through her hair, and returned to the taproom before the gentlemen had well begun their ale. They rose on her entry and this time it was Mr. Pontefract who sprang forward gallantly to hold her chair.

Anne took one sip of the ale and left the remainder, but the bread and cheese proved to be surprisingly good, and she revived sufficiently to ask curiously, 'Pray enlighten me. Why are you two gentlemen traveling together?'

Sir Mortimer sat back, lit his pipe, and replied offhandedly, 'I suggested that we should journey together, as it transpired that we both intended to visit the metropolis. We heard about the mill when we stopped for luncheon and decided to make a slight detour.'

Anne shuddered delicately. Aware of an irrational feeling of disappointment, she inquired haughtily, 'Then your journey had nothing to do with me?'

Sir Mortimer raised his eyebrows and suppressed a grin as he observed the petulant droop of her lips. He said calmly, 'My dear young lady, why should it? Your cousins were somewhat perturbed by your abrupt departure and I felt that my presence created an undue burden at such a time. Also I had promised my sister to return to London for a ball which she is giving next week, and it was always my intention to leave Lyme in good time for that event.'

Mr. Pontefract had been straining his ears, listening intently to this last remark. He now intervened roughly. 'Don't be deceived, Anne. I'll wager Vane isn't telling you his true motives, not by a long shot. When I arrived to visit you on a social call, your cousin Jack had already gone chasing off to Bristol in search of you and this fellow's curricle was at the door.'

He cast Mortimer a look of acute dislike. "Tis my belief he offered me a seat to keep me under his eye, for what reason I cannot imagine, since you are under my guardianship. The Prawne women were all in a flutter, much too agitated to keep a secret, if that was what you wished! They had your letter lying on the table and from it I deduced that you had gone to London to seek out that schoolmistress you think so much of, Chance or Chaunce, or whatever her name is. I informed your cousins that I had not wished to make a scene last night at the Tremaines, but that I had a legal claim and would not shirk my duty. It was then that Vane offered to take me up in his curricle, in order to come up with you as soon as possible, for I did not relish the thought of you traveling so far, fearing that you might fall in with undesirable company. And when we heard about the fight and realized what a mixed bunch of folk would be about, I knew that I should attend the mill, to be on hand to protect you in case of need.' His dark eyes gleamed with triumph as he added complacently, 'And so it has proved.'

Anne half-turned in her seat to face her tormentor. Two angry red spots glowed on her pale cheeks as she tossed her head. She retorted, icily, 'You are presumptuous, sir. And ... and disrespectful towards my cousins, whom I love dearly. If I must, I will return to my own family, but I totally reject your claims on me; your behaviour has forfeited any legal rights you may have and I will never marry you. I would die first!'

Mr. Pontefract was unmoved by this impassioned speech. 'No need to be so melodramatic, silly chit. Any court of law will uphold my authority. Isn't that so, Vane?'

'I regret, I was not paying attention. I was considering

what should be done. Obviously Miss Fairleigh cannot remain here; the crowds will be returning from the mill quite soon and I imagine a number of the spectators will stop here to quench their thirst.'

Roused from her other preoccupations, Anne exclaimed in dismay, 'My baggage is still on the coach. It must not go without me!' She stood up, much agitated, and the two men followed her example.

Sir Mortimer said coolly, 'Perhaps it will be best if you rejoin the coach. Wait here, if you please, while I settle the shot and bespeak my curricle. I will escort you to the coach and see you safely on your way.'

Anne nodded miserably, unaccountably hurt by his well-bred indifference to her plight. He strode over to the bar and pounded the worn surface with perhaps unnecessary force. When this did not achieve the desired result, he stamped through the back door leading to the stable yard, leaving Anne with Simon Pontefract. She bit her lip in vexation and eyed her guardian warily. She perceived that he was much incensed by the peremptory manner in which Sir Mortimer had taken command of the situation. His hands were clenched and his dark eyes flashed dangerously. Anne felt a certain sympathy with his reaction, but prudently stepped back and busied herself with adjusting her bonnet and drawing on her gloves.

'Confound him, insufferable fellow,' muttered Mr. Pontefract, along with several other epithets which Anne judged it wisest to ignore. 'If only I had brought my carriage,' he burst forth at last, his impotent rage subsiding as he became aware of Anne's silent presence.

He regarded her thoughtfully, his expression softening as he noted her pale face and large eyes filled with apprehension. He said gently, 'Anne my dearest girl, how could you run off and leave me? Had you no thought for my predicament, for the position in which you placed me? Your friend Mary told her parents such a taradiddle of nonsense that those Lovelaces nearly turned me out of their house. It took all my powers of persuasion to convince them that I would not harm a hair of your beautiful head.'

'Oh, yes, I know that your persuasive powers are considerable. Mr. and Mrs. Lovelace now believe me to be virtually unhinged,' responded Anne bitterly.

There was a faint sound from the corner by the fire, but neither Anne nor her companion noticed, so intent were they on one another. Mr. Pontefract advanced slowly towards her. She felt paralyzed; she wanted to run, but she could not move. Abruptly he pulled her to him, his fingers dug into her shoulders, and she could smell the ale on his breath, as he pressed his lips against hers. She struggled futilely for several moments, but realizing this was fruitless, she forced her body to relax and stood limp and passive in his arms. At once he released her and stood back.

The settle creaked as an elderly gentleman of large proportions rose, grunting, to his feet. At the same moment Mortimer reentered the taproom, whistling cheerfully. He stopped in mid-tune, his sharp glance traveling from Anne's flushed and indignant face to Simon's grinning one. Sir Mortimer found the grin particularly offensive.

'He kissed me!' exclaimed the affronted young lady.

The third member of the party muttered defiantly, 'Don't be missish, girl. What else should a man of flesh and blood do when left alone with his betrothed?'

Oblivious to the stranger, who was standing quietly watching the proceedings, Sir Mortimer regarded the pair before him with a cynical eye. 'Seems to me there may be a misunderstanding here, Pontefract,' he suggested lightly.

'Nonsense. Mind your own affairs, man,' blustered the ardent suitor.

'He only wants me for my fortune. He does not love

me. His behaviour was reprehensible – unpardonable!'
cried Anne.

Goaded, Simon Pontefract swung round on her
menacingly. Sir Mortimer leapt to protect Anne, caught
his head on a beam and staggered unsteadily, clutching
his forehead. Gamely he struggled forward, but Mr.
Pontefract was quick to perceive his advantage. He
squared to meet the onrush of Anne's champion, fists
upraised. With unerring aim and lightning speed, he
caught his opponent neatly on the jaw. There was an
unpleasant crack as bone met bone and Sir Mortimer
measured his length on the floor without a murmur.
Standing over his recumbent form, Simon said blithely,
'My apologies, Vane. I infinitely regret the necessity, but
needs must and, er, so forth.'

Sir Mortimer blinked and groaned; Mr. Pontefract
turned briskly to Anne. 'Come along,' he commanded,
'We will borrow Vane's curricle. His injuries are not
serious and I will send his groom in to attend to him.'

Anne stood her ground, regarding him with an
expression of mingled fury and disdain. When she did
not move, Simon's face became correspondingly grim
and determined. Anne had a fleeting vision of herself
being bundled unceremoniously across his shoulder like
a sack of potatoes. Whether such an indignity would
indeed have occurred must remain a matter of conjecture, for an unexpected diversion was created by the
elderly gentleman in riding boots, who interposed his
bulky cane purposefully between Mr. Pontefract and his
prey. The gentleman addressed Anne jovially.

'Josiah Henderson at your service. What's to do here,
young lady?'

'Oh, sir,' gasped Anne, injecting a world of loathing
into her tone, 'This man was seeking to force his
attentions on me and when Sir Mortimer sought to
intervene he hit him – as you can see.' She gestured to
indicate the inanimate form a few yards distant. She

continued, 'I am Anne Fairleigh and my home is Fernditch Hall in the county of Somerset. I was on my way to London when the coach suffered an accident ...' She paused, wondering how best to explain her present predicament.

Mr. Pontefract decided that he had been ignored long enough. He said irritably, 'This is a private matter, sir. I am Miss Fairleigh's guardian and also her betrothed.'

Her new defender bent his beetling brows on Anne's face. She shook her head pleadingly. He moved closer and possessed himself of one small hand, which he pressed in a comforting manner. She felt an instinctive liking for the gentleman, with his grizzled side-whiskers and neat, old-fashioned dress. Mr. Henderson frowned at Simon and said bluntly, 'For shame, sir, to have exhibited such violence before a lady.'

Sullen and defiant, the younger man was about to protest, but Mr. Henderson silenced him by remarking, 'No need to explain. I myself overheard and witnessed sufficient to comprehend the situation.' He turned to Anne with a courtly bow and added, 'Didn't think it my place to intervene at first. I was half-asleep when you came in, bin up since the small hours with a difficult case of a widow and her son. The lad's accused of highway robbery and I'm the local magistrate, ye understand, missy. Anyway, to cut a long story short, I sent my man, Jem, off to watch the mill while I attended to business and arranged to meet him here. My duties having been discharged to the best of my ability, I sought refreshment and then indulged in a post-prandial nap, from which I was roused by yonder unfortunate gentleman thumping vigorously to summon attention. He departed for the kitchen quarters and while he was absent you, young lady, mentioned the name Lovelace.'

Anne nodded, puzzled and intrigued. Mr. Henderson went on, 'Now I have distant connections of that name. My wife's brother, George Gower, is married to Ralph

Lovelace's sister Mary. We are a close-knit family and although we do not meet as frequently as I would wish, we correspond regularly. In recent months there has been much speculation in the family letters concerning the whereabouts of a young lady, a friend of Ralph's daughter, also a Mary, his daughter, I mean. Dear me, how complicated this all is! It seems that Mary's friend was staying with the Lovelaces, prior to her wedding, but she ran away and left no hint of her destination. Naturally Ralph was much concerned; he felt partly responsible for her flight and immediately contacted all his trusted connections in an effort to trace her.'

Mr. Henderson stopped and eyed Anne shrewdly. She exclaimed impulsively, 'But Mr. Lovelace was not at all responsible –' Then, realizing that she had been trapped, she paused in dismay.

'Don't look so stricken, my dear,' said Mr. Henderson kindly, 'I knew who you were as soon as you told me your name. I once had the pleasure of attending a lecture given by your father at Ralph's club. A truly eminent scholar; we dined with him after his talk. Not really in my line. Horace was it, or perhaps Virgil? I'm more interested in the future than the past, but he was a stimulating speaker. I was sorry to see his obituary in the *Post*. If my memory serves me correctly, you also attended that lecture, Mr. Pontefract?'

It was Simon's turn to be taken aback. He nodded and felt for his eyeglass, through which he surveyed Mr. Henderson in dawning recognition. After a moment he dropped the glass and executed a graceful bow. Unwillingly Anne admired the smooth manner in which he masked any feeling of discomfiture. He straightened and said politely, 'Pray accept my sincere apologies for failing to know you at once. The very different circumstances and my overmastering concern for Miss Fairleigh's welfare must serve as my excuse.'

Mr. Henderson replied curtly, 'I, too, am concerned

for this young lady's welfare. Tell me, missy, where have ye bin hidin' all these weeks and what has the other young man to do with the matter?'

Anne reflected inconsequentially that Mr. Henderson must be a good Justice of the Peace; his questions were sharp and to the point. At the mention of Sir Mortimer, she glanced guiltily in her erstwhile champion's direction. He was beginning to stir. Anne ran across the room and fell on her knees by his side, crying remorsefully, 'Oh, how thoughtless we have been. Please help me, sirs, I fear he requires medical aid. Look, his face is bleeding and his eye is swollen. Perhaps his wound has reopened.'

Anne's urgent plea brought both men to join her. Simon carried with him the ale which Anne had not drunk and splashed it liberally on Mortimer's face. Mortimer sat up, choking and spluttering. He was a sorry sight. The ale and blood mixed together and ran down to stain his neckcloth and waistcoat; in fact his habitual sartorial elegance had deserted him and Mortimer was uncomfortably aware of the blemishes, as he attempted ineffectually to staunch the flow, with one badly stained silk handkerchief.

'Dem!' he said.

Mr. Henderson looked him over in silence, his eyes twinkling. Anne suppressed an inane desire to laugh, bit her lip, and said, 'Mr. Henderson, allow me to present Sir Mortimer Vane of Shawcross Manor. Mr. Josiah Henderson.'

'Who the devil ...?' Mortimer looked up, winced, and raised a hand to his throbbing brow.

'Oh, do lie back. Would you like us to summon a physician? Let me put my pelisse under your head.' Gently, Anne pushed him back on the makeshift pillow. Still on her knees, she appealed to Mr. Henderson. 'Dear sir, this gentleman is a gallant soldier who has been visiting my relatives, the Misses Prawne of Lyme Regis. I met him while staying under their roof.'

Mr. Henderson meditated profoundly for a moment, his lips pursed to aid concentration, one hand clasping the stout cane, the other drumming on a chair back. His keen gray eyes came to rest on Mortimer. He addressed his firmly. 'Well, sir, I am a magistrate and was acquainted with Miss Fairleigh's father. She has need of my protection and it seems to me that your eye and other scratches could benefit from the ministrations of my good wife. I propose that you both return with me to Natherscombe House, which is but a few miles from here on the Lyndhurst Road. My man, Jem, should be here shortly with the carriage.'

He turned to Anne. 'As for you, missy, it would be a pleasure to introduce you to my wife and daughter if you would care to accept our hospitality for tonight. Mrs. Henderson is a real lady; some folks say she married beneath her, but we've bin wed nigh on thirty year come Michaelmas Day and barely a cross word spoken between us. You put me in mind of her when she was a girl, the same dark curls and sparkling eyes.'

Anne smiled and answered warmly, 'You are very kind to a stranger, sir. I am reluctant to trespass on your generosity, but I fear there is no good alternative. I cannot remain here.' She hesitated, 'I wonder if perhaps the coach is mended.'

A new voice broke in on their deliberations. 'If'n ye means the stage, miss, 'tis in the stable yard. Come in jest ahead o' me, but it won't be leavin' yet awhile, for one of the horses is lame and some of the tracings need repair.' He turned to Mr. Henderson. 'Here I be, master, an' ye owes me a crown piece, sir.'

'Ah, Jem, ye rascal, you've come in a good hour,' exclaimed the gentleman, fishing in his pocket for a coin. He regarded his manservant between narrowed lids, holding the coin in the palm of his hand.

The man grinned. 'I told ye yon Chris was too slow to ketch a cold, now didn' I, sir?'

'So The Sledgehammer won?' Mr. Henderson queried ruefully.

'Aye, Mr. Josiah, jest like I said. There was some nice footwork. Chris the Cobbler had the edge for skill, but the claret flowed pretty freely, the Cobbler lost two of his ivories an' in the end The Sledge'ammer felled 'im wiv a blow that would've felled an oak.'

Mr. Henderson sighed. 'Hum. Pity about the local man. But the clarets been flowing here, too, Jem.' He handed over the crown and stood aside to reveal Sir Mortimer, who was struggling yet again to rise. Mr. Henderson stepped forward to assist him and Jem hopped nimbly to take his other arm. For the first time, Anne noticed that the man had only one leg, but he was a lean, wiry little body, and strong for his size.

Between them they soon had Mortimer propped in a chair. The invalid grunted his thanks and then asked Jem abruptly, 'Old soldier?'

'Yessir,' responded the man, instinctively knuckling his eyebrow. 'India, sir, under Sir Arthur as he then was. Afore your time, I expect, sir.' The two men exchanged knowing smiles.

'How is it that military men always recognize one another?' pondered Mr. Henderson.

Jem looked sheepish and Sir Mortimer, recalled to a sense of his surroundings, said with dignity, 'I am much recovered. If you will be so good as to summon my groom, I will escort you to Natherscombe House or to a respectable inn, whichever you wish, Miss Fairleigh.'

Anne looked at him doubtfully. 'I don't think you are well enough to drive, sir,' she said, glancing at Mr. Henderson for support. He agreed and gestured to the other end of the room, which was rapidly filling with spectators seeking refreshment after the fight.

''Tis over-late to be journeying and there's some rough elements in this throng. I'd say you're safer with me and Jem tonight.'

Mortimer stiffened. 'Are you suggesting I'm not capable of protecting this lady?'

'Yes,' replied Mr. Josiah bluntly.

'What about me?' interposed Mr. Pontefract, peevishly aware that the others had all but forgotten his existence. 'I'm Anne's guardian.'

'Your conduct in that capacity is open to serious question, and besides, no man who gives me a black eye is riding in my vehicle,' observed Mortimer, in a tone which brooked no argument.

'I imagine the stage will soon be repaired,' said Mr. Henderson placidly. 'I suggest you avail yourself of the seat left vacant by Miss Fairleigh.'

This remark reminded Anne that her carpetbag had been abandoned in the coach. Jem was ordered to extract Anne's possessions, find Mortimer's groom, and bring Mr. Henderson's carriage to the door with all possible speed. Sir Mortimer bowed to the inevitable with secret relief. His head ached abominably and he felt sick and dizzy. He allowed himself to be tucked up with a rug in the carriage, while his groom followed obediently with the curricle. He soon fell into an uneasy slumber, while Anne and Mr. Henderson conversed quietly and kept a watchful eye on the afflicted gentleman.

Mr. Henderson probed the intricacies of Anne's story with characteristic shrewdness and by the time they reached Natherscombe House, he had a very fair understanding of the situation.

Meanwhile, left alone at Tricketts Cross, Mr. Simon Pontefract kicked his heels and imbibed several more tankards of strong, home-brewed beer. Thus fortified, he devised various cunning stratagems to win Miss Fairleigh. Mr. Pontefract was not a man to admit defeat easily.

IX

Natherscombe House

A few moments later Mr. Henderson descended upon his household like a small tidal wave, carrying all before him. He sent a groom running to assist Sir Mortimer and bounded up the shallow, well-worn steps, sweeping Anne in front of him through the open door. He greeted his butler, tossed his hat and cane on a side table, and bellowed for his wife at the top of his lungs. There was a flurry of footsteps and muffled voices above stairs. Satisfied, the master of the house turned and strode back to Anne, who had been divested of her bonnet and cloak by a tall, spare individual with a pale, austere face and long, bony fingers.

Anne's host flung open a door on the right of the paneled hall and they entered a large, low-ceilinged room, comfortably furnished and fragrant with the scent of roses. A log fire was burning brightly in the stone fireplace and cheerful tapestries hung on the walls. The curtains had not yet been drawn and Anne noticed a deep window seat, littered with cushions and books. Mr. Henderson beckoned Anne to the fire; she was about to comply with this suggestion when a light step sounded and a young woman, perhaps in her late twenties, appeared.

Mr. Henderson did his best to frown. 'Here you are at last,' he said gruffly. 'Not a soul about to welcome us – unless you count that beanpole, Tompkins. A fine reception, indeed!'

'Hush, Papa, you know how sensitive he is!' The young lady advanced to kiss her father, smiling mischievously. He returned the salute heartily, then said, 'This is my daughter, Drusilla, Miss Fairleigh. Miss Anne Fairleigh, m'dear.'

'How do you do, Miss Henderson?' Anne held out her hand. The two ladies appraised one another as they shook hands. Anne saw a tall, angular woman, with a plain, but interesting face. Miss Henderson had been blessed with her father's square jaw and mobile, humorous mouth, hinting at a character possessing qualities of stubbornness and determination. The somewhat harsh lines were softened by a quantity of thick, wavy brown hair and serene violet-blue eyes, set wide apart.

Miss Henderson's smile deepened as she returned Anne's regard. She greeted her gently, accepted her calmly, and, to Anne's relief, wasted no time on questions. Instead she addressed her fidgeting father. 'Mama will be down directly, Papa. She merely ran to put on a fresh cap when she realized we had a visitor.'

'Two visitors, my gel,' corrected Mr. Josiah cheerfully, as the cadaverous Tompkins ushered Mortimer into the room. Drusilla was unable to repress a gasp as the glory of the newcomer's black eye and bloodstained apparel met her startled gaze.

Sir Mortimer rose nobly to the occasion. 'My profound apologies for this unexpected intrusion, ma'am,' he began, bowing with grace and sweeping the floor with his curly brimmed beaver.

'Nay, lad,' broke in his host, unceremoniously, 'No need for that. We bid you welcome to Natherscombe House. 'Low me to present my daughter, Drusilla. Sir Mortimer Vane.'

Before Miss Henderson could do more than acknowledge the introduction with a curtsey, the door opened once more to admit a plump, sturdy little figure, dressed in a purple high waisted round gown, several years behind the mode and displaying iron gray curls in surprising profusion beneath a becoming cap. The little lady was speaking in a rush of words as she crossed the threshold.

'Josiah, my love, you might have told me you intended to bring us guests. But no matter, welcome, my dears. Poor young sir, what has happened to your eye? Did you attend the dreadful mill? I'm forever telling my husband you find nought but rough company in such place. Not that you are rough yourself, sir, far from it, as I can see very well, even without my spectacles. Drusilla, run and tell Polly to find a raw steak and send up warming pans to the pink and blue bedchambers – or, perhaps we need but one bedchamber. Are you man and wife, my dear?'

Anne shook her head quickly and Mr. Henderson raised his hand, saying firmly, 'Hold your horses, Charlotte. This lady is Miss Anne Fairleigh and this is Sir Mortimer Vane. Explanations can wait until our guests are comfortable. It has been a long day.'

Mrs. Henderson blinked twice, then nodded briskly. 'Of course, Josiah. Drusilla, show Miss Fairleigh to the pink chamber, and I'll have her bag sent up.'

'I'll go with Sir Mortimer, Charlotte. Let us but rid ourselves of our dust, while you see to our dinner and we'll join you shortly.'

Mrs. Henderson ran to kiss her husband on the tip of his nose, pulling him down from his greater height to do so. Then she stepped back, her eyes twinkling. 'I do so love a masterful man!' she exclaimed. 'It shall be as you say. Dinner in half an hour. Away with you now.'

She shepherded them all before her into the hall, indicated the stairs and candles with an airy wave of her pretty, soft hand, and tripped daintily over the flagstones which led down the long corridor to the nether regions.

On the first landing the stairs divided. The gentlemen took the right fork, while Anne followed Miss Henderson to the left. The ladies went halfway along a passage and entered a spacious chamber, filled with modern furniture and hung with pink draperies. The room smelled sweetly of lavender. Correctly interpreting Anne's surprised expression, Miss Henderson said, 'Papa will have nothing changed downstairs. He likes things to be old and comfortable, but he gives Mama a free rein here.'

'It is delightful,' replied Anne sincerely, as she absorbed the simple, elegant furnishings, softened to comfort by a thick, rose-pink carpet; the walls adorned with pink-and-white striped paper and the marble washstand, where stood a china basin and ewer ornamented with rosebuds.

Miss Henderson crossed the room to check that there was hot water in the jug and clean towels on the rail. Satisfied, she smiled pleasantly and said, 'It suits you, with your dark hair and creamy complexion. I cannot abide pink for myself – too insipid! Do you have everything you need, Miss Fairleigh?' She indicated Anne's carpetbag, already open on the bed.

'I believe so. You are very kind. Pray call me Anne. I do so hope we may be friends,' suggested Anne impulsively. 'I believe you are connected by marriage to my dearest friend, Mary Lovelace of Bristol.'

Drusilla nodded, her eyes widening as she absorbed fully Anne's identity and linked her with the young lady of the family correspondence. Tactfully, she made no direct comment, merely saying, 'Yes, indeed, although I have not seen Mary for some years, but I hear news of her in Mama's letters. I should be happy to be your friend, Anne. I confess I have frequently felt lonely and in need of congenial company. One can be very isolated in the country. My only brother died of the smallpox when I was six and Mama was terrified that I would contract something and be carried off, too, though I'm strong as an ox. Therefore, she refused to send me away to school. Now most of the girls my age are married, with children in the nursery. Papa offered to send me to London for a season, but I am so plain and naturally reserved I knew I would not take and I persuaded him it was not worth the expense and disruption to the household, for Mama would have felt obliged to go with me. I count myself fortunate to have such kind and loving parents and my life is quite full with reading and domestic duties, so I should not repine, but ...' she sighed, brushed her skirt with long, tapering fingers in an eloquent gesture, and finished smoothly, ' ... But this is not the moment for confidences. I'll leave you in peace.'

She moved towards the door, but Anne caught her hand, exclaiming, 'You do not see yourself as others see you. I will not allow you to malign yourself unjustly. Your countenance has far too much animation to be called plain! I know how it is when one is too much alone – one broods and loses all sense of proportion. I did go to school, but my home was very quiet. My mother died many years ago. I have no brothers or sisters and recently I lost my father, so I envy you your charming parents.'

Observing the older girl's eyes to be bright with unshed tears, Anne gave her a quick, affectionate embrace and released her, saying lightly, 'I must make haste. I think even charming parents do not care to be kept waiting for their dinners!'

Drusilla grinned, nodded, and departed, leaving Anne to make her toilette. Her wardrobe was limited, but she rummaged in her bag and unearthed a simple gown in jonquil crêpe de Chine, clean, but crumpled. She shook it out and slipped it on. Then she let down her hair, which was tangled after the day's confinement. She brushed it hard and threaded a yellow ribbon through the curls to give some semblance of order. Fearing the worst, she avoided the looking glass, rummaged again for her old black velvet slippers and completed her preparations by tucking a lace handkerchief in her sash. Breathing rather fast, she descended the stairs as the dinner bell rang.

In the sitting room she found Mortimer discoursing with the family. Anne noted with amusement that he had not wasted his time; his appearance was in every respect *comme il faut*, although his visage still bore the marks of earlier combat.

Mrs. Henderson came and took Anne's hand to lead her into the small circle, saying kindly, 'My dear, you are most welcome. Everyone in the family has been concerned for you. But let us eat first and we can talk later.'

Dinner was an ample meal and the travelers did full justice to the efforts of Mrs. Henderson's cook. The atmosphere of the house was informal; the servants were polite, but obviously considered as people rather than furniture by Anne's hosts. The conversation flowed easily, touching on a wide range of subjects. They did not always agree, but good humour prevailed. Anne stoutly defended Lord Byron, supported, somewhat unexpectedly, by Mrs. Henderson, while the gentlemen condemned him as a vain fribble. Mr. Henderson declared roundly that he was a poet of no great distinction and had received a great deal of totally unmerited attention because of his rank and so-called "romantic" life-style. Almost choking over her soup in her indignation, Anne demanded to know whether the gentlemen had ever read any of his lordship's works.

'Yes, indeed,' retorted Mr. Josiah, before Mortimer could do more than throw up his hand in protest, 'I bought that nonsense *Childe Arthur*, or *Childe Harold*, or whatever it was, for Drusilla, and a very dreary time I had of it thumbing the pages on my way back from town. Give me Sir Walter Scott anyday. I prefer his prose, but if it's poetry you want, what can surpass *The Lay of the Last Minstrel* or *Marmion*, hey, young lady?'

Anne accepted this challenge with enthusiasm and held forth for several minutes on the superior poetic gifts possessed by Lord Byron. Drusilla listened intently and when Anne paused for breath, she said thoughtfully, 'I believe Lord Byron is undoubtedly a greater poet than Sir Walter Scott. He is a genius, in fact, but I do wish he would not dabble in politics.'

Sir Mortimer smiled at her across the table. 'He is the darling of Whig society. No social function is complete without him. You feel he should be above such petty involvements, Miss Henderson?'

'Most definitely,' responded Drusilla, laughing.

Mrs. Henderson sipped her wine meditatively. 'I really do not see how we can compare the two men at all sensibly; they are such very different personalities and their works are not at all in the same style. Sir Walter is more interested in history.'

'My dear Charlotte,' interjected her husband, tapping the table for attention, 'please pass the saltcellar. Scott writes to amuse and entertain. He thinks of his readers. Byron is a conceited fellow who spends too much time thinking about himself and his feelings. But you are right, as usual. Aside from the fact that they are both poets and see the world through "romantic" spectacles, they have very little in common.'

Everyone laughed and agreed to differ.

The talk drifted to the recent arrival of the Duke of Wellington in London and thence, by degrees, to Sir Mortimer's time with him in the Peninsula. The Hendersons showed genuine interest in his army career and by dint of unobtrusive questions, succeeded in drawing out their rather prickly guest, so that Anne scarcely recognized the cool, reserved gentleman she had known in Lyme. He seemed quite unconscious of his scar or his bruised eye, as he described, with a wealth of amusing anecdote, his life as an aide-de-camp.

'Did the Duke keep a good table, Sir Mortimer?' inquired Mrs. Henderson curiously.

'Not half so good as yours, ma'am,' Mortimer replied promptly, as Tompkins supplied him with a second helping of roast venison. 'In the ordinary way his chef, Thornton, produced beef, mutton, potatoes; potatoes, mutton, beef. The Beau loved his cup of strong black tea and there was always good champagne and claret on hand, but in general the victuals were unremarkable.'

Anne caught Sir Mortimer's eye; she raised her eyebrows delicately.

'Why do you call him "The Beau"? I have always understood that his nose destroyed any pretensions to handsomeness,' she remarked provokingly.

Mortimer swallowed the bait at once. He lowered his gaze to his wineglass and idly twirled the stem. 'Wellington's features are most distinguished, Miss Fairleigh.' He spoke defensively and Anne assumed an expression of polite attention. He continued, 'Wellington never wore military uniform except at formal reviews, but he was habitually neat and plain in his attire. He wore a white stock rather than the more usual black one and a cocked hat without the cock's feathers.'

Anne decided to refrain from teasing him further. 'I must bow to your superior knowledge,' she said sweetly.

Mortimer's lips twitched sardonically. He bent his head and addressed himself to his vegetables.

'It is a pity we cannot see the Duke for ourselves, Anne. Then we could form a more definite opinion. The portraits I have seen in the monthly magazines are undoubtedly flattering and probably as misleading as the caricatures,' Drusilla concluded fairly.

Anne, seated next to her new friend, could not resist the temptation to reply mischievously, 'Whom would you rather meet, Drusilla, the Duke or Lord Byron? I vow I cannot decide.' They debated the point back and forth with animation.

Mr. and Mrs. Henderson exchanged indulgent smiles, noting with approval the friendly relationship established between the two young ladies and the fact that they were already on first-name terms. Sir Mortimer did not deign to take part in the discussion, but listened with an aloof, world-weary expression well-calculated to irritate Miss Fairleigh.

Nettled, she said directly, 'You find our discussion trivial I think, sir.'

In a tone of ineffable boredom he replied politely, 'Not at all.'

'For love is heaven, and heaven is love,' observed Mr. Henderson, unexpectedly, his piercing glance resting on each young person in turn. Three puzzled faces met his regard, awaiting enlightenment, but his wife experienced no such difficulty.

'You are thinking of Scott, *The Lay of the Last Minstrel* are you not, Josiah? Such a wise man. And you, too, of course. But while we are on the subject of trivia, would you care for some apple pie, my dear?'

Again they smiled at one another; a smile of deep affection and understanding, which made them appear surprisingly youthful. Anne, intercepting their look, thought how wonderful it must be to be so in harmony with another human being.

'If it's well-stuffed with cloves and spices. I can't abide watery apples,' grunted Mr. Henderson, sniffing the air suspiciously, while the butler and a little maidservant passed the plates and set out custard and cream, to accompany the pudding. It evidently passed muster, for it soon disappeared. The servants withdrew and Mr. Henderson folded his napkin, pushed back his chair, and beamed at the company.

'Now, Miss Fairleigh, Sir Mortimer, I trust you are not in a hurry to leave us. I recommend a quiet day with a

rod by the lake, young sir. Miss Anne needs a respite to
reflect on her position. And I know 'twould give my
daughter great pleasure to have time to become better
acquainted with you, missy. I will send word to Bristol,
to assure the Lovelaces that you are in safe hands.'

The ladies added their entreaties; surrounded by so
much warmth and kindness, Anne wavered and allowed
her polite objections to be overcome.

Not so, Sir Mortimer. The stern path of duty stood
plain before him and he was not one to shirk it, despite
the fact that his head throbbed and his jaw ached. He
said firmly, 'I thank you for your hospitality, but I
regret that I am obliged to convey Miss Fairleigh to her
cousins in Lyme. They will be worried about her
well-being. When I return on my way to Town, perhaps
I can avail myself of your generous offer.'

Anne's lips set mutinously. 'If you regret it, why do it,
sir? I am not your responsibility and I have no intention
of returning to Lyme. I will write to my cousins and
assure them of my safety, but I am determined to go on
to London.'

There ensued a moment of tense silence, while they
glared at one another across the table. Then Sir
Mortimer said frostily, 'Very well, I see you are
determined to be obstinate and continue capering
wildly about the countryside, disregarding those who
care for you.' He caught himself, startled by his own
vehemence; uncomfortably aware that Miss Anne
Fairleigh could rouse his hackles as no female had ever
done before – not even Stephanie, in her youth. Of
recent years he had been famed far and wide among his
friends for his good-natured indifference to the fair
sex. He drew a deep breath and said more calmly, 'I
presume you have relatives or friends waiting to receive
you in Town?'

The angry glint in his eye subsided. He turned to his
hosts with an apologetic smile, saying bluntly, 'Forgive

my ill manners. This situation must seem very strange to you, as I confess it is to me. I suggest you enlighten us, Miss Fairleigh.'

His crisp, no-nonsense tone did nothing to allay Anne's seething resentment. Lifting her head and fixing her gaze on some distant object, she responded coolly, 'I have already explained my circumstances and intentions to Mr. Henderson. I am most grateful, Sir Mortimer, for your efforts on my behalf, but I see no necessity for you to involve yourself further in my affairs, when 'tis plain you find me a nuisance and a hindrance to your plans. I wish you would be on your way and leave me alone. I can manage perfectly well and I prefer to be independent. Men are so organizing and – and overbearing,' she concluded wrathfully, wishing that her voice did not shake and her hands would stop trembling.

'Well, of all perverse females, this takes the cake!' exclaimed Mortimer in disgust.

'Hey, hey, hold hard, lass,' Mr. Henderson intervened, glancing helplessly at his wife, who leapt quickly to her feet and put a comforting arm round Anne's shoulders, saying, 'Come, my dear. You're very tired and everything will seem clearer in the morning. Let us leave the gentlemen to their wine and we will have a nice dish of tea before you retire. We only want to help and I'm sure I speak for Sir Mortimer, too. Drusilla.'

'Yes, Mama.' Miss Henderson rose obediently and the gentlemen courteously followed suit. At the door Anne paused to say, 'Good night, dear Mr. Henderson, my heartfelt thanks for all your kindness. Sir Mortimer.'

A brief, impudent curtsey accompanied her last words and Mortimer muttered 'Minx', as the door closed. The older gentleman nodded astutely, then passed the decanter with a jocular recommendation to 'Drink up, sir, and drown your sorrows.'

Mortimer frowned, took a hearty gulp, and lounged

back in his chair. In companionable silence the two men went through the solemn ritual of filling and lighting their pipes. They puffed until a satisfying cloud of smoke rings wreathed above their heads.

Mr. Henderson tapped the stem of his pipe on the table. 'Don't be too hard on the lass,' he advised. 'She's over-young for the problems she's had to face, and her experience with men has not been of the best, but I like her spirit.'

'Her head is crammed full of notions of independence. I suspect Mary Wollstonecraft's writings sit with her Bible on Miss Fairleigh's bedside table,' replied Mortimer bitterly. He relit his pipe, grinned ruefully, and added, 'She and m'sister, Hester, would get along wonderfully. Before I joined the army back in 1804, Hester and I were always arguing about the status of women in our society, and I must admit that many women's talents and abilities are stunted through lack of outlets for their energies. Hester solved the problem by writing novels and supporting herself and my mother after our father died in debt. My fortune was tied up and I was still a schoolboy. Eventually she married very happily, but she persists in her scribbling, "to keep her mind alive", so she says.'

'Bless my soul, now I know why the name Vane struck a chord in my memory. M'wife, sir, is an avid reader of Miss Vane's works. I always have to look out for a new volume when I attend the Winchester Assizes. Drusilla, now, she's a great reader, too much so, strains her eyes. She's mighty taken with Miss Austen. I enjoyed her *Pride and Prejudice* last year myself, though I would hate to think all the ladies are as observant of the foibles of mankind as that young woman. But Miss Vane is married, ye say?'

'Why yes, she still writes under her maiden name, but she's been the wife of Hugo Jermyn, my Lord Montfort, these ten years.'

Mr. Henderson absorbed this information with interest. 'I know of Montfort. Read his speeches in the Lords every week in the *Gazette*. Very sound. A Sussex family, I believe.'

Mortimer nodded. 'His estate at Huntsgrove borders on my own Shawcross.'

'And are ye thinkin' to set up as a farmer now the wars be over?' pursued Mr. Henderson.

Mortimer grimaced. 'If they are. It's hard to think of the great Boney locked up like a caged lion on Elba.'

'Aye, and just as dangerous. He still has quite a following in France, I gather.'

The two men fell to talking of the wars and the political situation as the wine passed back and forth and the candles burned low. They were just about to separate for the night, when Mr. Henderson said casually, 'Ye'll stay tomorrow and give that eye a chance to simmer down, lad. We can discuss matters then. But I will say this – Miss Anne needs protecting from that Pontefract fellow, who's of a mind to wed her for her money.'

Mortimer wrinkled his brow thoughtfully. 'Her cousins, the Prawne ladies, explained the situation to me briefly before I left Lyme in pursuit of Miss Fairleigh. Simon Pontefract arrived as I was setting out and I thought it safer to offer him a ride than to leave him to his own devices. I did not realize Miss Fairleigh was an heiress until she accused Pontefract of being a fortune hunter when we came up with her at the inn just before the fight. She had been using the assumed name of Miss Milton in Lyme and I thought she was a poor relation. I did not connect her with the Somerset family. Her grandfather and my father were gambling cronies. Old Sir Edwin was a hard-living man, a fearless huntsman and a rake who saw three wives into their graves. I met him once or twice; he had a tremendous sense of humour and I think his son, Anne's father, was a great

disappointment to him, being bookish and sickly. But I
daresay I may be wrong, it was a long time ago.'

Mr. Henderson sighed. 'I don't know your society
gossip, lad. I grew up in the north. I made my pile in the
cotton trade and married the squire's daughter. It was a
different world. Mrs. Henderson's mother was a
Fortescue and she hated living in Lancashire. Through
her my Charlotte inherited this house and we moved
south soon after Drusilla was born. Now I have my
investments and enough brass to be a respected pillar of
the community, but I'll never be accepted, not the way
Charlotte and Drusilla are – trade, ye see – not that I
care a jot so long as the womenfolk are happy. I have my
fun and stir up these Hampshire families with my plain
way o' speaking.'

Sir Mortimer grinned. 'I count it an honour to have
made your acquaintance, sir.' He blinked owlishly and
said a trifle thickly, 'I can't believe Mith Fairleigh –
Anne, is the Fernditch heiress.'

Mr. Henderson shook his head and said with careful
distinctness, 'Forget it, sir. Perhaps we've said too much,
the wine loosens the tongue. It'll all sort itself out in
time. Are ye minded to court her yourself, lad? Forgive
an old man's curiosity, but I've taken a rare liking to the
wench, and so has my Drusilla, and she don't make
friends easy, more's the pity, being more inclined to
laugh at folk than to love them.'

Sir Mortimer sobered abruptly. 'I scarcely know Miss
Fairleigh,' he began. His eyes met his host's and
something in Mr. Henderson's kindly regard obliged
him to say honestly, 'I thought she and my friend Jack
Davenport would make a match of it, but now I'm not so
sure. I suspect she gave him his congé and I am hoping
he will console himself with Miss Meg Oliphant, an old
family friend. However, as you said, sir, Miss Fairleigh is
very young and beautiful and she should meet many
eligible men before she makes her choice. It would be

unpardonable of me to take advantage of her inexperience. I am too old for her and in any event she finds me repulsive.' He tapped his scar meaningfully and Mr. Henderson observed with concern the deep, painful hurt in his expressive eyes. Unable to endure the other man's sympathy, Sir Mortimer raised his glass and said lightly, 'Do not distress yourself on my account, sir. We should not suit. You saw how the sparks always fly between us. I assure you we spend more time in quarreling than in rational conversation.'

Mr. Henderson rose stiffly. He looked down on Sir Mortimer and replied tranquilly, 'So did Charlotte and I; so do all young lovers. You're oversensitive, lad, and fear rejection. Well, don't be too long making up your mind. She'll have the young men flocking like bees round a honey pot when she gets to London, if I'm not mistaken, for she has a face to match her fortune.'

Sir Mortimer favoured Mr. Henderson with one of his rare, sweet smiles and said with commendable dignity, 'This is absurd. The sooner I return Miss Fairleigh to the protection of the Misses Prawne and discharge my obligation, the better for all concerned.'

He stalked across the room to close the window. Mr. Josiah chuckled as he snuffed the candles, 'I reckon Miss Anne will have a word to say on that subject in the morning. Good night, Sir Mortimer, sleep tight!'

No reply was vouchsafed to this sally, and the two men retired to their respective chambers, treading softly so as not to disturb the sleeping household.

X

London Bound

Mortimer passed a restless night, filled with disturbed dreams in which the face of Stephanie Tremaine would suddenly dissolve into the face of Anne Fairleigh, who smiled and beckoned as she rode ahead, always out of reach; the early morning mists swirled and a man stepped out from a little copse of beech trees. He ran forward, waving his arms; the horse shied and reared, tossing the rider to the ground, where the lady lay very quiet and still.

The man looked up at Mortimer. 'She's beyond your protection for good,' said Simon Pontefract triumphantly.

Mortimer woke with a start to find the sun shining brightly between the blue velvet curtains and a maid standing by his bedside presenting him with a cup of steaming hot chocolate. She said cheerfully, 'Good mornin', sir. 'Tis six o'clock and I'm to tell you the master's waitin' below with rods and tackle.'

He sat up gingerly, wincing at the pain of his bruised eye, which felt about twice its normal size. His head throbbed and he groaned, clasping his hand to his brow.

'It's a luvly mornin' sir. You drink this and I'll fetch you some nice, 'ot water to shave with,' said the girl encouragingly, as she handed him the cup.

It was indeed a perfect summer's day, warm, with a light breeze. Mortimer's jaded spirits revived in the open air and he and Mr. Henderson returned at noon, sharp-set from their angling exertions. The ladies had not been idle in their absence, but had arranged all between them; however, they prudently suppressed their enthusiasm and listened with unwonted interest to a detailed description of the finer points of catching a carp, until the needs of the inner men were satisfied.

Mr. Henderson was more attuned to devious female wiles than the younger gentleman and after a little he became suspicious. When he heard his daughter, who had learned how to fish almost in her cradle, ask Sir Mortimer how much bait he used, followed by Anne remarking ingenuously, 'But when does one know it is time to reel in something?' he gave vent to a loud guffaw.

'Doing it rather too brown, my dears,' he exclaimed, adding, 'Come, Mrs. Henderson, I want a word with you in private, if you please.'

The conjugal tête-à-tête took a little time and when Mr. and Mrs. Henderson emerged from their sanctum in the library, they found that the young people had gravitated to the garden, where they were seated on a rug in the shade of a large willow playing with the kitchen cat's latest litter. At least Anne and Drusilla were playing with the kittens, who were pouncing on dangling bits of ribbon and string. Sir Mortimer was propped comfortably against the tree bole, puffing his pipe and keeping a wary eye on the kitchen cat who sat beside him, her tail lashing gently to and fro.

'You're making Judy uneasy, Drusilla. Pray, put the kittens in the basket and while you're in the kitchen ask Tompkins to bring us some tea and my parasol if you please, dear,' requested Mrs. Henderson, settling in the wicker chair which her husband produced for her comfort.

Drusilla gathered up the furry brood and disappeared through the arch into the kitchen garden, with Judy stalking majestically in her wake.

'I shall fall asleep if I sit here for long,' murmured Mr. Henderson, closing his eyes and lifting his face towards the sun.

His wife leaned across and tapped him energetically. 'No, you will do no such thing, sir. The tea will be here directly and we have something to discuss when Drusilla returns.' She felt Sir Mortimer's keen gaze and said hastily, 'Look, Anne, over there by the sweet peas, do you see that beautiful butterfly? What is it, Josiah? I can never remember names, but I think it so cruel to stick pins through them and put them in glass cases. I wonder why people do it.'

They speculated idly on the motives of butterfly collectors until Drusilla reappeared with refreshments.

When everyone was served, Mrs. Henderson broached her proposal. She began by saying that she and Drusilla were now in Anne's confidence and shared her view that a return to Lyme would be inadvisable at present. Her bright, birdlike glance swept round the circle and came to rest on Sir Mortimer, who was frowning ominously. She said persuasively, 'Mr. Henderson and I are agreed that we should go to Town and hire a house for a month or two, so that Drusilla can enjoy the sights of this special season, and it would give us great pleasure if Anne would accompany us as our guest. It would be much more amusing for Drusilla if she had a friend to go about with and it will do her good to get her head out of her books and laundry lists. We suggest that we wait here for a week or two, until lodgings can be arranged, and in the meanwhile we can send to Lyme for your belongings, Anne.'

Anne hesitated. 'You are so kind, dear Mr. and Mrs. Henderson. There is nothing I should like more than to accompany you and Drusilla to London. But you have already done so much and I cannot put you to further expense on my behalf,' she paused and added delicately, 'Perhaps if you would permit me to travel to

Town with you, I could visit you while staying with Miss Chaunce.'

Mr. Henderson intervened, saying bluntly, 'I know that is what you said to Mrs. Henderson this morning, but she and I have put our heads together and feel you would be safer under our roof. You will more than repay us if you gad about with Drusilla and leave us old folks free to put our feet up. I shall come home for the harvest, mind.'

His wife shook her head reprovingly, 'Speak for yourself, sir. Of course the young ladies will need a chaperone and I am more than ready for a little gaiety myself. Now, Anne, are you convinced that your presence is indispensable to our well-being? Had it not been for your opportune arrival, I should be stuck here in the mud with my two country bumpkins for the entire summer, with no prospect of a change of scene. We all need to acquire a little town bronze to fortify us for the winter!'

Anne laughed happily. 'Very well. Since you put it so, I think it would be churlish to refuse. I will write to my cousins tonight and perhaps I can also write to my lawyer and have some funds forwarded to me here.' She flicked a ladybird from her wrist and surveyed Sir Mortimer from beneath her lashes. After a moment she inquired, 'You have no objection, I trust, Sir Mortimer?'

He removed his pipe from his mouth and returned her regard levelly. He shrugged. 'I am not your keeper, Miss Fairleigh. You present me with a fait accompli which I must perforce accept.' He looked up at the Hendersons, who were peering at him anxiously through the trailing leaves. His expression softened and he sprang lightly to his feet, moved aside the branches, and squatted on his heels beside Mrs. Henderson, proffering his teacup.

'More tea, please,' he demanded, grinning impishly. 'You have just rid me of an almost intolerable burden

and to celebrate my new-found freedom, allow me to
offer my services in the small matter of accommodation.' He sipped his fresh brew, blithely ignoring
Anne's outraged exclamation.

Mr. and Mrs. Henderson exchanged relieved smiles.
'Thankee, lad,' said Mr. Henderson, 'but 'twill be no
light task to find something suitable, I rackon. It's not
that we're difficult to please, but from what I read in the
newspapers it's unusually crowded in London this
month with all the festivities for the peace and the
Centenary of the Hanoverian Succession and so forth.'

Mortimer nodded imperturbably. 'Not for nothing
was I one of Wellington's aides. I can find accommodation in a desert or on a mountaintop, if necessary ...'
Satisfied with the impression he had made, he relented
and added, 'And if I fail, my sister is past mistress of the
art of finding needles in haystacks.'

Amid the general merriment which ensued, only Mrs.
Henderson looked perturbed. She prodded the ground
with her parasol and Sir Mortimer leapt back in mock
alarm. 'It's all very well for you, young man, but we have
no claim on your sister and cannot think of troubling
her in this matter,' she protested.

Sir Mortimer smiled down at her. 'Dear ma'am,
Hester will be delighted to help. She is the best and most
good-natured of females. Just tell me what you require
and for how long and it is as good as done.'

He brushed aside their thanks and suggested a walk
before dinner. Anne and Drusilla went with him, not
needing to run indoors for wraps in the late-afternoon
sunshine. They crossed a stile and followed a
right-of-way diagonally through a field of waving
wheat. On the far side they joined a cart track which led
to the village, conversing in a desultory, undemanding
fashion as they meandered along. When they reached
the village green, Anne exclaimed in delight at the
prospect. They halted by common consent to absorb the

view of neat cottages, their gardens bright with flowers. On one side the cottagers were obliged to traverse little bridges over a fast-running stream to enter their homes; on the other an avenue of ancient elms led to the church and the inn, side by side on a little mound. Some benches were ranged outside the inn, overlooking the stocks on the green, with the churchyard and lych-gate nearby. Several children were paddling in the stream and a woman came to the door of the nearest cottage to call them in. She saw Drusilla and waved eagerly.

'Excuse me. That is Mrs. Sutton, our washerwoman. I promised to let her know when Judy's kittens were ready for adoption. I won't be a moment.' Drusilla smiled and walked swiftly across the green.

Mortimer and Anne ambled on slowly. He sighed deeply. 'I shall miss the country,' he said wistfully, 'but I shall look forward to seeing you in London.' He hesitated, then added, 'The Hendersons seem like very good people, but your – our – acquaintance with them has been very brief. I trust, Miss Fairleigh, that you will look upon me as a friend to call on in time of need.'

He spoke so earnestly that Anne's heart missed a beat. She quickened her step and when she did not reply immediately, he persisted, 'And even if there is no need, you will allow me to call and bring my sister to meet you? I believe you will like one another.'

Never before had Sir Mortimer felt so uncertain of his welcome; he had spent his youth fending off eager damsels with easy indifference while obstinately cherishing his passion for the unattainable Stephanie. In a moment of acute perception he realized that he no longer cared a fig for Lady Tremaine; how Hester would be amused by his predicament! Anne was silent for so long that he wondered if he had unwittingly blundered; perhaps she suspected that his desire to see her again was motivated by a brotherly concern for her in lieu of her cousin Jack. Would she regard his

continued presence as unwarranted interference in her
affairs?

Some such thoughts did indeed flash through Anne's
mind as they reached the end of the tree-lined avenue
and emerged in the sunny courtyard of The Maypole.
The ancient inn sign creaked above their heads, causing
her to jump, easing the tension between them. She
giggled and looking up, caught an unguarded
expression of tenderness in his deep-set hazel eyes. For
a timeless space the tall, lithe man and the slender girl
stood facing one another, oblivious to all else. Then,
faintly, they heard Drusilla hailing them. In a
spontaneous gesture, Anne extended her hand, saying,
'Thank you, Sir Mortimer. It will give me great pleasure
to meet Lady Montfort when we arrive in Town.'

She had forgotten that she was not wearing gloves. Sir
Mortimer took her proffered hand and kissed it,
releasing it unhurriedly as Drusilla joined them, puffing
in her haste. She was in time to witness the little
exchange and raised her brows, but made no comment,
and met Sir Mortimer's impassive stare with a bland
smile of innocence.

Anne walked back to Natherscombe in a daze; from
time to time she furtively rubbed her hand behind her
back, feeling again Sir Mortimer's warm clasp, while her
companions discussed the kittens, the weather, local
beauty spots, and other innocuous subjects. There was
no further opportunity for private conversation that
evening and Sir Mortimer left on his house-hunting
mission early the next day.

He succeeded so well in this endeavour that the
Hendersons and Anne were able to follow him to
London only two weeks later. They arrived in the
metropolis at the beginning of August and established
themselves in a commodious house in Henrietta Street,
a fashionable residential district, close to the main
shopping thoroughfares. On the morning after their

arrival, Anne and Drusilla went walking to explore the neighbourhood, accompanied by Drusilla's maid, Tillie. They visited Layton and Shear's modish shop and Drusilla made several purchases, but Anne was reluctant to buy anything until she received her allowance from Bristol. The young ladies returned invigorated by their expedition to find that Sir Mortimer had called in their absence to assure himself that everything was to their liking.

'He left a few minutes ago,' reported Mrs. Henderson, adding complacently, 'He said all that was proper and showed a pleasing concern for our comfort. He also advised us not to go near Hyde Park or Kensington Gardens for a few days, as the big fairs to celebrate the peace and the Centenary are still in progress and there is much drunkenness and dissipation. Sir Mortimer conveyed Lady Montfort's good wishes and requested leave for her to wait upon us tomorrow. I believe we have her ladyship to thank for this house, if truth be told.' She nodded wisely.

Mr. Henderson looked up from his perusal of the *Morning Chronicle* and surveyed the ladies over the top of his spectacles, his bushy eyebrows much in evidence. He agreed with his wife's conjectures. He prodded his newspaper with one stubby finger.

'It says here, my dear, that all kinds of accommodation are at a premium and lodgings cannot be obtained for love nor money. It must have taken considerable influence to secure a house in this quarter, cramped though it is. Nay, I daresay it is spacious for a Town house, but I always feel hemmed in by squares and iron railings. I think I will take a stroll to the Park and see the situation for myself. It says here somewhere – ah, listen to this, "Since the delirium began the pawnbrokers have more than trebled their business; clothes, furniture, and, worst of all, tools, have been sacrificed for the sake of momentary enjoyment;

industry of every kind has been interrupted, and many hundreds of starving families will long have to remember the era of the Park Fêtes." There will be some rioting and discontent before all this simmers down.'

Mrs. Henderson was not unduly alarmed by this account. 'There are always some foolish people who are not happy unless they go to excess, but I think the articles exaggerate. I expect you will find it is an indirect attack on the Prince of Wales. I understand he has expressed a desire for the continuance of the Fair.'

Drusilla supported her mother. 'The poor man is very unpopular with the press. It will be a good thing when the Princess of Wales leaves the country. The Prince was hissed by the mob when the Allied Sovereigns were here in June and I expect he is trying to curry favour by encouraging these festivities.'

'The Princess is not an ornament to her sex. Her style of dress is vulgar and she talks like a fishwife. I pity the poor young Princess Charlotte, torn between two such ill-assorted parents,' pronounced Mrs. Henderson, in a tone which brooked no opposition.

'We will agree to differ, my dear,' responded her husband good-humouredly. He folded his paper, rose, and stretched his stiffened limbs, adding, 'And now, if you will excuse me, I will seek some exercise and what passes for fresh air in this benighted city.'

He departed, leaving the ladies to enjoy a comfortable gossip, while thumbing through the *Ladies Monthly Museum* and other magazines to acquaint themselves with the latest modes in colour and design. After luncheon it came on to rain, so they spent a quiet afternoon writing notes to their friends and settling in to their new abode. The gentleman of the house returned in time for dinner well-satisfied with his jaunt. He had met a fellow member of the Winchester Assizes and they had drunk a glass or two of wine together at the club.

In Mr. Henderson's opinion the Fair would soon be

over – the Park was a shambles, with booths, swings, roundabouts, wild-beast shows, and other diversions. The grass was much trampled and littered with the remains of the fireworks displays. It was time the Home Department stepped in to restore law and order. In answer to Drusilla's eager question, he said cautiously that he thought the usual fashionable promenade had taken place, but the damp had discouraged the crowds.

After dinner Mr. Henderson called Anne aside and pressed a roll of banknotes into her hand, saying kindly that Drusilla had noticed her reluctance to purchase anything in the shops. Anne demurred, saying that she could manage very well until her allowance arrived, but Mr. Josiah gently insisted. At length Anne gave in, on the strict understanding that it was a loan, not a gift. She knew that her clothes, while very adequate for the country, lacked the modish touches required in Town, and she did not wish her hosts to blush for her appearance. She retired early to her room, where she was soon joined by Drusilla, and the young ladies spent a pleasant half-hour before bed in planning the necessary additions to their wardrobes.

The next morning the three ladies dressed carefully in expectation of their visitor and Mr. Henderson also elected to remain at home, under pressure from his wife. Mrs. Henderson was a sensible woman, and she knew that Lady Montfort was extremely well-connected and moved in the first circles. She also admired her books and had a fondness for her ladyship's brother. For all these excellent reasons she was anxious to create a good impression when Lady Montfort came to call. She fussed and fidgeted until her husband, chafing in an unusually high neckcloth and tight waistcoat, told her that she could "do the pretty" without him and civility be hanged, whereupon she immediately became calm and set herself to coax him into a more agreeable frame of mind, reminding him that his only daughter was as yet unwed and twenty-six years old and was it asking too much for him to donate one morning and some trifling discomfort to her future welfare? She succeeded so well that when they quitted their chamber he chucked her under the chin and told her she was remarkably well-preserved for a matron with a full-grown daughter. She dimpled and pecked him on the cheek, happily aware that her gown of pale gray, edged with lilac, was indeed becoming.

They found Anne and Drusilla awaiting them in the drawing room, Anne in white muslin, sprigged with small red dots, and Drusilla in blue which matched her eyes. Mrs. Henderson barely had time to compliment them on their appearance and straighten two china dogs on the mantelpiece before Lady Montfort was announced. Tompkins stood back and they saw an elegant lady, clad in the first stare of fashion, who advanced quickly across the room to shake hands with Mr. and Mrs. Henderson. Drusilla and Anne made their curtsies and she smiled graciously upon them.

There was a moment's stiffness, swiftly dispelled by her ladyship, who sank down on the sofa indicated by her hostess, dislodged a cushion, bent to retrieve it, and exclaimed cheerfully, 'Oh my goodness, always so clumsy, do forgive me. Are you comfortable, do you like the house? I found it by the greatest good fortune – a friend of mine has been ill and was obliged to go into the country to convalesce. I think you will find it quite central and convenient. We live just around the corner in Portman Square and I love this neighbourhood, although it is getting very built up and my husband and sons are longing to be at Huntsgrove, which is our home in Sussex. However, we are fixed here for at least another month. I expect you will wish to be at home for the harvest too, sir?' She looked directly at Mr. Henderson, who relaxed visibly at the prospect and gave an assenting grunt, beaming warmly upon this unexpectedly understanding female.

'We are much in your debt, Lady Montfort, for finding us accommodation. It was indeed a kindness for complete strangers,' intervened Mrs. Henderson quickly.

Hester shook her head emphatically, causing the feathers on her high-crowned bonnet to wave alarmingly over one eye. She pushed them aside impatiently, saying, 'Truly, ma'am, 'tis I who am in your debt for your hospitality to my brother. Mortimer has told me so much about you that I do not feel we are strangers. His poor eye is much improved, did you not think when you saw him yesterday? Such a foolish boy! He has been well-roasted by his friends since he returned to Town, for all the Duke's aides have been fêted enough to make their heads spin, and Mortimer resorted to a patch for a few days until the bruise subsided. It made him look very sinister and all the young ladies thought it vastly fetching when he appeared at Lady Loughborough's drum, but he was not amused and took refuge in the card room, which I consider very poor-spirited. I have hardly seen him since; he refuses to stay with us, you must understand. He is putting up at Fenton's Hotel, where they serve "a capital English dinner", so he tells me. He cannot endure the uproar in our house, with my two naughty boys racing about, Hugo with his political friends, and my literary circle, but he has promised to dine with us on Tuesday and I hope that you will join us. It will be a quiet party, I assure you, with Dickon and Harry safely locked up in the nursery.'

Mrs. Henderson accepted the invitation gracefully. Having done his duty, Mr. Henderson seized the opportunity to excuse himself when Hester inquired if the ladies needed any introductions to milliners or dressmakers. He executed a low bow and Lady Montfort smiled as she gave him her hand. Watching silently, Anne decided that she liked the way her ladyship made no attempt to hide the gray streaks in her abundant brown hair and the crinkles round her gray eyes added to the attractiveness of her mobile, well-formed countenance. However, she was unable to discern any marked resemblance to Sir Mortimer in her features or manner. Lady Montfort was much livelier and more forthcoming than her brother, Anne concluded, observing the usually reserved Drusilla responding readily to her ladyship's genuine interest in her home and country life. After a little Hester turned to Anne and inquired if this was her first visit to London.

Anne hesitated, then said humorously, 'Well, no, your ladyship, I came several years ago with my father, but since we spent almost the whole time in the museums and antiquarian bookshops, I cannot say that I saw very much of the metropolis. I do not recall entering any other kind of shop, except once, to purchase some tooth powder.'

The mention of bookshops reminded Mrs. Henderson that she was in the presence of an authoress. 'Sir Mortimer told us that you are the lady novelist, Hester Vane. He is so proud of you. I have just read *Gideon's Grange* and could not put it down for a moment. Drusilla will tell you I was quite immune to family life when I was immersed in the volume. Are you writing another tale at present?'

Hester laughed aloud, but replied composedly, 'Dear Tim! I would give much to have heard him. Normally he does not boast of my writing exploits to his military friends, for fear they will imagine I am an eccentric bluestocking. But, yes, ma'am, I am now working on a new volume, *The Candelabra Tree*, which is to be a modern tale, not Gothic. However, it is hard to find time during the season and it has been virtually impossible recently with so many social demands. I do most of my scribbling in Sussex, during the winter months, when Harry is at Eton and Dickon in the schoolroom.'

'How old are your sons, Lady Montfort?' asked Mrs. Henderson.

'Nearly nine and nearly seven, but I must not start talking of my offspring or I will become quite boring and be here all day,' said Hester, rising and drawing on her gloves. Drusilla rang for Tompkins to show her out and, while they waited, Hester promised to send them a formal invitation to her dinner party. 'Just a small affair, with perhaps a little dancing,' she said gaily. She looked attentively at Anne and Drusilla and added, 'Mortimer will be happy to have the company of conversable young ladies of his acquaintance, instead of the empty-headed, but eligible females that I am continually throwing in his way, to no avail.'

She took her leave, with a soft rustle of silk and swish of feathers, and the ladies of the household sat down to discuss their visitor over a dish of tea.

XI

Delights of the Metropolis

About ten o'clock that evening Anne was sitting up in bed, diligently making her first entry in the journal which she had purchased earlier in the day. The ladies had had a very exhausting, but entirely satisfactory foray to the milliners' and haberdashers' establishments along Oxford Street and Anne had just listed her purchases and expenditures in some detail. She bit the end of her pencil meditatively and added at the foot of the page: 'Sir Mortimer Vane called again while we were out and left a message inviting us to drive with him in the Park tomorrow at five. I think I will wear my new bonnet, lined with ponceau satin. Lady Montfort's milliner claimed that ponceau means poppy-coloured – I can't remember – anyway, it is dark red.'

There was a light tap on her door and Drusilla entered. Anne closed her book and patted the side of her bed invitingly. Drusilla perched on the end and tucked her feet under the coverlet; the two girls smiled at one another affectionately.

'I feel as if I have known you forever, although it is less than a month since we first met. So much seems to have happened in such a short time,' said Anne reflectively.

Her friend nodded with understanding, her long braids swinging loosely as she pulled up her knees and rested her chin on them.

'Are you happy with us, Anne?' she inquired gently.

'Oh, exceedingly. You and your parents have been more than kind. Everything would be quite perfect, if only ...' she hesitated, and Drusilla prompted, 'Yes, if only ...?'

Anne suddenly looked very small in the big bed, her eyes enormous and vulnerable in the shadowy candlelight. 'I do so wish I did not always look over my shoulder for dread of seeing Simon Pontefract. I know he will not give up easily, for I'm sure he is desperate for money.'

'Perhaps he wants you for yourself; is it possible that you have misjudged him?' suggested Drusilla.

Anne denied this vehemently. 'He is quite old, thirty-five or even forty. He told me that it would be a business arrangement. I have heard that he had a mistress and I cannot believe he loves me.' She blushed furiously, but met Drusilla's eyes steadily.

Drusilla replied calmly, 'Love is not everything. From what I have observed it is frequently a most miserable state to be in. Your father approved of Mr. Pontefract, did he not?'

'Yes, but he would never have approved if he had known how Simon tried to coerce me. Indeed he did, Drusilla,' Anne insisted, seeing the older girl's skeptical expression. 'He was a savage beast,' she finished hotly.

'He does not sound exactly the answer to a maiden's prayer,' observed Drusilla dryly. 'Does he have no redeeming features?'

Honesty obliged Anne to reply, after a moment, 'I was not averse to him at first. He is handsome in a dark sort of way, and witty and well-traveled. He promised me a comfortable life and position and considerable freedom if I married him, but he seemed to feel no need for mutual regard beyond the most commonplace. It was only after my father died that he frightened me; one night he kissed me violently, not just my lips. I felt

smothered, suffocated, and – and besmirched!' She
shuddered.

Drusilla probed delicately, 'Would you say that he was
acting out of character?'

Anne's eyes grew round. 'He certainly seemed out of
control. Perhaps I angered him by my resistance; if a
debtor's prison is looming before him ...' She fell silent,
pondering the incident from a fresh aspect.

Drusilla suppressed a smile and replied, 'In that event
one cannot altogether blame him for seeking to wed
you, but I must say I think it very foolish of him to make
no push to engage your affections first. I am no doubt
framed in a more pragmatic mould than you, Anne. To
me an offer of comfort and security from a man who is
not quite an ogre appears quite tolerable after years of
being on the country shelf. I confess I had not realized
how dull my life was become till the change of scene and
bustle of London brought it forcefully home to me.'

'Simon Pontefract is the nearest thing to an ogre that
it has been my misfortune to encounter,' retorted Anne,
but her lips curved and it was clear to Drusilla that she
was fast recovering her equanimity.

'I think I will reserve judgment until – and if – I
should meet the gentleman. A monster is something
quite out of the common way; you have piqued my
curiosity,' said Drusilla lightly, adding, 'At least Sir
Mortimer's manners are unexceptionable. It is a polite
attention to invite us to drive with him, don't you agree?'

This cunning remark had the desired effect; Anne
was instantly distracted. 'I would not call his manners
unexceptionable. He can be absurdly aloof and
stand-offish. I would say rather unpredictable,' said
Anne, her eyes narrowed and fixed on a distant object.

Drusilla nodded easily. 'If you say so, my dear. For
myself I take it kindly that he has introduced us to his
sister and I know that the connection will give me quite
a different view of the beau monde. Of course, I

understand that his attentions are chiefly for you, the cousin of his old friend,' she concluded slyly.

Roused, Anne sat up and threw her pillow at her friend in mock fury, crying, 'I adamantly refuse to be provoked, for you are an incorrigible tease and are well aware besides that Sir Mortimer is much attached to your parents and yourself. He thinks I am a nuisance and is wearing the willow for another lady, if I do not miss my guess.'

Laughing, the two girls collapsed in a crumpled heap on the pillow. Drusilla forbore to press Anne further, being well-satisfied in her earlier conjecture that Anne was by no means as indifferent to Sir Mortimer as she would appear. For herself, she liked him very well, but had no illusions that she was the object of his attention. She rose, gave Anne a quick, warm hug and left her to straighten her disheveled bedclothes and make one final entry in her journal: 'Can it be true that his attentions are chiefly for me? I doubt it much.'

She doubted it even more the following afternoon. Sir Mortimer arrived at the appointed hour and handed both ladies into his curricle, Drusilla going first, so that she sat in the middle. It was a tight squeeze, but the day was warm and the ladies wore their lightest garments. Drusilla was glad of her parasol to protect her fair skin from the sun's rays, but Anne, looking very fetching in her new straw bonnet with its poppy-coloured ribbons, declared that she never troubled about freckles and could easily dispense with a sunshade. Mortimer and Drusilla conversed animatedly, but Anne felt unaccountably tongue-tied and shy. 'How well they suit,' she thought despondently, unable to think of a single intelligent comment to offer on the subject under discussion, which happened to be Southdown sheep.

They entered the park by the Grosvenor Gate and proceeded at a sedate walking pace amid the press of vehicles, riders, and pedestrians all bent on seeing and

being seen in the fashionable promenade. Several
military gentlemen on horseback hailed Mortimer
familiarly and cast admiring glances in Anne's direction;
her spirits began imperceptibly to rise. Mortimer
responded by touching his whip to his hat, but edged his
horses forward purposefully. His friends' faces fell
ludicrously and Mortimer grinned.

'All good fellows, but dreadful rattlepates. I daren't
linger, for I promised Hester to be at the other end of
the drive by five-thirty.'

Anne glanced eagerly about her. The grass was much
trampled and littered with debris in the aftermath of
the Fair, but it was ignored by the polite society, which
kept to the walks and concentrated on the human
scenery rather than nature.

'There is Lady Montfort,' she said suddenly,
indicating an elegant barouche drawn up in the shade
of a tree about a hundred yards distant. Seated beside
Hester was an angular, rather dashingly attired lady,
with bold, dark eyes, who beckoned imperiously on
seeing Mortimer.

'Oh lord,' he sighed, as he skillfully maneuvered
towards the barouche, "Tis Sally Jersey and I see the
Duke making his escape.'

'Wellington,' breathed Anne. 'How I should like to
meet him.'

Mortimer drawled, 'I daresay it can be arranged, if
you wish it. I didn't know you cared for military men.'

Anne tossed her head and replied haughtily, 'All
ladies admire the Duke. He is something quite
exceptional.'

'You must tell him so,' retorted Mortimer. 'He'll be at
Hester's dinner party on Tuesday. But now, Miss
Fairleigh, you must meet Lady Jersey, who is ten times
more intimidating than old Hookey, but a great friend
of m'sister's. Can't think why, she's a dreadful gossip,'
he finished in a muttered undertone, as he drew neatly

alongside the barouche. He greeted Lady Jersey and his sister. Hester introduced Anne and Drusilla and the ladies exchanged views on the weather. Sally Jersey addressed an obviously flirtatious remark to Sir Mortimer, with much fluttering of eyelashes and twirling of her pretty striped parasol, and Anne was surprised and not a little disgusted at his expert response, which sent her ladyship into peals of laughter.

Anne was seated on the side of the vehicle nearest to the barouche. After a few moments of badinage, Lady Jersey shot a sharp glance at Anne and said gaily, 'Beware of this young devil, Miss Fairleigh, he could charm a nightingale from a tree. I understand he left a string of broken hearts across Spain.'

'Indeed, ma'am, I expect he felt that there was safety in numbers,' she replied coolly, lifting her little nose.

Lady Jersey let out a hearty guffaw, Mortimer stiffened, and Drusilla intervened hurriedly, 'I imagine any member of the Duke's entourage was obliged to be civil to the local nobility. I understand the Spaniards are very punctilious in their manners.'

Not a whit disturbed, her ladyship replied tranquilly, 'I was not thinking of the nobility, my dear, but we'll let it pass. You must both come to Almack's and survey more of our military scene; it is good to have all these young sparks back from Spain. It really adds luster to the cluster this season. I'll send you vouchers on condition that you bring this rogue along to escort you and bring you unscathed through the perils of the fray. Lud, I become quite military in my metaphors. It comes of talking to our new Duke.'

They chatted inconsequentially for a little longer, Lady Jersey chaffing Sir Mortimer on the need to appear at Almack's, the apogée of polite society, where one's presence guaranteed acceptance in the highest social circles. Anne noted the amused quirk of Hester's eyebrows when Mortimer replied without a blink that he'd thought of looking in on Wednesday. Hester met Anne's gaze and the two exchanged smiles.

On the way home, Drusilla remarked inadequately, 'How very vivacious Lady Jersey is.' By no means lacking in town bronze, Drusilla suspected that the meeting with Lady Jersey had been arranged between Lady Montfort and Sir Mortimer to obtain the coveted vouchers for Anne and herself. She added, 'She was also very good-natured. I had always understood that the patronesses of Almack's were all quite draconian.'

'Countess Lieven is the worst, being foreign, she stands on her dignity, but Mrs. Drummond Burrell and Princess Esterhazy are also formidable "grandes dames". Sally is by far the most agreeable and she has a special weakness for a uniform,' said Mortimer smugly, leaning forward to observe Anne's reaction.

To Drusilla's relief she failed to rise, merely nodding and remarking practically, 'Ah, yes, her Peninsular heroes, I think she called you. Well, in this instance her preference seems to have worked to our advantage and we are grateful to you, Sir Mortimer, for bringing about the introduction.'

'Hm,' grunted Sir Mortimer, reddening, 'I'm sure Mrs. Henderson could have obtained vouchers for you through her acquaintance. I merely hoped to speed the process as I've promised to attend on Wednesday. In any event, 'twas all Hester's doing. I had forgotten how important such things are until she reminded me. As far as I'm concerned, spending an evening at Almack's requires more heroism than storming half a dozen fortresses in Spain. But Hester has a way of getting what she wants. May I hope to see you there next week? Do you like to dance, Miss Henderson?'

'I am very fond of the exercise, but of course I have been accustomed to dance in the country, where everyone is acquainted,' answered Drusilla, a shade doubtfully.

Anne caught the note of disquiet at the prospective ordeal and said comfortingly, 'I daresay many young ladies who come to Almack's are in the same position. But even if we do not dance very much, it will be entertaining to see the company and I like to listen to good music.'

'Yes, indeed,' smiled Drusilla, recovering her habitual poise.

Before Sir Mortimer could intervene to improve on this somewhat depressing view of the promised evening's entertainment, he was accosted by two of the gentlemen they had seen earlier on horseback; both sported neat military moustaches and were exceedingly upright in their carriage.

'Tim, old chap, well met,' boomed a fair-haired gentleman, with merry blue eyes. He was accompanied by a tall, wiry man in a dark green riding coat. They shook hands vigorously with Mortimer, who was clearly delighted to see his friends. The older rider in green looked quizzically past Mortimer to the ladies and gently admonished his companion, 'Peace, cherub, let us absorb these visions of loveliness in reverent silence until Vane deigns to introduce us.' He took off his hat and gazed solemnly at Anne and Drusilla. Recalled to his duty, Mortimer presented Lord Johnny Ponsonby and Captain Jeremy Grattan, both of the Rifle Brigade, adding nonchalantly, 'Good fellows in their way, but not to be trusted on the dance floor.'

Discomfited, Lord Johnny blushed and shook his fist at Mortimer, saying, 'Don't believe a word of it, ladies. Unjust and untrue – why I'm as at home in the ballroom as in the saddle, ain't that so, Grattan?'

Captain Grattan ignored this appeal; he gave a crooked smile and inquired how Mortimer came to be in Town. He had heard that he was rusticating with Jack Davenport in Dorset. Lord Johnny did not waste his time. He engaged the ladies in conversation and secured a promise from each of them to dance with him at the coming Assembly and allow him to vindicate himself after Vane's treacherous slander. They parted on good terms, Sir Mortimer engaging to dine with his friends the next evening. On the way home, Anne meditated on the close bond which army life seemed to produce between very disparate characters.

The ladies did not see Sir Mortimer again for several days. They did some indispensable shopping in the Pantheon Bazaar; went with Mr. Henderson to an equestrian display at Astley's Amphitheatre; attended a performance of *Hamlet* at Drury Lane, where they renewed their acquaintance with Lord Johnny and met his sister and aunt; and partook of a sumptuous, but tedious dinner at the house of Mr. Henderson's Winchester colleague. Anne's allowance arrived from Bristol, much to her satisfaction, and on Sunday she accompanied the Hendersons to Divine Service in St. Paul's Cathedral. It was here, while walking in the nave near the west door, that they encountered Mrs. Georgiana Upcroft, a childhood friend of Drusilla's, who was much gratified to be recognized by Miss Henderson. Mrs. Upcroft was dressed from head to toe in somber black and leaned on the arm of her much older husband, a hollow-cheeked individual, with a lawyer's stoop and pallor. They both had the stern eyes and ascetic faces which frequently indicate religious fervour and Anne thought they seemed out-of-place in the brightly dressed, fashionable congregation which worshipped in the Cathedral. They looked as if they would be more at home in a nonconformist chapel. Anne's instincts soon proved correct.

'Of course, we do not usually attend service here,' Mrs. Upcroft explained to Drusilla. 'We go to the Wesleyan chapel near our house in Eagle Street, but the topic of today's sermon was particularly pertinent and we thought to do a little special pleading in certain quarters on behalf of one of my charitable concerns, the female prisoners in Newgate.'

Drusilla expressed polite interest and Mrs. Upcroft, nothing loath, expatiated at some length on the plight of the unfortunate women who were incarcerated in the infamous institution. 'They exist in dirty, overcrowded cells. Indeed the conditions are indescribable and must be seen to be believed. Many of the women live like animals and their small children play amid the filth and get bitten by the rats,' she said earnestly.

Mrs. Henderson shuddered and tried to give the conversation a livelier turn. 'And do you have children of your own, Georgiana? Since your parents passed on we have had no news of your movements.'

Mrs. Upcroft winced and cast a furtive glance at her husband, who was deep in talk with Mr. Henderson. She lowered her voice and said sadly, 'No, ma'am, the Lord has not seen fit to bless us, but I know that it is His will that I should atone for my sins by ministering to the poor and needy. In others' misery I can forget my own insignificant sufferings and, in truth, there is much work to be done. Perhaps you would care to go with me and see for yourself, Drusilla?'

Mrs. Upcroft ignored Mrs. Henderson and Anne, fixing her unwavering stare on her friend. Mrs. Henderson was not best pleased at the suggestion, but her daughter, after a brief moment of hesitation, said firmly that a prison visit would be exactly the right antidote to her present life of frivolity and dissipation. Georgiana gave a little crow of satisfaction and insisted that Drusilla should come to tea at the earliest possible date, to discuss the project. She graciously included the other two ladies in her invitation and Mrs. Henderson agreed reluctantly to go on the following Wednesday.

'You are too soft-hearted, my child,' she grumbled, when they were safely out of earshot. 'Why do you want to go that nasty place? You will pick up lice or worse still, some dreadful disease and we shall all catch it and what good will that do for anybody, I wonder!'

Drusilla laughed and taking her mother's arm, set herself to reassure the older lady, insisting that she would take the greatest possible precautions and would wear her oldest clothes.

'They are all left behind in the country, you stubborn girl,' protested Mrs. Henderson.

Josiah Henderson came, unexpectedly, to his daughter's defence. She would come to no harm with Georgiana, he contended, and it would be an interesting experience for her. He reckoned Georgiana was more than a match for a roomful of prisoners and their attendant wildlife and he did not propose to lose any sleep on the matter. This statement effectively ended the subject and Mrs. Henderson, recognizing defeat, allowed her mind to be diverted in more fruitful directions.

On Monday the promised vouchers for Almack's were delivered by Lady Jersey's footman, sending Mrs. Henderson into transports of happy anticipation. The ladies sustained a call from Lord Johnny and Captain Grattan, but otherwise passed the day quietly in order to be rested and refreshed for the week's engagements. Despite this period of relaxation, Anne was a prey to nerves on the following evening when she joined the family party for the short drive to the Montfort house in Portman Square.

Mr. Josiah, squeezed into uncomfortably tight pantaloons and a square-cut tailcoat, handed the ladies into the carriage and complimented them on their fine appearance. Mrs. Henderson smoothed her lilac skirts complacently and smiled at the girls seated opposite, with their backs to the horses. Anne thought Drusilla looked uncommonly well in a gown of deep blue china crêpe, with a lighter blue flounced petticoat peeping out, but she was uncertain about her own robe of yellow sarcenet, trimmed with apricot, and wished she had not allowed Tillie to dress her hair so high; she was sure that the rosebuds tucked in among her curls would wilt in the middle of dinner, giving her a pathetic, drooping appearance.

However, these doubts were soon forgotten in the cordial warmth of their reception. Anne appreciated the unassuming way in which Hester set her guests at ease and admired her tall, handsome husband, with his arresting green eyes and restrained good taste, in the style of Mr. Brummell.

At dinner, Anne was placed beside Mortimer. They were seated about halfway down the long table, which tonight accommodated some twenty persons, including His Grace, the Duke of Wellington, who had the chair of honour on Hester's right. Drusilla was next to a very intense young man, who seemed to spend much of the evening reciting his own, rather bad, poetry.

'Dear Drusilla,' said Anne to Mortimer softly, under cover of the general hum of sprightly conversation, perhaps induced by the excellence of Lord Montfort's cellar, 'She is so tolerant of all kinds of people. I'm afraid I should laugh if someone gave me poetry over my meat!'

'That is no doubt why Hester placed you at my side, Miss Fairleigh. She is very good at summing up people's characters and she clearly saw you needed a firm rein!'

His twinkling eyes belied his words; Anne's own eyes sparkled in response, but she pursed her lips and said with dignity, 'Lord Johnny Ponsonby and Captain Grattan paid us a call yesterday. They spoke very highly of you, sir, but the Captain was convinced that you would fail to appear at Almack's on Wednesday. He said that in all the years he had known you, he had never seen you there and it was his understanding that you only attended balls under strict military orders, in the line of duty. He was so skeptical that Lord Johnny instantly laid a wager with him on the subject.'

Anne tilted her head inquiringly, dislodging a rosebud, which Sir Mortimer caught neatly as it fell. He pocketed it calmly and said, without rancour, 'Impudent puppies. A fine way to show respect for their senior officer. However, Grattan will lose his wager, for I promised Sally Jersey and my word is my bond, whatever the cost. I must admit there is an element of truth in Grattan's charge; may I hope to ameliorate my prospective sufferings by engaging you for the supper dance – unless Ponsonby is before me?'

Anne accepted this invitation a trifle distractedly; she was trying to decide whether her dinner partner had abstracted the rosebud for reasons of gallantry or to save her embarrassment. His demeanour offered no clue; it was perfectly correct, but quite impersonal. Their conversation ranged over various topics, including music, painting, and books and, when Anne rallied him, saying that she had not realized that a soldier would have time for much reading, he replied, 'Oh, Hester was very good at keeping me supplied with literary nourishment. When I was wounded, or otherwise beset with the various afflictions of campaigning, I found solace and an escape from boredom in books. I delved into the classics with an enthusiasm I had never imagined possible while at Oxford.'

Mortimer did not share Anne's preference for modern poets, but they found enough common ground to render them almost immune to their surroundings, until a scraping of chairs indicated that the ladies were about to withdraw. Anne jumped up, guiltily aware that she had shamefully neglected the portly gentleman on her left, who had eaten his meal in stolid silence. Politely, Mortimer held her chair and her heart fluttered queerly as she met his quizzical gaze. He put up his hand involuntarily to hide the ugly, disfiguring mark on his face and Anne experienced a sudden longing to pull his hand away and replace it with her own. Trembling, she backed away and he watched her with an enigmatic expression until she disappeared from view through the tall double doors.

Anne sought temporary refuge in the dressing room, where the ladies had left their wraps. She bathed her face in cool water and regarded her appearance critically in the tall looking glass. She was surprised and reassured to find nothing amiss; indeed, an impartial observer might justly have claimed that she looked beautiful, with an indefinable glow of inner happiness and excitement. Anne saw simply that her flowers had not wilted and her gown had not creased as much as she'd feared. Her poise recovered, she descended to find Drusilla at the pianoforte and Hester dispensing tea and coffee.

Anne approached the tea table and Hester gave her some tea, and said cheerfully, 'Excellent, now everyone is served and I am at leisure to enjoy myself. Do sit here my dear and tell me if the Duke came up to your expectations.'

'Well, I only spoke a few words with him before dinner, your ladyship,' replied Anne cautiously. 'He was very affable, but we exchanged the most commonplace civilities and I thought he seemed preoccupied. I do not think I formed any definite opinion of his character.' Fearing that these remarks would seem an inadequate assessment of the Great Man, she added, 'I expect one must see him in his own milieu on the battlefield to form a true impression.'

Lady Montfort nodded understandingly. 'Few people warm to him on first acquaintance and I think he is not in spirits tonight. He confided to me that he has dined richly every night for the past week and the indulgence has taken its toll on his constitution. His will may be made of iron, but his digestion is another matter,' she concluded with a smile.

Anne sipped her tea. 'Sir Mortimer is very devoted to him, I believe,' she said tentatively, introducing the subject which was uppermost in her thoughts.

Hester agreed. 'My brother was in a privileged position as an aide-de-camp. He spent several years campaigning at the Duke's side and worked closely with him on a daily basis. I think Arthur reciprocates Mortimer's esteem and affection.' She paused and glanced about her, alert to the comfort of her guests. It appeared that the other ladies were quite content and deep in conversation. Hester looked shrewdly at Anne. It had not escaped her attention that her brother had taken an unusual interest in Miss Fairleigh and his efforts on her behalf had been quite extraordinary, not least among them his apparent willingness to attend an Almack's Assembly, a dubious entertainment which Hester had heard him condemn in no uncertain terms on numerous occasions. The bond between brother and sister was very strong, but on the subject of this young lady he had been quite provokingly reticent. He had told her the bare bones of Anne's story and had given Hester to understand that his attentions were merely to oblige Anne's cousin, Major Davenport. Hester had accepted this explanation at face value when Mortimer first returned to town and asked her to help him find lodgings for the Hendersons and Miss Fairleigh, for he had not the slightest idea how to go about such a task. This evening was the first opportunity she had been afforded to observe Mortimer and Miss Fairleigh together for any length of time; her duties as hostess had not been conducive to prolonged study, but she felt tolerably convinced that her hitherto unimpressionable brother entertained more than a passing tendre for the elusive young lady at her side. She had wondered briefly if Drusilla Henderson had replaced Stephanie in Mortimer's affections, but he had spoken freely of Drusilla, praising her good sense and good nature.

When she asked about Anne, he became dumb as an
oyster. With considerable restraint, Lady Montfort
wisely decided to wait and see. She now exerted herself
to draw Anne out by talking of her brother.

'I was very set against it when Mortimer decided to
join the army,' she began reminiscently. Anne entered
into her sentiments very satisfactorily and by degrees
Hester adroitly led the talk to Anne's own background
and youthful experiences. The two ladies soon
established that they shared a common outlook in
several important respects, not least a similar sense of
humour and a great fondness for animals.

'I understand you narrowly avoided witnessing a
prizefight,' ventured Hester. Not wishing Anne to
construe this as a criticism, she added quickly, 'It is
something I have always wished to do. I'm sure it would
provide me with so much interesting material for an
incident in a novel. One can imagine, but it is not at all
the same; one lacks the significant details which lend
authenticity to the account. I did persuade Hugo to
teach me to fence, but my mind wandered at a vital
moment and he almost ran me through, or would have
done had we not had buttons on the foils, so we have not
repeated the experiment.'

'You mean you would like to *observe* a prizefight, not
to take part?' queried Anne, amused.

Hester grimaced, her expression reminding Anne of
Sir Mortimer for the first time. 'Oh, yes, did I not make
it clear? You must think me very unconventional, but I
have always resented the sharp divisions between the
sexes in terms of behaviour and aspirations.'

They were getting along famously when the
gentlemen joined them, effectively ending their
tête-à-tête. As she moved among the various groups,
Hester reflected wryly that she was no wiser concerning
the extent of the relationship between Miss Fairleigh
and her brother; she had detected not the faintest trace

of "hero-worship" in the young lady's comments, and yet she was obstinately convinced that her instincts were not at fault. No doubt Hugo would tell her to be patient and await developments and, above all, to avoid matchmaking. Having made this praiseworthy resolution, she went forward to the piano and suggested a little impromptu dancing.

Several couples took the floor in a small area where the carpet had been rolled back for the purpose. Anne was partnered by the Duke himself and enjoyed the experience more than she expected, for he was neat and quick on his feet and unbent sufficiently to make her think him quite human after all, despite his cold gray eyes and awesome reputation. Sir Mortimer danced with Drusilla, then retired to drink his coffee without approaching Anne. Chagrined, she performed a lively polka with Lord Montfort and did not once glance in Mortimer's direction.

Soon afterwards the Duke took his leave and the rest of the company followed his example. Anne returned to Henrietta Street with much food for thought, most of which she did not confide in her journal, noting briefly: 'Grand dinner in Portman Sq. Had a long talk with Lady M., very charming in amber silk; Danced with the Duke of W. and Lord M. Lost a rosebud ...'

On some subjects, Miss Fairleigh also could be "dumb as an oyster".

XII

Further Developments

With the resilience of youth and the prospect of novelty, Anne and Drusilla were up betimes the next morning and had been waiting for half an hour when Mrs. Henderson made her appearance, somewhat heavy-eyed, but ready to accompany them to make the promised call on Georgiana Upcroft. Anne took an eager interest as they drove to a part of the city which she had not previously visited. The great squares and spacious parks of the fashionable West End were left behind and they entered an area of older houses and narrower streets. The well-kept residences conveyed an impression of solid respectability; it was here that one found the dwellings of the rich merchants, doctors, lawyers, and other rising members of the professional class.

Unlike sleepy Mayfair, which was barely astir at this hour, the streets were bustling with life. A brewer's dray blocked the entrance to Eagle Street, which was their destination. The heavy cart had been involved in a collision; its contents were spilled far and wide and the driver was giving vent to a string of colourful imprecations as he struggled to unhitch his powerful, but placid horse, cheered on by a motley crew of street urchins and errand boys. After a few moments, Mrs. Henderson remarked decisively, 'Well, I do not propose to sit here all day. Let us walk.'

She dismissed the carriage, charging Coachman Jem to return for them in exactly one hour, and tripped daintily across the road, neatly sidestepping the rapidly

159

forming puddles of beer, which had leaked from several splintered barrels. They skirted the crowd of onlookers and Anne suddenly felt her skin prickle with the uncomfortable sensation that she was being watched. Her bonnet was a large one; she turned her head slowly from left to right, but could see no one special, only the usual hawkers, a lady walking with her dog, a closed hackney cab and, at the far end of the street, an organ grinder surrounded by children with their nursemaids. She hurried to catch up with Mrs. Henderson and Drusilla, who had stopped at a door a little farther down. Drusilla plied the shining brass knocker vigorously.

Mrs. Upcroft greeted them briskly, apologizing that her husband, James, had but just quitted the house with an unexpected visitor, a Bristol merchant who was an important client.

'You might have seen them,' said Georgiana, as they ascended a steep staircase, 'they went off in a hackney not five minutes ago.'

'I don't think so,' puffed Mrs. Henderson a trifle breathlessly as they reached the landing. She smiled kindly at their hostess. 'Do not concern yourself, my dear, we do not expect to see the gentlemen in the morning when they have affairs.'

'Anne knows Bristol well,' remarked Drusilla, as they disposed themselves in a handsome, austere room, which Anne found chilling after the cheerful clutter of the Henderson household.

Georgiana turned politely to Anne. 'Then perhaps you have met Mr. Pontefract, Miss Fairleigh? With his many interests, I'm sure he must have a wide circle of acquaintances in Bristol society.'

Jerked abruptly from her contemplation of the room by Georgiana's pronouncement of that name, above all others which she least wished to hear, Anne stammered, 'Why, er, yes. I am acquainted with him. Mr. Pontefract was accustomed to do business with my father.'

She hoped that this would suffice and did not dare

look at Drusilla. However, Mrs. Upcroft said brightly, 'What a small world it is, indeed. We entertain him frequently. It's odd he's never married, but I hear he may be hanging out for a rich wife.'

Her sharp, unwavering eyes fixed themselves inquisitively on Anne's face, avid for information. Anne wondered uncharitably why so many "good" people should also be mischief-making gossips, but unwilling to antagonize Drusilla's friend, she replied noncommittally. Mrs. Upcroft could not leave the subject alone, but pecked at it like a hungry pigeon.

'He is such a well-bred, handsome man, so distinguished and so very easy in ladies' company, not at all like my poor James, who is so painfully shy, except with his dry-as-dust legal friends.' As she spoke, her countenance was marred by a discontented frown and her lip drooped petulantly.

Anne and Drusilla exchanged glances of mingled pity and embarrassment, but Mrs. Henderson evidently did not approve of such frank criticism of one's husband, particularly before unmarried ladies. Deftly she steered the conversation into safer channels, by asking Georgiana to describe her prison work.

The question caused Mrs. Upcroft to reveal a different aspect of her character; Anne began to understand Drusilla's attachment to the lady. 'At present I conduct a regular weekly sewing class, but we have all kinds of plans. I am not alone in my endeavour, there are a number of ladies involved, including a Quaker lady, Mrs. Elizabeth Fry. I share Mrs. Fry's view that we are merely scratching the surface; legal reforms are urgently necessary to ameliorate the situation in our prisons and I am trying to persuade James to take action, but so far I have been unsuccessful. He says he will not meddle in matters which do not concern him, but I know his true reason is that he does not wish to alienate certain wealthy clients who are much opposed to any change in our penal code.'

Refreshments appeared, brought by a skinny, sly-faced wench who informed her mistress pertly that cook was tipsy and the buns burnt and what should she say to the fishmonger's boy who had not been paid for three weeks? Mrs. Upcroft scolded her harshly for her impertinence, but the girl flounced out insolently and slammed the door.

Mrs. Henderson raised her eyebrows and pursed her lips at such behaviour, but their hostess blandly poured coffee as she resumed their interrupted discussion. Anne was obliged to admit that Georgiana exhibited real enthusiasm and displayed no distaste for the harsher aspects of prison life, saying matter-of-factly that she always had a good bath to rid herself of any little creature she might have picked up and she liked to take small treats for the poor children.

Promptly on the hour, Mrs. Henderson stood up to leave, saying that they must not keep the horses standing. Drusilla arranged to come again on Thursday to go with Georgiana to Newgate and Mrs. Upcroft apologized to Anne for being unable to include her, remarking that the number of visitors was restricted, but perhaps another time ... Anne strove valiantly to hide her relief and offered to send some trifles for the children.

Mrs. Upcroft thanked her effusively, declaring, 'Any little thing would be most welcome. If I may suggest, they would enjoy marbles, wooden toys, scraps of material or old clothing. Very few of them can read, but a few appreciate picture books.'

Anne emerged thoughtfully into the sunshine, happy to be released from the oppressive atmosphere of Mrs. Upcroft's house. It was clear that the lady's marital situation left much to be desired; even marriage with Simon Pontefract would be preferable to Georgiana's fate!

In the carriage it appeared that Drusilla had been following a similar train of thought. She observed to her mother, 'How changed she is. I recollect Georgiana as a carefree country girl, caring naught for anything but her latest gown and beau.'

Mrs. Henderson shook her head sadly. 'One cannot be too careful in one's choice of a husband. I fear the Upcrofts have few tastes in common and there is a great disparity in age. Georgiana is a disappointed woman. It is a condition not conducive to domestic felicity,' she concluded trenchantly.

'Why did she marry Mr. Upcroft?' inquired Anne, puzzled.

'Oh, there is little choice in our district,' responded Drusilla simply. 'James was older and doing well in his profession and when her favourite beau, Dick Allen, was killed at Salamanca, Georgiana became very listless. James, who had long admired her, seized his opportunity, her parents approved, and she drifted into matrimony to escape from the country and its memories.'

'How tragic,' murmured Anne with a shiver, thinking how precarious life could be for a soldier.

Mrs. Henderson decided to change the subject. 'So Mr. Pontefract is in Town,' she remarked, glancing at Anne dubiously.

'Yes, I fancy he may have seen me as we walked down Eagle Street. You may recall a hackney cab passed us and I had a most unaccountable feeling that someone was watching me; then Mrs. Upcroft told us that her husband had just left with Mr. Pontefract,' replied Anne uneasily.

Mrs. Henderson leaned forward and patted her hand comfortingly. 'No need to distress yourself, my dear. The gentleman must have realized by now that his suit is unwelcome to you. I expect he will respect your wishes and do his utmost to avoid meeting you.'

Anne sighed. 'I hope you may be right, ma'am. I wish he had not come to London.'

Nothing further was said until the young ladies were alone after luncheon, Mr. and Mrs. Henderson having gone to inspect the fine jasperware newly arrived in Wedgwood's showrooms. To occupy an idle hour, Drusilla invited Anne to her chamber to help her select some items to take to amuse the prisoners' children. They sat on the floor and rummaged in a large trunk, putting aside in a pile the objects to be discarded.

'If only I had known,' said Drusilla regretfully. 'The attic at home is full of jumble, for Mama cannot bear to throw anything away. But fortunately I brought far too many things with me and some of them are very outmoded. Here, put this hairpiece and necklace on the pile.' She handed them to Anne and leaned back against the bedpost. 'I did not quite like to mention to Georgiana that we were going to Almack's this evening. I felt guilty to be so gay and – frivolous.'

'Why?' Anne shrugged and met her friend's eyes directly, 'Did you think she would be envious? Or that she would not approve?'

Drusilla half-smiled and half-sighed. 'You are severe. But you are right – a mixture of both, I think.'

Anne rested on her heels and peered into the trunk. 'Do you truly wish to visit Newgate?' she asked over her shoulder.

'No, I confess I dread it,' owned Drusilla softly, 'but I cannot hurt Georgie; we were close friends for many years and although I do not feel the same affection for her now, I do pity her.'

'That husband of hers has much to answer for,' observed Anne sagely.

'Do you think we shall do any better? Marriage is a lottery,' Drusilla spoke with uncharacteristic cynicism and Anne regarded her sympathetically, but refused to encourage her mood.

'We must give the matter our earnest consideration so that we can make a rational choice; if all else fails we can live together as eccentric old maids,' she said flippantly. 'Now tell me, Drusilla, what qualities do you require in a husband?'

'Kindness and consideration. I suppose – to be treated as a person, not an appendage. Someone in whose company I like myself and feel at ease,' reflected Drusilla.

'You do not think looks are important, or a sense of humour?'

'Yes, of course, but there are few such paragons, even in London, and one must be reasonable and not set one's expectations too high. After all, what do I have to offer in return?'

'A sweet and loving disposition,' said Anne promptly. 'You must not underestimate yourself, my love.' She had moved to sit on the daybed and was curled in unladylike comfort, with her feet tucked up and her head supported by one slender arm; her dark, unruly hair fell forward over her face in a shining mass, shading her eyes and highlighting her small, pointed chin.

Drusilla tried and failed to repress a slight twinge of envy.

'You're an unusual girl, Anne,' she remarked wistfully, 'Beautiful women do not commonly bother with plain ones.'

Disconcerted, Anne jumped up and went over to the wardrobe; she fingered the gowns, her back to her friend. After a moment, she turned, saying, 'Don't be a ninny, Drusilla. You *are* down in the dumps today! My problem will be to know when someone wants to marry me for myself and not for my inheritance. Come and show me which gown you have decided to wear to the Assembly.' She pulled out a richly ornamented dress in emerald green and held it up for inspection. 'You have not worn this one yet, but I think you would look very fine à la militaire with gold braid and netted buttons.'

Drusilla shook her head doubtfully, but came forward and pirouetted slowly round the room, holding the dress up before her. After some debate, she conceded that Anne's choice was the best one; they were hunting through her jewelry box to find some matching earrings when Tillie appeared to say that Mr. and Mrs. Henderson had returned and tea was being served in the drawing room.

*

Anne's own selection for her début at Almack's was a polonaise long robe of white gossamer net over a rose satin slip, accompanied by white dancing slippers and gloves. She wore no jewels, but a single, gold chain and threaded a pink ribbon through her hair, which was loosely dressed in the Eastern style.

The young ladies entered the already crowded rooms in Mrs. Henderson's wake and followed her nodding ostrich plumes through the throng with some difficulty. Mr. Henderson had sensibly elected to remain at home, but as they were leaving, he presented Anne and Drusilla each with a dainty, painted fan; to his wife he gave a small box, enameled in the French fashion with tiny fleurs-de-lis to hold her pills, in case she should get a headache. Anne's fan tapped delicately at her side and she longed to open it, for it was not easy to look curiously about her and keep her eyes demurely lowered at the same time.

They successfully cleared the first hurdle, which was the receiving line conducted by several representatives of the committee of seven aristocratic ladies who ruled Almack's with absolute authority. Tonight they were welcomed by Lady Jersey and Countess Lieven, the wife of the Russian ambassador, who surveyed Anne haughtily through her lorgnette and pronounced her "charming" in a guttural French accent. They made their curtsies and passed on into the ballroom of this exclusive temple of the ton, both young ladies rather pale and tense, suffering from a sudden onset of nerves as they endured the critical stares and supercilious smiles of a sea of faces. Calmly Mrs. Henderson shepherded her charges through the press of people, which magically gave way before her small, stately figure. Her firm guidance had a beneficial effect and gradually Anne's vision cleared and she was able to focus on individuals.

The evening began well. No sooner were the ladies seated than Mortimer's two friends, Johnny Ponsonby and Jeremy Grattan, appeared to claim their promised dances. Mrs. Henderson nodded graciously and the

couples took their places, Anne going first with Lord
Johnny, followed by her friend and Captain Grattan. In
no time Anne was calling Johnny by his first name and
treating him as familiarly as she had treated Jack
Davenport in Lyme. She was reminded of Jack and asked
Johnny if he knew him well. It transpired that they were
good friends and Johnny sat beside her and talked of
Jack and life in the Peninsula when Anne was obliged to
sit out for a waltz.

Warmhearted Lady Jersey was not unmindful of Miss
Fairleigh's predicament. She observed that Anne and
Drusilla correctly remained seated during this daring
dance and when the next lilting waltz struck up, she
approached with Sir Mortimer and Captain Grattan in
tow and presented them as suitable partners, thus giving
her official sanction for the young ladies to take part in
the exercise.

'Here are two of my best dancers come to request the
honour of leading you out,' she said kindly.

Obediently the gentlemen executed low bows; the
ladies curtsied and placed their right hands lightly on the
proffered arms and Lady Jersey waved them away with
an impatient flick of her wrist and sank down beside Mrs.
Henderson with a sigh of relief.

The unaccustomed proximity had an inhibiting effect
on Miss Fairleigh, causing her to move with unnatural
stiffness. When they had twice circled the floor in silence,
her partner glanced down at the top of her head and
remarked gravely, 'I hope you admire my waistcoat. My
tailor assures me that blue forget-me-nots on white satin
will soon be all the rage, but perhaps you have not seen
the design before: I like to be a trifle ahead of the pack.'

Anne smiled fleetingly, but muttered through clenched teeth, 'I can't speak, Sir Mortimer. I'm counting my
steps.'

'Nonsense. Relax and follow me and, for heaven's
sake, stop calling me "sir" when I distinctly heard you
address that rattle Ponsonby as Johnny on a much briefer

acquaintance.'

Anne's step faltered and she felt Mortimer's hand tighten on her waist. She shivered with a delightful thrill of pleasure and involuntarily pulled slightly away. Misinterpreting her movement, he avoided her eyes and thus failed to see the radiant glow which suffused her countenance. Before he could stop himself, he heard his own voice saying harshly, 'Or do you find me so distasteful that you need to preserve the barrier of formality between us?'

The dance ended with a final flourish; Anne's face was as white as her dress, but she rallied when he released her and replied heatedly, 'There can be no familiarity between us while you persist in misunderstanding me, Sir Mortimer.'

She sketched a rapid curtsey and almost ran from the floor, leaving her partner pale-faced and grim-lipped, the target of many curious eyes.

Anne retreated to her seat and fanned herself vigorously. Mrs. Henderson was deeply engaged in conversation with a purple-clad dowager and after a perfunctory smile, left Anne in peace. Halfway through the pre-supper dance, which had been promised to Mortimer, Anne began to feel better and to regret her hasty words. When everyone started to drift towards the refreshments, she longed for some tea; she was much relieved when Drusilla, who had observed the incident from afar, came seeking her.

'Lord Johnny and Captain Grattan have joined the line for some beverages and I said we would find a table. Come quickly, before they are all gone,' urged Drusilla, half-turning to retrace her steps. Anne caught up with her and seizing her hand, whispered, 'Sir Mortimer?'

'He's in the card room with a face like a thundercloud,' according to the Captain,' laughed Drusilla, adding bracingly, 'Dear Anne, thunderclouds blow over.' Then she wisely changed the subject, for Anne's eyes were bright with unshed tears.

A few sips of tea did much to restore Anne's morale and she even managed to toy with a stale cake.

'One certainly does not come here for the refreshments,' muttered Johnny, munching bread and butter with gusto, if not enthusiasm.

Anne's three companions exerted themselves to distract her. The two gentlemen were acquainted with almost everyone present and obligingly pointed out various notable personages, vying with one another to recount amusing anecdotes and several times causing Anne and Drusilla to hide their giggles behind their fans. That dandified man with the spindly legs and orange-and-apricot striped waistcoat was also a brave officer, who owned an enviable pack of hounds and was a bruising rider; the young sprig beside him with the impossibly high cravat was a minor poet, who would make short work of Anne's winged eyebrows, given the smallest encouragement; and the lady in apple green, with the oddly spaced patches, was the wealthy and eccentric Lady Victoria Lennox-Dabney, who had nearly died of the smallpox and had driven away any number of suitors by her unfortunate habit of constantly reliving the experience.

'That's m'sister, Sophie, sitting by Lady Montfort,' said Johnny at length, indicating a plump, but pretty, fair-haired damsel in a gown of celestial blue, who waved cheerfully when she caught her brother's eye. Lady Montfort also glanced in their direction and inclined her head with a smiling nod.

'Sophie likes Lady M's books, ye know,' confided Johnny, a look of puzzlement transparent on his open face.

'So do I,' said Jeremy Grattan unexpectedly. 'Mortimer had them in the Peninsula. I remember sitting in a small boat, ostensibly fishing, but in fact wiling away an idle afternoon most pleasantly with *The Master of Crumbling Keep*. In spirit I was transported back to Sussex and felt quite homesick for the remainder of the day.'

'Is your home in Sussex, Captain Grattan?' asked Anne.

'Yes, Miss Fairleigh. My father is vicar of a small parish near Lewes.'

'Good evening, Miss Henderson, Miss Fairleigh, gentlemen,' Lady Montfort's soft voice caused the two officers to leap to their feet as she paused by Anne's chair on her way back to the ballroom.

'We were just telling Johnny that he must read your books, Lady Montfort,' said Captain Grattan mischievously.

Correctly interpreting the young man's hissing, indrawn breath, Hester smiled upon Lord Johnny and said kindly, 'Gothic tales are not to everyone's taste. Don't worry, I promise not to grill you on your reactions next time you call.'

Johnny blushed and stammered that he was not much of a reader, but would be most happy to cast an eye on the written page for her ladyship's sake. Lord Montfort, who had been listening to this exchange with a sardonic glint in his brilliant green eyes, intervened to spare the hapless Johnny further embarrassment. Under cover of the general badinage, Hester said quietly to Anne, 'Is Mortimer not with you? My wits must be wandering. I was certain he told me he was engaged to you for the supper dance.'

Anne hesitated. The music had commenced and there was a general shuffle to return to the main Assembly room. She found herself walking by Lady Montfort's side and said, flushing uncomfortably, 'Your ladyship was not mistaken. Sir Mortimer and I had a slight misunderstanding earlier in the evening and – and I have not seen him since,' she finished lamely.

Hester frowned. 'That is not like him. I know I am partial, but I have never thought him capable of being so ill-mannered.'

'Oh, he was not uncivil, or if he was, it was all my fault,' broke in Anne, miserably.

Though mightily intrigued, Hester saw her duty plainly. She must *not* meddle. Instead she said gently, 'Forgive me for raising the matter. It was not my intention to distress you. Let me make amends for my family's unpardonable behaviour by introducing you to "Cupid" Palmerston, who dances divinely and talks all the time. He is a very interesting man. He was the first to dance the waltz at Almack's, with Countess Lieven.'

She left Anne in the gentleman's safe, but undemanding company. He whirled his partner expertly up and down the length of the floor, conversing fluently and amusingly, but requiring no more response than the occasional nod or smile. Gradually Anne relaxed and performed more gracefully and confidently than she had ever done before. The other dancers gave way as they flew round and round, spinning and swaying as if they indeed had wings on their heels. Through a dazed blur Anne thought she saw Mortimer's scowling visage emerge from the card room, but she had no opportunity to look again for some minutes, and then he had disappeared. However, other gentlemen had begun to notice the attractive Miss Fairleigh and for the remainder of the evening Anne was so besieged with invitations to dance that she began to wonder cynically if word of her fortune had preceded her. Shaking off this disturbing thought, she danced until her feet ached and her head swam, but seek as she might, she saw no more of Sir Mortimer and found it difficult to respond with more than a mechanical smile, and a murmured apology that she was very tired, to Mrs. Henderson's generous remarks on the drive home that she had been the success of the evening.

XIII

The Spectre of Newgate

'You are making a mountain out of a molehill,' observed
Drusilla next day, drawing on her gloves. Anne merely
shook her head and gazed at her book, all the light
quenched in her dark eyes.

Drusilla left her to her melancholy thoughts and
proceeded to her friend Georgiana Upcroft's house, for
this was the day she was to visit Newgate Prison. She was
accompanied by a young footman, who carried a sizable
bundle of clothes and other comforts for distribution
among the women and children. She must remember to
ask Georgiana the best method of handing out the items
equitably; she did not want to provoke jealousy or even
fighting between the inmates.

When shown once more into the austere drawing
room which had so repelled Anne, Drusilla found her
friend entertaining a gentleman who rose and met her
eyes with a bright, confident stare as Georgiana
introduced them. 'Drusilla, may I present Mr. Simon
Pontefract of Bristol. Miss Drusilla Henderson, one of
my oldest friends,' Mrs. Upcroft's sharp face wore an
expression of alert curiosity. For a moment there was
silence, except for the steady tick of the mantelpiece
clock, which seemed unnaturally loud in the stillness.
Drusilla experienced a pang of annoyance; obviously
this meeting had been arranged, for Mr. Pontefract
must be aware of Anne's presence under her parents'
roof and she blamed her friend for placing her in such

an awkward situation. She inclined her head slightly in acknowledgment of his presence, but did not extend her hand. Instead she looked at him carefully, noting with immediate approval that he was a well-proportioned man, with a strong face, neatly attired in buff pantaloons and a square-cut, dark blue tailcoat. He endured her quiet scrutiny unflinchingly until Georgiana broke in to say, 'Well, I must beg you to excuse me for a moment while I fetch my pelisse. Time presses. My husband will be with you directly, Mr. Pontefract.'

She sounded flustered and Drusilla's lips tightened as her friend hurried away, leaving her alone with the object of Anne's distress and dread. She determined to put her theory to the test. Unceremoniously interrupting Mr. Pontefract's polite remarks concerning the festivities in London, she said abruptly, 'I believe, sir, we have a mutual acquaintance, Miss Anne Fairleigh?'

Simon Pontefract's brow contracted in a quick frown at this frontal attack, but then a sardonic grin replaced the grimmer expression. 'You suspect my motives in seeking you out, Miss Henderson?' he asked frankly.

Unaccountably she wished that she was not wearing her oldest and plainest bonnet and mantle. She pushed the unworthy thought aside and retorted cautiously, 'Why should it be a matter for suspicion, Mr. Pontefract? I am unaware that I have accused you of "seeking me out", as you put it, but your quick assumption suggests that offence may be the best method of defence, from your point of view.'

Drusilla folded her hands composedly in her lap and raised her face inquiringly. Mr. Pontefract flung up a hand in a gesture of self-defence and laughed aloud, but his eyes grew keen. He crossed the room and seated himself close beside her, saying urgently, 'Cease fencing with me, ma'am. I admit I would like to speak with you, but Mrs. Upcroft will return at any moment. Will you forgive my incivility on a matter of mutual interest and consent to another meeting in the near future?'

Drusilla regarded the gentleman meditatively, resisting the impulse to move farther away, although his proximity disturbed her more than she cared to own. She found it difficult to reconcile the earnest man before her with her preconceived image, derived from Anne's description, and was inclined to think she had exaggerated the darker side of his character. Her practical mind did not consider fortune-hunting or the absence of love between a couple as criminal offences, although she did think he had been rash to make rough physical advances to a girl half his age, no matter how desperate his financial plight.

'Do I pass muster – will you trust yourself to Miss Fairleigh's ogre for a second meeting?' The plaintive voice was belied by the twinkling eyes.

Drusilla nodded briskly, as footsteps sounded in the passage.

'I will be in the gallery at the Royal Academy at four tomorrow. Do you care for Turner's paintings?' she finished significantly as Mrs. Upcroft reentered the room.

'Not a great deal, but on your recommendation I will certainly take the opportunity to reacquaint myself with those on exhibit at the Academy,' responded Simon with an emphatic nod.

Satisfied that he had understood, Drusilla rose and departed with Georgiana. As she waited for the footman to bestow Mrs. Upcroft's gifts in the carriage, she glanced up at the window of the room they had just quitted and saw Mr. Pontefract watching them. He raised his hand and Drusilla smiled back cheerfully, feeling strangely drawn to the man – he represented something outside her experience of country gentry or town aristocrats – he had a dynamism about him and she wondered why Anne had failed to respond to it. She found herself anticipating their next meeting with

pleasure and listened with but half an ear to Georgiana's
prattle as she commented on the comfort of the
Henderson carriage compared with the hired cabs she
was usually obliged to take; suddenly Drusilla's
companion caught her attention. 'I shouldn't be
surprised if Simon Pontefract finds himself in Newgate
or The Fleet one of these days. James says the man is a
reckless gambler.'

'Indeed?' said Drusilla coolly. She had not yet
forgiven Georgiana for forcing the meeting upon her
and she did not wish to encourage her malicious tongue.
To Drusilla, Mr. Pontefract seemed a sensible
humorous, decisive man of experience, no more
Georgiana's "reckless gambler" than he was Anne's
"sinister, heartless adventurer". 'Have a care, Miss
Henderson,' she mentally apostrophized herself. She
decided to reserve judgment and diverted her
companion's thoughts by inquiring closely about the
conditions she might expect to find in Newgate.

Although Georgiana told her at length that the jailers
were ignorant, cruel, and corrupt; the government
loath to institute reforms, and the prisoners half-starved
and despairing, nevertheless Drusilla was unprepared
for her overwhelming sense of revulsion when she
entered the great, gloomy, castellated building designed
by the architect George Dance. She hoped she was not
going to faint as she followed Mrs. Upcroft and the
turnkey along dark corridors to the women's quarters.
Her skirts brushed the dank walls and she trod
delicately on the herbs strewn to protect the inmates
from the foul fumes which caused jail fever. The odour
of unwashed, crowded humanity was all-pervasive, but
once inside the large room where the women and
children were assembled, pity overcame her disgust and
Drusilla made haste to follow Georgiana's directions,
handing out small packets of sweets or toys to the eager,
outstretched little hands. One child, a boy with

enormous dark eyes and a sallow, unhealthy pallor, attracted Drusilla's attention. He hung back as the other children clustered round her, pushing and scrambling; she saw that he was leaning on a roughly made crutch. Drusilla reserved a wooden cart and horse for him and when the group had dispersed to examine their spoils, she approached him holding out the toy. He stared at it, taking in the glory of red-painted wheels which revolved as Drusilla spun them. Slowly he put out one finger and ran it gently along the smooth wood. Drusilla took the string and wound it round his thin wrist, pressing the toy into his palm. 'Cor, lumme, fer me, miss?'

She smiled and nodded, 'Yes, just for you.'

His eyes shone as he stuffed the cart in his ragged shirt and hurried to a far corner to examine his treasure in peace.

Drusilla straightened and brushed away a tear, forcing down a strong desire to do battle with the English legal system, which condemned innocent children to share their parents' fate in this noisesome, squalid, disease-ridden hole.

The phrase "I have ta-en too little care of this" kept running through her mind as she moved diligently among the women sewing, helping them cut and alter garments for themselves and their children. She realized that the prisoners who had been allowed to join the needlework group were the most docile and well-behaved; she was only seeing the tip of the iceberg. The majority of the women were quite young and many were thin and undernourished; some worked in dogged silence, straining their eyes in the dim light, while others were eager to talk, asking Drusilla about the newest modes and showing surprising interest in the affairs of the Prince Regent. They begged her to bring some fashion magazines next time she came and one or two requested writing materials; as they gained in confidence they suggested other needs: pins, needles, a cake of soap, a comb. Drusilla made a list and promised to do her best to obtain the articles.

She had no opportunity to speak privately with any of the women, but several spoke quite openly of their lives and of the sequence of events which had brought them to their present situation. One woman had been desperate to feed her starving children after her husband was arrested at a political demonstration and she had stolen a pound of liver from a butcher's shop; another, better spoken than the rest, was a respectable widow who had struggled to run a bakery in Pudding Lane, but she had run into debt with the high price of bread and the grain suppliers had forced her into bankruptcy. One unfortunate woman did not know why she had been arrested; she thought it was a case of mistaken identity, but had been held without trial for three months.

Drusilla listened incredulously to these tales of woe; how could the authorities put such cases in with hardened criminals and what effect must it have on the children to mingle with thieves and prostitutes during their most impressionable years? Newgate was mainly a prison for criminals, but anyone owing money was liable to be sent there for months and even years if they were unable to find means to repay. In the prevailing conditions, it was obvious that many of the inmates' characters and habits were bound to deteriorate seriously during the period of their incarceration.

Towards the end of their allotted time, Georgiana took out her Bible and read aloud the story of Ruth. Drusilla did not think it particularly appropriate, since the audience was unable to follow anybody at present, but it appeared that she was mistaken, for one poor girl burst into tears, crying that everything would have been as it should be if only she had drawn one of the lots to accompany her husband to Spain and those seated by her nodded their heads in sympathy.

'Only six wives for every 'undred soldiers in a regiment was given a "to go" ticket, ye see miss. The ones left be'ind don't get no allowance, not a penny. It's crool 'ard fer those wiv no family ter go back 'ome to an' often there's a baby on the way,' explained a middle-aged woman called Mary, who saw Drusilla's puzzled expression.

'But that's dreadful. I mean, it may be sensible to limit the number of camp followers, but those left in England should be given some support.' Drusilla was horrified.

Mary shrugged. 'This world's chock full o' injustice. This institution's full o' discharged soldiers 'oo can't find a way ter make an honest livin'. There's no work an' some says arl the grand folk can't ferget the troubles in France and are mortal afeard o' revolution an' riotin'.'

When the ladies finally regained the sanctuary of the carriage, the women's thanks still ringing in their ears, Georgiana commented, 'It's pitiful how grateful they are for any little kindess.'

Drusilla nodded and leaned back, thankfully closing her eyes. It had been a harder day than any she could remember. Georgiana was also tired and mercifully silent. Battered by unusual thoughts and sensations, Drusilla reflected that in one day she had been attracted to a reckless adventurer who was unacceptable to friends as different in character and outlook as Anne and Georgiana, and also had had her whole country-bred views on social order and the essential rightness and justice of the English penal system undermined. 'I'm weary and fanciful,' she decided, summoning common sense to her aid.

The carriage stopped at Georgiana's door. On the step, Mrs. Upcroft turned for a parting admonition, 'Be sure and bathe thoroughly and disinfect your clothes. I appreciated your company and aid, but I could not answer to your mama if you contracted some jail fever. You are fatigued, so I will not keep you. Good-bye, Drusilla. I hope to see you again soon.'

Left alone, Drusilla frowned, winced, and laughed.

More solemn thoughts were banished and for the
remainder of the drive, she longed for a hot scented
bath and tried to ignore a strong desire to scratch
herself! On her arrival, she was relieved to hear that her
parents had departed to spend the day in Richmond
with an elderly aunt and Miss Fairleigh had been invited
to take luncheon with Lady Montfort; Tillie had but just
returned from accompanying her to Portman Square.

Drusilla followed Georgiana's instructions and wall-
owed luxuriantly in the tub, while Tillie took her
garments to be laundered, holding them at arm's
length. The maid reappeared to help her mistress dress,
having first inspected her hair and combed it carefully.

'You was fortunate, Miss Drusilla,' she said with a sigh
of relief, 'I can't see nothin' untoward, but we'd best
keep a close watch for a few days yet.'

Drusilla shuddered, but agreed reluctantly to this
suggestion.

'Now, Tillie, I feel quite famished. Could you bring
me a tray up here, just some soup and perhaps a
sandwich. I think I'll rest for a little while until Miss
Fairleigh gets back.'

After her meal, she lay down upon her bed and slept
soundly for two hours. She was awakened by a light tap;
Anne's head came round the door and Miss Henderson
sat up, feeling much refreshed and disposed for
conversation.

'Come in. You look like the cat that ate the cream –
quite different from the forlorn waif I left this
morning,' remarked Drusilla, amused.

It was true Anne's eyes were sparkling as she
plumped down beside her friend and pulled off her
bonnet, but she said penitently, 'I beg your pardon for
being such a miserable wretch. Will you forgive me?'

'Only if you tell me what has happened to effect such
a miraculous transformation,' teased Drusilla.

Anne paused to collect her thoughts. She began,

'Well, soon after you left, Lady Montfort's footman came to bring me an invitation to luncheon. It was to be quite informal, just the two of us and perhaps his lordship, who was working at home on estate matters this morning. When I arrived she was playing at skittles with her sons and I joined them in the garden. We had a merry game for about half an hour and when the boys were summoned for their nursery meal, we sat by the lily pond and talked. She began by saying she had been for an early ride with Sir Mortimer, who had described the unhappy incident between us last night at Almack's and blamed himself for provoking me and for his subsequent incivility in failing to take me in to supper. She seemed much vexed and I assured her that I was also at fault for losing my temper; my reaction had been out of all proportion to the offence. I explained that I had just heard that my feared guardian and would-be husband had come to town. This intelligence and the natural trepidation which I felt on making my first appearance at an Almack's Assembly had combined last night to make me nervous and oversensitive. It was really a very trivial matter and I felt so ashamed.'

'And what did Lady Montfort say?' inquired Drusilla curiously.

'Oh, she was very kind and understanding. She observed that in certain situations one frequently makes remarks which are instantly regretted. She said that I was like a character in a Gothic novel, running away from my wicked guardian! But she pointed out that unlike many unfortunate heroines, I do have family and friends to protect me. We had an interesting discussion on the necessary ingredients for a Gothic novel over luncheon. I had not thought about it before, but it is true, there are many common themes in such works.'

'For instance?' prompted Drusilla.

'Any number of things: dark family secrets; exotic foreign settings; ghosts; terror and dread; sinister fathers or brothers; murder and death, with undertones of the old religion in ruined abbeys or monasteries; and heroines who are weaker physically than the male characters, but who represent reason and civilization in conflict with the powers of evil and the supernatural.'

'I would never have suspected that Mrs. Radcliffe was such a deep thinker,' replied Drusilla lightly.

'I doubt if she is,' returned Anne, 'but Lord Montfort analyzed his wife's stories for me over lunch quite exhaustively. I was so fascinated I barely ate a morsel. Indeed, Drusilla, it will be quite some time before I can read a Gothic tale again seriously.'

'I wonder why it is that literary criticism invariably detracts from one's enjoyment of a work,' meditated Drusilla. 'But we are digressing. Did anything else of importance occur?'

'Perhaps,' Anne dimpled. 'Lady Montfort gave me a message from Sir Mortimer as I was leaving. He wants to take me for a drive tomorrow. I said that I would go: I hope it does not rain. Do you think it will?'

Drusilla smiled and prophesied that it would not. Anne's arrangement suited her very well, for it would leave her free to meet Mr. Pontefract. Drusilla did not tell Anne of the rendezvous planned with her guardian, for she thought the knowledge would distress her unnecessarily; she decided to keep her own counsel.

Anne rattled on, 'We talked a little about prisons as well as novels. Lord Montfort is most concerned to introduce prison reforms and to ameliorate the harsh penalties for lesser offences, but he has been so much abroad with the peace discussions that he has been able to do nothing as yet. You must talk to him. I was thinking of you so much. Was it a very unpleasant experience?'

Drusilla reflected. 'Yes and no. I was quite proud of myself; I did not faint and I was not overcome with nausea, although the stench was appalling. I thought if

Georgiana could do it, then so could I. It is no doubt spiteful of me, but I confess I did not care for Georgiana's condescending manner. She was so obviously "doing good" that I half-expected the women would reject her overtures, but they seized the "gifts" with pitiful eagerness and most of them listened to the Bible-reading attentively. Of course the warden stood by the wall the whole time, holding a whip or stick, I'm not sure which, and that must have had a restraining effect. Bye-the-bye, Lady Montfort's children might have some old toys they could spare, or clothes. The need is very great.' She described the little boy with the crutch, the soldier's wife in tears, and her conversation with the prisoner Mary.

'I think you are very brave,' said Anne warmly at the end of this recital. 'I felt guilty remaining in comfort this morning while you went to face suffering and misery.'

'Nonsense,' said Drusilla soothingly, 'I spent most of my time sewing and I know how you hate to sew. If you want to ease your conscience you may come with me to purchase writing materials and ladies' fashion journals, which I promised to take next week.'

Anne nodded. 'Of course, but I still feel inadequate. May I come with you next time? I know you think me a featherbrained romantic, but I do wish to help.'

Drusilla smiled, but said cautiously, 'I think you a delightfully imaginative creature and very far from being useless, but the number of visitors is strictly limited and it may not be possible. We'll see.'

Anne gazed out of the window at a blackbird chirping with a worm in the tree outside. She said dreamily, her dark eyes intent on the bird, 'You know, Drusilla, if you face things squarely, you will often find your fears dissipated.'

Drusilla moved to tidy her hair. 'Do you have any particular "thing" in mind?' she asked over her shoulder, brushing vigorously.

Anne went to join her and fiddled with the articles on the dressing table. After a moment she met her friend's eye in the mirror and said slowly, 'I could say prisons, or Lord Montfort, or any number of frightening places or persons, but I was thinking that I have been brusque and unkind to Sir Mortimer because he made me feel uncomfortable and – and because I was repelled by his scar, although I would not admit it; did not even know it until he accused me of it last night. Lady Montfort hinted delicately that he is very sensitive about it and I was wondering, Drusilla, do you think perhaps he idealized Stephanie Tremaine as a substitute – I mean, because she was beyond his reach and he could not come close to her?'

Miss Henderson shrugged in disbelief. 'It's possible, but pardon my skepticism, Anne. In the polite world we live in, marriage is not always an insuperable barrier.'

Anne sighed impatiently. 'I know, but I believe I am right, nonetheless.'

Drusilla stood up and said gently, 'Don't fret so. You always knew that beauty is not skin-deep, else why are you my friend? I suspect, my dear, that Sir Mortimer is a special case with you, not amenable to reason.'

As they made their way downstairs to the drawing room, she added, 'Action is the solution. We've been too much isolated in the country with our books and our imaginings. Having acknowledged this, I intend to become much more active. My experience today reminded me that it will not do to turn aside from suffering and pass by on the other side. Oh, dear, I sound like the Dean last Sunday. Let us make haste to find some tea to console you, while I bore you with my moralizing.'

Anne giggled, but whispered, as Mr. Henderson appeared in the hall below, 'Thank you, Drusilla, you're a great comfort.'

And the two young ladies reached the bottom of the stair in greater harmony than ever.

XIV

Anne and Mortimer Go Sightseeing

'Anne, my dear, you will strain your eyes reading such fine print. Would it not be better to move over here by the window?'

Anne closed her book and smiled at Mrs. Henderson and Drusilla, who were sewing by the open window and enjoying the warm breeze, which stirred the curtains and filled the air with the scent of roses. The older lady bent forward to select a thread from her workbasket.

'What are you reading?' she asked, 'such a bookworm, always visiting the circulating library and a different volume every time I look at you.'

'This one is a translation from the French of St. Pierre, ma'am. It is called *Paul and Virginia* and it is interesting because the tale is set in the French slave colony of Madagascar. But you are quite correct, the print is very small; the advantage is that the book is also tiny and I can slip it in my bead bag, ready for any idle moment.'

Mrs. Henderson shook her head in mock despair. 'Well, you will not be needing it this afternoon, I vow. When do you expect Sir Mortimer?'

Anne consulted the timepiece on the étagère. 'My goodness, quite soon!' she exclaimed, 'in about half an hour. I must run and get ready.'

She had begun to gather her things, when Tillie entered with a letter for her. Anne sat down again, remarking happily, 'It is from my cousin, Letitia. Such wonderful news, Jack is to marry Meg Oliphant. You recall I told you I met her at the Tremaines' dinner party and liked her very well. You remind me of her, Drusilla, except that she is taller. Oh, I am sure they will suit. They have known one another since childhood, but had drifted apart when Jack was in the army. It seems the wedding will be quite a large affair and my cousins are coming to Town to do some shopping. How delightful, you will be able to meet them.' She paused and skimmed the rest of the letter quickly, then looked up laughing. 'Cousin Ippolita has appended a note at the end, saying that Letty can think of nothing but shops, but she hopes to see me and some good plays and they intend to leave Jack to his own devices for a week or two.'

'When will the ladies arrive in London, Anne? Do they have a place to stay?' inquired Mrs. Henderson practically.

Anne studied her letter more closely. 'Dear Letty's hand is very spidery and hard to make out. Ah, yes, here it is. They hope to be settled at Gordon's Hotel in Arlington Street on Saturday and will send word of their arrival at the first opportunity.'

Mrs. Henderson approved their choice of hostelry. 'Quiet and comfortable, my dear. Much better than a noisy staging inn. Josiah and I put up there some years ago now and we were very satisfied with our room, although the dinners are plain. The Misses Prawne must dine with us as soon as it can be arranged.'

'Thank you, ma'am,' said Anne sincerely, folding her letter carefully.

Mrs. Henderson waved aside her thanks. 'It's nothing, child, I enjoy company. Now, run upstairs and make haste. Gentlemen do not like to be kept waiting.'

Anne rose obediently, but lingered at the door. 'Are you sure you will not go with us, Drusilla?'

'Not today, Anne. I forgot to tell you I am engaged to meet a friend at the Royal Academy later this afternoon. May I use the carriage, Mama, or shall I take a hackney cab?'

Fortunately for Drusilla, her mother and Anne

assumed she was meeting Mrs. Upcroft; Mrs. Henderson gave her permission for Drusilla to take the carriage just as the doorbell rang and the two young ladies sped upstairs to adjust their toilettes for their respective outings.

Some twenty minutes later, Mrs. Henderson stood beaming and waving her sewing at Anne and Sir Mortimer from the small balcony of the drawing room.

'What a delightful woman Mrs. Henderson is!' exclaimed Sir Mortimer, as he gave his horses the office to move and the curricle pulled into the line of traffic, with the groom and the maid Tillie up behind. Tillie was very nervous in the light, high vehicle and concentrated almost exclusively on retaining her seat, giving vent to muffled shrieks from time to time.

Anne agreed with Mortimer's remark. 'Yes, indeed. I feel myself very lucky to have been adopted by such an affectionate household. I loved my father dearly, but I did sometimes long for a more lively family. Papa was such a bookworm. Our housekeeper used to say he was quite different in his youth and when my mother was alive.' She sighed wistfully.

Mortimer glanced reflectively at his companion. She was gazing at the sky and he thought what an enchanting profile she possessed, her chin resting on the lace frill of her apple-green spencerette, with her bonnet loosely tied and perched well back on her curls.

Unaware of his scrutiny she said dreamily, 'Do you ever look for pictures in the clouds, Sir Mortimer? See, there, straight ahead, a beautiful white whale blowing bubbles in a blue sea.'

Mortimer scanned the heavens blankly and was surprised by a sudden chuckle from Anne.

'No, no, sir, not directly above us. But, pray keep your eyes on the road or we shall run over that sleek cat rolling in the gutter. Are you fond of cats? Do you remember Judy and her kittens at Natherscombe? I hope they all found good homes.'

Bewildered and pleased by her bantering tone, Mortimer grinned, his hazel eyes alight and his face crinkling in what Anne privately considered an excessively attractive manner, even the mark stretching from his right eye to the corner of his mouth seemed to relax and blend in the warmth of her approbation. Deftly avoiding the fat feline, Mortimer threaded his way slowly along Oxford Street.

'Where are we going? This is not your usual groom with you today?' asked Anne.

'No, this is Possum, who has come along to play propriety, but I warn you he is deaf as a post. I borrowed him from my brother-in-law. My own groom is in bed with a severe cold in the head. But I thought I would take you for a different drive today. I want to show you some of my favourite parts of the City.'

The vehicle swung round the corner of Oxford Street into Park Lane. Anne shuddered, thinking of the numerous felons who had met their fate on Tyburn Tree. Sensitive to her mood, although he kept his eyes on the way ahead, Mortimer said gently, 'Does the site distress you? We will return by another route, if you please. But Tyburn is no longer a place of execution, you know.'

'No, but Newgate is. It distresses me to think of a fellow human being's death as an excuse for a public entertainment. I know criminals must be brought to justice, but I feel it should be done in decent privacy,' replied Anne, frowning at the leafy trees which fringed Hyde Park on their right.

'I believe the theory behind a public hanging is that such an example will deter prospective criminals, reminding them of the awful fate in store if they are caught,' responded Mortimer quietly.

Anne was unconvinced. 'I still maintain it is a barbarous custom. I have never witnessed a public execution, but from what I have read and seen in pictures it appears that such an event is an excuse to indulge the baser, crueller instincts of human nature. Most people who watch these affairs cannot be criminals; they come in the same spirit in which they go to see a bull-baiting or a cockfight or even a pugilistic display. Surely one should begin at the other end and try to prevent crime by improving the lot of poor people? But, as a soldier, I do not expect you to agree with me.'

Uncertain how to reply, Mortimer reined his horses to a walk, before saying meditatively, 'That last remark was meant to provoke, I doubt not, Miss Fairleigh, but I shall not rise to your bait. As a soldier I believe in firmness and justice, but not, I would stress, in unnecessary brutality. I suspect that we share a common bond in our fondness for animals. Don't forget that I grew up much under my sister's influence and Hester loathes blood sports, while her husband is making himself extremely unpopular in some quarters by his agitation for penal reform. There should be greater distinctions between types of crime: between, for example, petty theft, highway robbery, and murder. I, myself, have seen the hardship suffered by the men returned from the wars, trained in violence and receiving little appreciation from their country for their years of service. Often these men have been wounded and can no longer perform the labours of an able-bodied person. Is it any wonder they turn to less orthodox methods to feed their families?'

Impulsively Anne laid one gloved hand on Mortimer's sleeve, exclaiming, 'You are quite right and I beg your pardon. I have been feeling guilty at doing so little, and Drusilla's account of her visit to Newgate has put the injustice and intolerable slowness of our legal system much in my mind. But it is not proper talk for such a lovely excursion. I did not mean to tease you. I vowed that I would be on my best behaviour today.'

'H'm,' Mortimer grunted. Then with the special smile which he kept for his sister and one or two close friends, he placed his free hand over Anne's; she felt a slight pressure and he released her, staring fixedly at the beasts' twitching ears. His voice was not quite steady as he

said, 'I like to know what you are thinking. Best
behaviour can be very inhibiting, and since we are being
frank with one another, may I apologize for my abomin-
able manners at Almack's the other evening. It was good
of you to consent to drive with me again, for I am aware
that I presumed too much on our acquaintance and there
was no reason why you should allow me to address you by
your first name.'

Touched by the lowering of his proud spirit, Anne said
resolutely, 'Please, Sir Mortimer, let us forget the incident. I fear I also must regret some hasty words. The
whole affair made me very unhappy, for I value your
friendship a great deal. I should like it of all things if you
would call me Anne.'

Bravely she raised her eyes to meet his, the horses
stilled to a halt and, for a long moment, they gazed at one
another breathlessly. Slowly, Sir Mortimer lifted her
hand to his lips. 'So be it, Anne,' he murmured.

The animals stirred restlessly, a dog ran out barking,
and Mortimer dropped her hand to restrain the startled
beasts. Overhead the birds sang joyfully; Anne clasped
her parasol with trembling fingers and a muscle twitched
beside Mortimer's firm mouth. Possum stared stolidly
the other way and Tillie emitted one of her shrieks.

They proceeded steadily eastwards, following a route
along Piccadilly, down the Haymarket, past Charing
Cross to The Strand. Sir Mortimer talked easily on
impersonal subjects and pointed out various places of
architectural or historical significance, while Anne
listened with interest. As they passed the Royal Mews and
entered The Strand, she exclaimed, 'Oh, I do love
London, and you are such an excellent guide. So much
better than reading a guidebook, for one cannot read
and look at the same time! I must remember all these
details to impress my cousins when they arrive.'

'Your cousins – do you mean Miss Ippolita and Miss
Letitia?' inquired Mortimer.

'Yes, I had a letter from them this morning. They are

coming to Town in a few days. They sent their kind remembrances to you.'

'Thank you. Does Jack come with them?'

'No. But I have such good news; he is betrothed to Meg Oliphant. You recall they met again after many years at Lady Tremaine's dinner party?' Anne bit her lip, regretting her careless words, as the memory of Sir Mortimer's different preoccupation that night came flooding back to her. In her distraction she failed to observe the sudden gleam in the gentleman's eyes. With unusual fervour he agreed that it was indeed excellent tidings and rejoiced privately that his old comrade had overcome his tendre for Anne so speedily.

A young lady and her mother whom Anne knew slightly through the Hendersons were walking along the pavement and waved to attract her attention. Anne bowed and waved in return, but her companion appeared oblivious and swung his vehicle into the far right lane to pass the church of St. Clement Danes, which he indicated with his whip, remarking, 'Did you know Samuel Johnson, the compiler of the great dictionary, worshipped regularly at St. Clement's?'

Anne shook her head silently. Mortimer glanced down at her and raised his eyebrows. 'Did you wish to stop and speak to those ladies?' he asked. 'Your acquaintances will think you are up beside a boorish fellow, a beast who keeps this beauty all for himself.'

'Nonsense,' replied Anne lightly, to hide the rapid beating of her pulse. 'They will think I am a selfish minx who will not share her dashing, military gentleman with other deserving ladies.' Then, fearing that she had been too fast, she added, with an attempt at nonchalance, 'Besides, it is impossible to have any rational conversation from carriage tops and I get very bored with polite gossip.'

His eyes twinkling, Mortimer begged mischievously, 'My dear Anne, don't spoil it. The first half of your speech has quite puffed me up in my own esteem.'

Fortunately she was spared the necessity to reply to this sally, for they had reached the gate of Temple Bar and Mortimer handed the reins to Possum. 'We will walk a little, if you please. Some of the most fascinating parts of the City can only be seen on foot.' Suiting the action to the word, he jumped down, ordered Possum to return in an hour and assisted Anne to alight. He kept her hand tucked within his arm as they strolled down Middle Temple Lane, and Tillie followed at a discreet distance, happy to be on firm ground once more. It was cool and shady in the narrow walk, hemmed in on both sides by the ancient stone buildings, the flagstones and cobbles worn smooth by the feet of centuries. Here they had left the fashionable world behind; as they progressed, the noise and clatter of Fleet Street receded and was replaced by an unhurried, but purposeful scene of barristers in wigs and flapping robes followed by their clerks, clutching heavy piles of books and papers, steadfastly pursuing their path from chambers to courtroom. Snatches of legal talk reached Anne's ears from open windows and doorways as they rounded several corners, went under an arch, and emerged in a sunny courtyard at the heart of the Inns of Court and Chancery. Here stood the old, austere Temple Church, founded by the Knights Templar.

'This is my favourite place in London,' said Mortimer quietly, as he pushed open the heavy, creaking door for Anne to enter the church. They stood a moment, letting their eyes adjust to the dim light and inhaling the musty damp smell of the old building.

'Oh, how lovely and peaceful,' breathed Anne, gazing at the tall windows which filtered the sunlight, the wooden pews, and the strange shape of the church, which was divided into two portions, a circular part called the Round, and an oblong.

'Come this way,' said Mortimer, taking her hand and leading her to the round portion on their left. 'This is the oldest part of the church. It is badly in need of repair, but

I want you to see the effigies of the knights.'

They passed some strangely carved stone heads and Anne shivered at the grotesque expressions of many of them.

'It was built in the late twelfth century,' Mortimer was saying, 'And over there was the chapel of St. Anne, on the south side, but only the crypt survives. By the wheel window is a tiny cell; it was the penitential cell and measures only four and a half feet in length by two and a half in breadth, so that the unhappy prisoner could not lie down except by drawing his limbs together.'

'It's worse than Newgate!' observed Anne, walking forward to bend down and peer at the chamber.

'At least they could listen to the services and music for entertainment. I believe one poor man died there in his fetters. His name was Walter le Bacheler. All the knights took vows of chastity and obedience to the order and for a time their reputation was very high. Look here at the effigies; many of them were renowned for their exploits in the Crusades to the Holy Land.'

'Do you know who any of the figures represent?' asked Anne, thoughtfully surveying the monuments to long-dead great men.

'Some of them are known, but others have not been positively identified. The one I always remember is the first figure on the left; that is Geoffrey de Mandeville, who was very bold and very bad. He was the son of a Norman baron who fought at the Battle of Hastings.'

'I like best the one with his dog at his feet,' said Anne, touching the faithful beast gently.

Slowly they made a tour of the church. Mortimer was very knowledgeable and spoke of the knights and their deeds with a professional appreciation. Anne was entranced and their allotted hour flew by.

They came once more to the creaking porch door. On the threshold Anne stopped and faced her guide with a radiant smile.

'Mortimer, I do thank you for showing me this special

place. I will never forget it – it was living history. That
sounds very inadequate, but I don't know how else to
express my feeling of taking a giant step back in time.'
'You express your sentiments perfectly. Your pleasure
was my reward; I saw the old building anew through your
eyes. And I like the sound of my name on your lips. I
wondered how long it would take you to say it!'
Anne blushed, but recovered and said tartly, 'Indeed,
sir, but familiarity breeds contempt, so they say.'
Mortimer grinned, appearing in no way discomfited
by this dire prediction. He replied simply, 'It is a risk
which I am willing to take. I fear we are pressed for time.
I had hoped to be able to walk through the gardens to the
river, but perhaps we can do that another day.'
They retraced their steps and found Possum waiting
dutifully just outside Temple Bar. Thankful that the
history lesson was over, Tillie relaxed and closed her eyes.
As they drove back along The Strand, Mortimer
inquired, 'Have you visited the Summer Exhibition at the
Royal Academy yet?'
'No, we are quite close to the Academy here, are we
not?' Anne glanced down the street.
'We will pass it in a moment. It is in Somerset House.
There are some good exhibits this year, but the walls are
too crowded and the mediocre is hung with the works of
gifted artists so that it is difficult to do anyone justice. It
seems to me that few people go there to admire the
creativity of the artists; they go to dissect the portraits,
asking "Who is that"? and "Is it like"?' Mortimer frowned
in distaste.
'You are very severe. Do you perhaps prefer paintings
which depict events in history, or landscapes in the
romantic style?' Anne teased him.
'I admire great art in any form; sculpture as well as
painting. But I cannot accept court artists, so-called, who
flatter or caricature to please a patron or lampoon some
unfortunate who cannot defend himself. Such skills are
all very well in their proper place – flattering family

portraits should be hung in private houses and satirical drawings belong in broadsheets, not in the Royal Academy. I feel that the President allows himself to be too much influenced by public whim and popular artists, and the truly great are frequently overlooked, ignored, or hung in some obscure position where one must crane one's neck or use a telescope to see them!'

'Such strictures cannot be allowed to pass unchallenged,' Anne began, 'I must see for myself. I will ask Drusilla, she was meeting a friend at the Exhibition this afternoon.' She stopped abruptly and gave a startled cry.

Preoccupied with the heavy carriage and pedestrian traffic, it was a minute before Mortimer could turn to discover the cause of her dismay. He found Anne looking back over her shoulder, her parasol waving precariously and her face very white.

'What is it? Have you seen a ghost?' he demanded in alarm.

'Oh, Mortimer,' she wailed, 'I have just seen Drusilla arm-in-arm with Simon Pontefract on the steps of the Royal Academy. What can it mean?'

'Are you certain? I cannot easily turn around here. Did Miss Henderson see you?'

'She waved her hand at me,' Anne spluttered.

Mortimer's scowl lifted and he said dryly, 'That does not sound as if she were doing anything of a clandestine nature. I am persuaded she will have a perfectly rational explanation. How did she know Pontefract? Could the meeting have been accidental?'

Anne shook her head and gave a puzzled shrug, 'She may have met him through her friend, Mrs. Upcroft, but she said nothing of it. Mrs. Upcroft's husband has business with Simon, but I have not seen him since that day in the New Forest.'

Mortimer nodded, grimacing ruefully, 'I remember it well. But reflect a moment. Miss Henderson is a sensible lady, who has your interests at heart. It was perhaps injudicious for her to meet Pontefract, apparently alone, but it may well have been a chance encounter.' Anne was still very pale and he added comfortingly, 'You are quite safe in London, Anne. It is quite impossible for you to be forced to wed the man against your will. We do not live in the days of the Knights Templar now, you know. This is the enlightened nineteenth century!'

'But he is a character from an older, darker age,' mused Anne, leaning back against the seat. Her colour improved and she continued hesitantly, 'I expect I have been very idiotic in this matter all along, but Simon has been a strong, though distant, presence in my life since I was a child. My father held him in such high esteem and I could not believe it when he pressed his attentions on me so violently and unexpectedly.' She paused, brooding on her grievances. 'And his behaviour before you at Tricketts Cross was so possessive, so humiliating. I was mortified.'

'A tactical error, certainly, but I can sympathize with his impetuosity,' said Mortimer. 'Youth and beauty allied to wealth are irresistible to many men, and the poor fellow probably realized it was then or never.'

Not displeased by this masterly analysis of the situation, Anne twirled her parasol meditatively for a few moments. Finally, she pronounced, 'You may be right. But I wonder what can have passed between him and Drusilla. So odd, I did not know they were acquainted. I suspect this is Mrs. Upcroft's doing.'

They had reached Henrietta Street and further speculation was impossible. Mortimer stopped by a flower seller, bright in scarlet and green, with an enormous tattered straw bonnet and a basket of country flowers over her arm. The gentleman fumbled in his pocket for some change and the impudent, sharp eyes of the flower girl sparkled. She approached the curricle, holding up an artfully tied bunch of red roses, trailing a red-and-white striped ribbon. She stood on tiptoe and Mortimer reached down; deftly the coins and the roses changed hands, while Anne watched, amused.

'Blessings on yer, kind sir,' the country girl's singsong echoed after them as they covered the remaining distance to the Hendersons' lodgings halfway down the street.

'You must have given her far too much,' laughed Anne.

Mortimer deposited the scented posy in her lap without deigning to reply. As he was helping Anne down, he hesitated a moment, his hands around her waist, her hands on his shoulders; the roses' ribbons tickled his ear. His mouth quirked humorously, 'It's good to know some of the best things in life can be bought!'

'Wretch,' muttered Anne, preparing to spring down.

'Ouch', cried Mortimer, as a thorn pricked him. However, he landed Anne gently on her feet. Side by side they ascended the shallow flight of steps.

The young lady bobbed a curtsey. 'Thank you for my roses an' the outin', kind sir. Y'r honour has blood on his ear. Would y'r honour care for a cup o' tay?' inquired Anne wickedly, mimicking the flower seller's accents.

'Or 'praps a drap o' summat stronger,' retorted Mortimer, as the butler opened the door. Hastily composing their features, Anne removed her bonnet and gave it to Tillie, who ran upstairs, brimming with gossip. Mortimer gave his hat and whip to Tompkins, 'Tea, please, Tompkins,' requested Anne, 'and some water – for the flowers.' She smiled mischievously at Mortimer, who had wondered for one hideous moment if the water were meant for him. Anne in high good humour sailed past the imperturbable manservant into the drawing room, still clasping her nosegay. That night she pressed some rose petals in her journal, to be cherished as a permanent reminder of an intriguing day.

XV

A Lady's Sense of Honour

That same evening, Anne and Drusilla had a brief moment alone before dinner. Anne seized the opportunity to tax her friend concerning her meeting with Simon Pontefract. Drusilla replied dismissively, 'It was nothing, a chance encounter through Georgiana at the Academy. He offered to escort me to my carriage and we were waiting for it to appear when you saw us.'

Mrs. and Mrs. Henderson chose this moment to join the young ladies and Drusilla sent up a silent prayer of thanks for her reprieve. She began to talk animatedly of various paintings, which she claimed to have studied in detail and was grateful that neither Anne nor her parents had yet visited the exhibit, since the pictures she described were almost entirely figments of her imagination. When her powers of invention were exhausted, she asked Anne about her excursion with Sir Mortimer and took care to ask sufficient questions to keep the conversation flowing throughout the meal.

Soon after the ladies retired to the drawing room, Anne complained that her head was throbbing. At once Mrs. Henderson was all motherly concern. 'My dear, you do not eat enough to feed a sparrow and I vow we have not been in our beds before midnight this past fortnight. It was very thoughtless of Sir Mortimer to keep you standing so long in that drafty old church. You must have contracted a chill. Go to bed at once and I will send Tillie up with a hot posset.'

Nothing loath, Anne submitted to being fussed and cosseted, but in the morning she awoke with a putrid sore throat, which developed into a severe cold. For several days she was confined to her bedchamber, too miserable to require much company, while Mrs. Henderson and Drusilla took turns to act as sick nurse. They canceled most of their engagements, for Mr. Henderson also caught the cold and he was a very demanding patient.

However, Drusilla's mother insisted that fresh air was a necessity and accordingly, on the first day of Anne's indisposition, Drusilla took her sketchbook and went with Tillie for a walk in the park. Here Mr. Pontefract saw her, seated under a tree, busily engaged in drawing a likeness of the maid as she fed the ducks.

He watched her silently for several minutes and at length she said, without looking up, 'You may look, if you wish, Mr. Pontefract. I have nearly finished.' Simon approached and squatted beside her. She smiled in a friendly fashion and he noticed with approval the way in which her eyes reflected the deep violet-blue colour of her dress. 'It is not destined for the Royal Academy, I'm afraid.'

He took the sketch and studied it. 'Perhaps not, but it is competently executed. Will you do one of me?'

He liked the fact that she consented immediately, without any false modesty or coquettishness. She chose to draw him in profile and they conversed amiably while she worked. She asked about his family and learned that he was an only child, born to elderly parents who had both died of the typhoid fever when he was at school. Drusilla listened with interest as he described his years spent as a poor relation, going from pillar to post between trade on one side and middle-class gentility on the other. In the end he could stand his humiliating position no longer; he ran away and took ship to the Americas, where he amassed a sizable fortune. On his return he settled in Bristol and invested in various shipping enterprises. 'And of late these ventures have not fared too well,' he ended abruptly, as a shower of raindrops began to fall.

Tillie came running and folded the rug, while Drusilla packed away her drawing materials.

'I hope you will be kind enough to complete the likeness?' begged Simon, impervious to the now steady rain. Tillie fidgeted, impatient to be off, but her mistress hesitated, surprised by the undertone of urgency in the man's deep voice.

'Of course, if you wish. I can add the final touches at home. Perhaps you would care to call in a day or two and I will give it to you. Anne is confined with a bad cold, so we have canceled most of our engagements this week, and if it continues to rain I shall have time to work on the sketch.'

Simon smiled at her enigmatically. 'Thank you, Miss Henderson.' On a sudden impulse, he bent and kissed her hand.

Drusilla blinked and her mouth lifted humorously at the corners. 'It is but a trifle,' she murmured and prepared to scamper after Tillie. The maid was hovering, poised for flight under the next tree. There came a sudden clap of thunder. 'Good-bye, sir, I must go. It is not wise to stand under trees during storms and Tillie is frightened.'

Simon was smitten with a troubling thought. He reached out to detain her; his hand clamped on her arm. 'Forgive me, I know you are getting very wet, but I hope you do not suspect my motives. I did not ask for the portrait to flatter you, or as a means of gaining access to Anne. But I do want it – very much.'

There was no mistaking his sincerity. Drusilla was touched by his earnestness. She said simply, 'Yes, I know, and I am very damp.' Then she picked up her skirts and ran, jumping through the puddles in carefree abandon. Much later, when she was soaking in a hot tub by the fire in her bedchamber, she gave a shriek and dropped her sponge. 'Oh, what have I done,' she wailed, 'Anne will never forgive me for inviting him to call!'

The rain did not abate until Friday, by which time Anne was sufficiently recovered to join Drusilla for tea in the drawing room. Sir Mortimer arrived with the tea tray and was greeted with cries of delight by the young ladies, who were in need of diversion after a dull week. Pleased by the warmth of his reception and cheered to find Anne downstairs, Mortimer challenged her to a game of dominoes. They had been playing for perhaps half an hour, with much good-natured squabbling, when another caller was announced. Drusilla looked up from her magazine and rose slowly, but Anne, on hearing the caller's name, scrambled to her feet in shocked astonishment, sending the dominoes flying in all directions. Mortimer pushed back his chair, but remained seated, watching the other three with detached amusement.

Mr. Pontefract proved equal to the occasion. He performed an elegant bow before Drusilla and drawled, 'My dear Miss Henderson. I hope I do not intrude. I came but to inquire for your health after your drenching in the park the other day. And Anne, I am delighted to see that you are restored to your accustomed self. Sir Mortimer.'

The two men acknowledged one another distantly, the recollection of their last encounter on the field of pugilism vivid in both their memories. Anne pulled out her handkerchief and sniffed vigorously. It was left to Drusilla to say politely, 'Thank you for your concern, sir. Fortunately, I suffered no ill effects. Do come and sit down and I will pour you some tea. I am at the urn today, as poor Mama is in attendance on my father, who is sick and irritable as a bear. Do you take one lump of sugar or two?'

'Two please, ma'am,' said Simon, with a grin. Anne's mouth opened and closed again. Everyone sat down and Drusilla gave Simon his cup.

'I believe I forgot to mention, Anne, that I met Mr. Pontefract in the park the other day,' she remarked conversationally. 'It must have been the first day you were ill and not inclined to listen to my chatter. Then it slipped my mind. Mr. Pontefract found me sketching by the lake.'

Simon's lip quivered. He said, 'Miss Henderson was gracious enough to promise me a drawing, when it was finished, Anne.'

Poor Anne spluttered and took refuge in her handkerchief once more. Drusilla said hastily, 'I have it here. One moment while I rummage for it.' She soon produced it. Simon set down his cup and examined the work carefully.

Anne craned her neck to see. She exclaimed, 'Oh, Drusilla, it is very like! You have captured his nose and the wave of his hair exactly, but ...' she hesitated.

' ... But she has made me much too handsome? Is that what you would say, Anne?' Simon helped her. The two ladies both blushed. He shook his head. 'I was not angling for compliments.' He glanced at each face in turn. His mood changed and he grew solemn. He addressed himself to Anne, who was seated on the sofa, with Mortimer beside her, casually swinging his watch fob between finger and thumb.

'Well, Anne,' Simon Pontefract began, standing stiffly before the empty fireplace, 'this is not easy for me to say, for I've never been one to admit myself in the wrong, but desperation may make a man foolish and my debts have mounted astronomically over the past months. Two of my ships were sunk in storms off the West Indies and other business ventures also failed in the recent depression following the end of the French wars. It was necessary to keep up appearances, but the hands of my creditors are at my throat and I am forced to flee the country or pass my days in a debtors' prison. Misliking these disagreeable alternatives, I have taken advantage of the promise which you rashly made to be my wife, under pressure at your father's deathbed. An understanding of my predicament may explain, though it does not excuse, my selfish pursuit of your sweet self. It was the old and not uncommon reason – that to marry an heiress was the only way to make myself solvent – and I have traded on that expectation to get loans and thus sunk further into the mire. You were the only young lady of wealth available in my hour of need.' Mr. Pontefract paused, then continued deliberately. 'After my conversations with Miss Henderson at the Academy and in the park, I realized that I have caused you much suffering and before taking to my heels and heading for exile, I am glad to have this opportunity to offer you my profound apologies for my barbarous behaviour.'

Very pale, a prey to the dangerous conflicting emotions of pity and indignation, Anne rose unsteadily to her feet and gripped Simon's hands, more for support than to give comfort.

To the incredulous amazement of the other three, she said resolutely, 'You do right to remind me that my dear father promised you my hand and fortune in marriage. I am a little older and wiser now.' Here she smiled at Drusilla and Mortimer and continued firmly, 'And although there is no love between us, it is plainly my duty to fulfil my father's promise and my own. I will wed you, if you still wish it.'

Goaded, Mortimer almost shouted, 'You can't do this, Anne. I thought you despised men's notions of duty and honour – you've told me so often enough.'

'Women are bound by their own notions of honour,

too,' retorted Anne, swallowing back the tears which threatened to overwhelm her. With pathetic dignity she said to her erstwhile suitor, 'Mr. Pontefract, perhaps you will be so good as to let me know your reaction to my proposal when you have had time to reflect upon it.'

She ran from the room, leaving Drusilla, Mortimer, and Simon Pontefract staring at one another in dismay.

'She can't do this,' choked Mortimer, pulling convulsively at his tight collar. 'She's going to wed me, but she doesn't know it yet. She's mine, do you understand, Pontefract, you can have her cursed money, with my good will, if that will ease her conscience – but there is no necessity to wed her as well!' He too stalked out.

'This is degenerating into a melodrama or a farce,' cried Drusilla, collapsing weakly on the arm of her chair. Common sense coming to her rescue, she conquered a slight impulse to give way to hysterics and looked up at Mr. Pontefract, the beginnings of a scheme surfacing in her mind.

'Dash it all, females are so perverse. I'd better be off to my ship without delay!' burst out Simon, running a hand through his dark hair.

Satisfied by this bewildered reaction, Drusilla asked abruptly, 'So you do not plan to take advantage of Anne's proposal?'

Simon hesitated, then seizing her hands in his, he said passionately, 'I have done many things in my life which would not bear close scrutiny, but since I met you I know there is only one woman in life for me and I cannot spend my days with a girl half my age, who lives with me in fear and loathing. If I possessed half the fortune which once I had, it would be at your feet, but as it is, I will remember that I was at least born a gentleman and will disappear, leaving Miss Anne to her jealous lover. Pray wish them happy and accept my humble prayers for your own happiness.'

He made to withdraw, but Miss Henderson clung to his fingers with a surprising strength. 'Not so fast, dear sir. I am quite worn down with chivalry and histrionics this afternoon. Do have another cup of tea. I have a plan to bring our young lovers together and to atone for past misdeeds you can help me, if you will. It need not delay you for long.'

Half-reluctant, half-curious, Simon sat down on the loveseat recently vacated by Anne and Mortimer. Soon he and Drusilla had their heads close together over the teacups and a muffled laugh or murmurous voice were the only sounds to be heard from the drawing room for some time.

In pursuit of her plan, Drusilla left Anne severely alone. Brooding unhappily in her chamber, Anne decided that her friend was angry at her apparently irrational behaviour. Drusilla probably thought that she had accepted the Hendersons' hospitality under false pretenses after her flight from Simon, for she had now expressed her willingness to marry him. She passed a lonely, sleepless night and determined in the cold light of early dawn that she must quit the Henderson residence. If she did not hear from Simon soon, she would go to Gordon's Hotel and await her cousins' arrival.

A note from Simon appeared with her breakfast tray. Grimly, she munched her toast and absorbed Mr. Pontefract's message. It was brief and to the point; he thanked Anne for her generous offer, which he accepted. He wrote that the pressing nature of his obligations made speed imperative and suggested an elopement to Gretna Green. He would make all the arrangements and would be waiting at the corner of Henrietta and Welbeck streets, at four-thirty the next morning. She was to bring one small bag and he begged her not to fail him. He was, her most faithful servant, Simon Pontefract.

She was becoming quite an expert in early-morning escapes, she reflected sardonically as she packed her bag. Her eyes felt hot and dry and her head ached. She had no difficulty in convincing sympathetic Mrs. Henderson that she felt unwell and needed a quiet day in bed. She pretended to be asleep when Drusilla peeped in and when Sir Mortimer called, he was obliged to spend a dejected half-hour making desultory conversation with Mr. Henderson as none of the ladies were available.

Ten minutes before the appointed hour the next morning, Anne crept downstairs. Her resolution was at a low ebb and she half-hoped someone would see her and stop her, but there was no one about, although she could hear faint stirrings in the servants' quarters, the hissing of a kettle, and the rattle of a poker in the kitchen range.

All went uncannily smoothly, no obstacle presented itself, and she found Mr. Pontefract already waiting, with a closed carriage and a sturdy pair of horses to pull it. Like a prisoner going to execution, she took one last look at the bright blue sky and entered the gloomy, chilly interior of the hired vehicle. The door slammed. Mr. Pontefract solicitously produced a rug to wrap around her knees, but did not burden her with talk. She huddled as far away from her betrothed as possible and stared blankly through the unwashed panes, heedless of their direction. At first a medley of street cries echoed in their ears, as the streets of London slipped away; from a great distance she heard the Cockney bootlace man's cheerful mispronunciation: "Lice, lice, penny a pair bootlice!", but she remained sunk in numb misery until they had left the residential areas far behind and were moving steadily through a landscape of farms and fields.

At length Mr. Pontefract asked Anne if she would care to stop for some refreshment.

She roused herself in surprise. 'Is it wise to linger? We may be pursued.'

'Oh, I think not. Who's to stop us? After all, I am your guardian,' said Simon blithely. 'In any event, we'll travel easier if we are comfortable and the horses well-baited.'

Anne peered vaguely through the window. 'Are we going in the right direction? Surely this is not the Great North Road?' she asked, her listlessness vanishing as she noted the strange absence of traffic and the narrowness of the road.

Simon replied calmly, 'No, this is not the North Road, but it runs parallel and is less frequented. Also it avoids the toll booths, which makes our journey both cheaper and harder to trace. I do not fear pursuit, in that I am confident of the outcome, but I wish to avoid any undue delay.'

They came to an inn situated in a small village on the outskirts of Epping Forest. Anne was glad to get down and stretch her cramped limbs. Simon ushered her before him into the taproom. His manner towards her was impersonal, almost avuncular. She began to relax, grateful that he had made no attempt to touch or caress her, and stood quietly waiting while he requested a private parlour and breakfast for himself and his "niece". The innkeeper's wife bustled out to welcome Anne and showed her to a chamber where she could freshen herself and remove the travel dust.

When the woman had gone she walked slowly to the little washstand, absent-mindedly bathed her face and hands and gazed at her reflection in the cracked looking glass. In truth, the irony of her predicament was almost ludicrous; this was the third time she had run away, but this time she had gone freely with the very man she had been fleeing on previous occasions. She combed her hair vigorously and gritted her teeth, oppressed by the enormity of her imprudent action. She could find little comfort in the thought that at last she was fulfilling her

duty and was also saving a man from the horror of
indefinite imprisonment. In her mind's eye she saw the
concerned faces of her cousins, the dear Hendersons,
and, most clearly of all, Sir Mortimer Vane.

In a state of abject wretchedness, she fumbled with
her hairpins, finally admitting to herself that the notion
of spending the rest of her life (or at least of his!) as
Simon Pontefract's wife was unutterably depressing.
She paused in the middle of the room to retrieve her
bonnet and shawl and said aloud, 'I'm half his age, I'm
independently wealthy, and I love another man. How
did I come to be caught in such a trap?'

With an impatient, despairing sigh, she straightened
her shoulders, lifted her chin, and went in search of her
betrothed. A chambermaid directed her to a low-
ceilinged, brown-paneled parlour, where she found Mr.
Pontefract seated at a table by the window, engaged in
pouring coffee from a pewter pot. He rose politely as
she approached and pulled out a high-backed chair with
wooden arms. When they were seated he inquired with,
to Anne, odious cheerfulness, 'Will you pour, my dear?
I vow there is nothing more charming to bachelor eyes
than the sight of a pretty woman across the breakfast
table.'

'I should have thought you would prefer an
unobtrusive manservant at your elbow and your
newspaper in front of you,' retorted Anne irritably.

He eyed her shrewdly, but responded with unim-
paired good humour, 'Not quite at your brightest in the
morning, I perceive.'

Anne missed the sharp glance, but accepted some hot
coffee gratefully. She stared out of the window and
tapped her foot in mute frustration.

'These muffins are very good,' said Simon, proffering
the plate. She took one reluctantly, but the warm,
appetizing fragrance piqued her appetite and the first
muffin was followed by another; both disappeared with

remarkable rapidity. Some feeling of inner well-being returned and she raised her head to look directly at her future husband. She found his face expressionless, the heavily lidded eyes contemplating her in hawklike fashion. Anne shivered. At once, Simon was all concern: Would she like the casement closed, very drafty, these old inns, but quaint in their way. He enjoyed the country as a rest cure, but of course, was really a city person by virtue of his profession. He discoursed easily on the rival merits of town and country life, asking her which she preferred, but not waiting for an answer.

Anne began to be vexed. Was this a sample of his future treatment, as if she were some decorative doll, with no opinions of her own? Mortimer had always given her comments due consideration, even if he did not agree with them. Unconsciously she sighed, then yawned.

'Do I bore you so soon?' asked her companion mendaciously, as he energetically attacked his ham and eggs. 'Don't worry, my dear. When we are wed I shall leave for the warehouse early and you can take your chocolate in your chamber in peace. We shall go our own ways.'

At the image conjured up by these dreaded words, Anne's tolerance snapped. She stood up wildly, as if waking from a dream, and cried, 'I'm sorry, Simon, I cannot marry you. I promise I will make over a large share of my fortune to you and I trust that will be adequate compensation. I must return to London at once, my friends will have discovered my absence, and they will be so worried for my safety.'

Apparently unmoved, Mr. Pontefract regarded the distraught female before him. Ostentatiously, he dabbed the corners of his mouth with his napkin. 'How fickle women are. My amour propre is affronted!' he remarked to the ceiling. Then, lowering his gaze, he addressed Anne sternly, 'And what of your sense of honour, of duty? I have not forgotten your eloquence on the subject, Miss Fairleigh.'

Anne stumbled to his side and fell on her knees beside his chair, her hands clutching his sleeve. 'Please sir,' she entreated, 'I am all you say. I have been foolish, thoughtless, and cruel, but I simply cannot proceed with this contract. I – I love another.'

Mr. Pontefract frowned and flicked some crumbs from his waistcoat. 'Indeed?' he said calmly. 'You are not the first to find yourself in that uncomfortable situation, my child.'

Anne nodded and sniffed valiantly. Abruptly, Simon relented. He leaned forward and kissed her soundly on the brow, then gripped her elbows and raised her from the floor with easy strength. 'For heaven's sake, Anne, what a monstrous, heartless tyrant you must think me. I like women, but I don't like them groveling at my feet. Now, pray resume your chair, you will soil that fetching gown. Drink your coffee and let us consider, rationally, what is to be done.'

But his kind tone and unexpected words swept Anne temporarily beyond the sober realm of reason. In her relief, she abandoned herself to an exquisite rush of sensibility and put her head on Mr. Pontefract's cream velvet chest, sobbing incoherently. To his credit he bore the onslaught nobly, standing rocklike and patting her shoulder soothingly as he ignored the imminent ruin of his favourite waistcoat.

Totally absorbed in this release of pent-up emotion, neither Mr. Pontefract nor Miss Fairleigh heard the arrival of a carriage in the yard outside. A few moments later the door was flung open unceremoniously and Sir Mortimer appeared on the threshold, closely followed by Drusilla.

'I'll have your hide for this, Pontefract!' declared Mortimer dramatically. He advanced into the room, flourishing his whip with menacing purpose.

XVI
Resolution

Thunderstruck, the runaway couple jumped apart; obeying an unchivalrous impulse, Simon prudently retired to the breakfast table and lit a cigar leaving Anne to face her irate pursuer alone.

With Anne so strategically placed, Sir Mortimer was unable to carry out his threat to horsewhip her abductor. Anne held her ground, her eyes riveted on his knuckles, which had whitened alarmingly with the intensity of his hold. 'Stand aside, Miss Fairleigh,' he commanded. 'The cowardly cur shall not find refuge behind a woman's petticoats!'

To the unbounded surprise of the two onlookers, Anne smiled radiantly at these scornful words. Sir Mortimer tried again. 'As for you, Miss Fairleigh, your absurd propensity for getting into scrapes is unequaled in my experience,' he began icily, but Anne seemed not to hear him. She came forward deliberately and put her hands over his, looking up at him with an expression so filled with adoration that he dropped the weapon of vengeance and clasped her in his arms crying fiercely, 'You're mine, Anne darling, do you understand?' He shook her to emphasize his point. 'I don't give a fig for your fortune, but I want you for my wife. Thank heaven I found you in time!' A shadow of doubt surfaced. 'I am in time, am I not?' he questioned, very low. His grip became painful.

Anne protested weakly, 'Mortimer, you are giving me

more bruises than Mr. Pontefract who has been the soul of courtesy.'

'Has he indeed?' Mortimer did not appear totally reassured, but Anne, clinging to his arm as if she feared he would vanish, insisted, 'Yes, truly. Just before you arrived we had agreed that we should not suit and that it was silly to let honour and duty stand in the way of happiness.'

'Oh!' said Mortimer blankly.

Having observed this touching scene in silent satisfaction, Drusilla now stepped forward, thinking it was high time to give a more practical turn to the conversation. Her intention was preempted by Mr. Pontefract, who stubbed out his cigar and rose to his feet, stretching his limbs in relaxed fashion.

'Women do so like a masterful man,' he informed the bewildered Sir Mortimer kindly. 'What Anne is trying, in her blundering way to convey, my dear Vane, is that she has decided to obey her instincts. She has put the world of reason aside and ascending to a higher plane, has placed her trust in love, in you, to be precise.'

Obedient to an imperative signal from Miss Henderson, Simon edged his way across to the door, taking care to keep the sofa between himself and Sir Mortimer. He need not have worried, for his rival and his erstwhile betrothed had eyes for no one but themselves and barely heard the soft click as Drusilla closed the door.

Mortimer held Anne at arms' length, studying her face intently. 'Tell me honestly, was Pontefract mistaken, or is it really so – that you have placed your trust in me? That you love me and are willing to marry me?'

Impatient with his obtuseness, Anne thumped him with her small fists, exclaiming, 'Oh, you dear aggravating man, of course I love you and will wed you! How can you be so dense?'

'Miss Anne Fairleigh, I was not the one who ran

away,' he pointed out with some asperity. He caught her hand and pulled her down beside him on the sofa, watching with delight as a vexed frown drew her winged brows together.

She said remorsefully, 'I've been such a goose. Love must send one's wits a-begging, for until recently I've always prided myself on my good sense. I really do not deserve such happiness.' Tenderly she reached up to trace the line of his scar with gentle fingers. 'I've been wanting to do that for so long,' she murmured smiling.

He kissed her fingers, then his eyes darkened as he looked down at her; he bent his head and kissed her on her parted lips, with a fervour which took her breath away. His embrace made the memory of Simon Pontefract's original passionate overtures pale in comparison, but this time she responded eagerly, trusting and unafraid. At length he drew back, saying huskily, 'Little tormentor. Promise me you will never run away again.'

Anne tilted her head mischievously. 'We-ll, not unless you beat me.'

She snuggled in his arms and he tightened his hold, muttering fiercely into her hair, 'With your misguided sense of duty, I shall probably be tempted to beat you, but I think you will make an excellent soldier's wife. After a little discipline, I imagine we shall rub along very tolerably together.'

Anne squeaked with indignation, then sobered and asked seriously, 'Do you think you will have to fight again?'

'Who knows, my love. Boney is still alive and from what Montfort tells me, the French military are his to a man. But, for the moment we shall retire to the country to my manor at Shawcross and cultivate rustic pursuits, if you have had your fill of town junketings.'

Promptly Anne responded, 'My dear sir, there is nothing I should like more, but I pray you be patient for a little while, so that I can entertain my cousins and thank milady, your sister, and Drusilla's parents for all their kindnesses.' Roused by another thought, she sat up and regarded Mortimer earnestly. 'Before we take any irremediable step, you must be aware that I shall be almost penniless, for I cannot in good conscience condemn Simon to a debtor's prison after my irresponsible behaviour.'

Overwhelmed by the ardour of his emotions, Mortimer dismissed Anne's inheritance airily. 'So long as I have you, my dearest, that is more than sufficient. Your fortune is your own to dispose of as you will.'

Anne sighed with relief. 'You are very good.' She jumped up and added lightly, 'And so agreeable. I have never known you so accommodating for so long a period. It seems unnatural. How may I provoke you?'

Mortimer stood, too, and clasped her hands behind her back, holding her close. Teasingly he replied, 'I have your measure now, Miss Fairleigh of Fernditch. 'Tis *I* shall provoke *you* by failing to take your bait.'

He kissed her again, but this time they were interrupted by Drusilla, who tripped in and smiled at them complacently.

'All is happily resolved, I see,' she glanced from one glowing face to the other and nodded.

Anne ran forward to hug her friend, exclaiming, 'Dear Drusilla, somehow I feel it is all your contriving that Mortimer arrived so opportunely. Indeed, now I think of it, I am convinced that you planned the whole affair to bring me to my senses. And Simon was your accomplice. He drew such a grim picture of matrimony that no one in their right mind could contemplate willingly entering such a state.'

Drusilla sank down on a chair and pushed a stray hairpin back in place with slightly trembling fingers. She laughed shakily and said, 'Well, Anne, you must tell me of it. I feel forewarned is forearmed. You see, I have just proposed to Mr. Pontefract, knowing that a man with his odd notions of honour would fear to be labeled a fortune-hunting adventurer a second time.'

'But you hardly know one another,' gasped Anne, in dismay, while Mortimer exclaimed simultaneously, 'Good lord, Drusilla, are you an heiress, too?'

'Not precisely,' returned the young lady, twisting her handkerchief nervously. 'I already have control of my fortune, which was left to me by my Great Aunt Emma. Of course, I will inherit from my parents eventually, but I hope that will not be for many years yet.' She beckoned to Anne to sit beside her and said gently, 'I do not know how long it took you to realize the strength of your attachment to Mortimer, but I have to confess something has happened to me which I never believed possible outside a fairy tale. For me, it has been a case of love at first sight – or very nearly. Perhaps we should say at second sight! I met Simon at Georgiana's and then again later and in the unusual circumstances connected with you, we discovered a depth of understanding which I had despaired of sharing with another soul.' She paused and added, half in jest, half in earnest, 'It took me some time to convince him that he would really be doing me a favour by removing me from the spinster's shelf. You must believe me, Anne, this has only just occurred. Simon knew nothing of it when he left London with you; he only knew that I would follow with Mortimer. We had not spoken of marriage between us until the last few minutes.'

Anne struggled for words. 'My dear, of course I believe you. I am immensely grateful to you, but, oh, Drusilla, are you sure ... Simon!'

As if on cue, Mr. Pontefract entered at the sound of his name. He raised his eyeglass and surveyed the ladies in amusement, Anne gaping like a flounder in confusion and Drusilla torn between tears and laughter at the effect her announcement had produced.

'May I suggest a chair, Pontefract?' offered Mortimer, upholding masculine solidarity.

Simon accepted this gesture of peace with a graceful bow. Slowly he dropped his glass and arranged his sturdy frame in a comfortable wing chair. Anne watched him in amazement, unable to reconcile this benign gentleman with the awesome being who had haunted her dreams for so long.

He addressed Drusilla firmly. 'You do yourself an injustice, my dear. I swear to you that no suspicion of a hint of your financial status has reached the town gossips. Even your friend Georgiana does not know, or she would certainly have told me. I assure you that your own charms (and, I cannot deny, an educated conjecture that you are your parents' only child and probable heiress) would guarantee that your destiny is not, and has never been, the shelf of spinsterhood. I am merely snapping you up before the town beaux realize what a jewel they have in their midst. I feel I should explain that I have no distaste for the word "adventurer" when genuinely applied, but in this case, where true sentiment is involved, I find I have a quite irrational objection to the appellation. Understand that I will wed you for yourself alone, Drusilla, and I will repay to you every penny which I borrow to set my business on a firm footing once more. This I solemnly swear in the presence of our two witnesses.'

He smiled fleetingly at Anne and Mortimer, then leaned forward and declared fervently, 'With you to encourage and aid me, I am confident it may be done, and then, if you wish, you shall give all or part of your fortune to those poor wretches in prison, where, but for the grace of God and your generous, gentle heart, I should myself shortly be languishing in hopeless misery.' His mouth twisted and he could not resist adding wryly, 'Unless, of course, I had fled into exile and died of some tropical fever.'

Anne sniffed and said a trifle sharply, 'Don't spoil it, Simon. You could always have gone to Canada!'

'Touché. A just reproof,' answered Mr. Pontefract, 'but don't forget, young lady, that I am still your legal guardian and you cannot marry without my consent.'

Anne stiffened and Simon crossed to her side and took her hand, 'Come now, can we not bury the hatchet? It would be hard for Drusilla if her closest friend would not speak a civil word to her husband.'

For a moment Anne hesitated, but her natural good temper reasserted itself. She said warmly, 'Forgive me. It was a spiteful remark. By all means let us be friends. I would rather have you for a friend than an enemy and besides, although I hate to admit it, I do like you, my lord guardian!'

Mortimer intervened with a grin. 'I vow 'tis incredible how fortunes are flying today, Pontefract. Before you and Drusilla joined us, Anne was telling me that her fortune is at your disposal also. My felicitations, you are about to become an extremely wealthy man!'

For once Mr. Pontefract's ready eloquence failed him. Drusilla leaped hastily into the breach. 'So much is not necessary, although we thank you both most heartily for your good will. Now, let us cease this vulgar talk of money, or I shall have hysterics.'

'Yes, I agree,' Anne came to her support. 'Would you like some refreshment before we return to town? I know it is early, but do you think we might drink a toast – it will fortify us to face our irate friends and relations. We cannot leave until you have told me how you arranged everything, Drusilla. Surely your parents objected when you left the house with Mortimer?'

'Oh, I ordered a picnic last night and told Mama that we were going with a party of friends. I stole into your room early to remove any note you might have left, Anne, and sent an urgent message to Mortimer at six o'clock this morning! He responded with quite remarkable alacrity to the news of your elopement. I showed him your note, you see, and we departed from the city at high speed, but in quite terrifying silence. Fortunately, he was so angry that he followed my directions without question and otherwise paid me no heed. I was glad I was not one of his horses, for he cursed them most ferociously – in Portuguese, I believe,' she finished, innocently directing an inquiring gaze at the Peninsular veteran.

Mortimer bowed. 'In Spanish, Miss Henderson, Spanish,' he reiterated, showing his teeth in an evil leer.

Drusilla shrank back in mock fright; Simon rang the bell for refreshments and Anne said teasingly, 'My hero! Imagine coming to my rescue on two occasions. So very noble!'

"Tis lucky for you, my girl, that love has a mellowing effect on a man's disposition,' observed her suitor calmly.

'Quite,' Simon nodded, as the landlord entered. 'What say you to some Spanish sherry wine? It would be appropriate, I think. Would you like something to eat, Drusilla?'

'Mm, I'm famished, I would like some ham and eggs, with toast and coffee,' she responded cheerfully. Mortimer seconded this order and they all repaired to the table in high good spirits.

Anne enjoyed her second breakfast much more than her first. At last she pushed away her plate and said meditatively, 'I confess I'm still a little puzzled to know how you found us, for we quitted the Great North Road some way off. Did you know this inn existed, Drusilla?'

Miss Henderson and Mr. Pontefract exchanged a conspiratorial smile. 'While you kept to your chamber yesterday afternoon, I met Simon at the circulating library and we consulted a guidebook. That part was not difficult. I own I experienced several qualms concerning my ability to persuade Mortimer to forsake the main route, but in the event my fears were groundless. He was so preoccupied that I think I could have indicated the Bath Road and he would have taken it! When we reached the fork, I cunningly suggested we ask a cowman if he had seen a vehicle of your description this morning. I was fortunate in that yours was the only carriage which had passed this way and this inn was the first respectable one on the side road, so naturally we stopped to make inquiries! The rest followed just as I had anticipated.'

'You're a devious, unscrupulous creature, Drusilla Henderson, and I'm eternally in your debt,' exclaimed Anne, bubbling with mirth.

'So say we all,' confirmed Mortimer, grinning.

Miss Henderson accepted these deserved tributes with a modest smile, but reminded the young lovers gently, 'Simon was also instrumental in bringing about this happy outcome. His altruism was truly outstanding, for recollect he was about to sacrifice his opportunity to win an heiress and he had no notion that there was another one waiting in the wings. He acted as he did at my behest and fully expected to depart into exile (or worse, if the delay proved fatal!) as soon as he had performed his good deed and brought you two together in a compromising situation, where all misunderstandings would have to be explained.'

Anne nodded and Mortimer's eyes glinted appreciatively as he lit his pipe. 'What a loss to the army that you were born a woman, Drusilla. You would have made a formidable strategist,' he drawled.

Simon leaned forward and put his elbows on the table, surveying his betrothed with a penetrating glare. 'You are quite right, Vane, and I suspect she had an ulterior motive which she has not so far divulged. You were testing me, were you not, Drusilla, to see if I kept my part of the bargain? Come now, admit that it crossed your mind that I might not resist the temptation to keep Anne in my power and go directly to Gretna Green.'

Miss Henderson had the grace to blush. She reached out her hand pleadingly. 'Forgive me, Simon. After all, I have known you for a very short time and it was only a very small doubt, quite without foundation, as you have amply proved. I am delighted to know tht you can read my mind so well; I shall be more on my guard in future.'

Simon covered her hand with both his own and said simply, 'I admire prudence, although it is not a virtue which I share; your cautious instincts will complement my rash gambling tendencies and we will make an excellent team. Let there be no more secrets between us, my dear.'

'We should drink a toast to that,' said Anne and Mortimer together. Everyone laughed. The bell was rung and wine produced. Solemnly the two couples felicitated one another and drank to long life and happiness.

When they were seated again, Anne asked inquisitively, 'Do you have any close family, Simon? You never speak of any relations.'

'No. I was an only child and my parents both died long ago. I have some distant connections in Warwickshire, but we lost contact after I went to America. I come from a respectable middle-class family, small country gentry on my mother's side and trade on the other.'

'Well, at least our backgrounds are compatible,' remarked Drusilla.

'You are the source of this country's prosperity; a suitable admixture of wealth and breeding,' observed Mortimer. 'I mixed with all ranks in the army and I assure you flexibility and movement between classes is essential to England's greatness.'

'Next, you'll be saying it prevented a revolution on the French model,' suggested Anne.

'It did, Miss Fairleigh, but I will spare you a dissertation on the subject, for I see you are not in the mood to allow your mind to be informed,' retorted Mortimer, puffing a cloud of smoke in her direction.

Anne coughed and changed the subject. 'However shall I explain what has happened to my cousins and your parents, Drusilla?'

Miss Henderson stood up, shaking crumbs from her gown, and reaching for her traveling cloak, she said, 'They will be so delighted that you have decided to settle down with such an eligible parti (Mortimer grinned and bowed ironically) that they will forget your regrettable penchant for running away and agree that it is a case of all's well that ends well. And consider, Anne, I have a far larger problem than you, for you have painted so lurid a portrait of poor Simon that I fear my parents will question my sanity.'

Anne frowned in thought. 'How complicated everything is. But I promise I will help you to persuade them; I will tell them that Mr. Pontefract in no way resembles my caricature, which would be better suited to a character from a novel. I wish I had not been quite so vehement in voicing my detestation, but never fear, Simon, we will overcome it and convince them that you are perfect for Drusilla and not a real-life ogre at all!'

Mortimer added helpfully, 'Yes, and I'll emphasize that poor Anne has read too many of m'sister's works and until recently related everything in life to tales of fiction, but that since coming to Town she is much wiser, if not older.'

Anne pouted, then giggled as she gathered her belongings together. In a happy haze the quartet set out for the metropolis, having exchanged partners for the return journey.

XVII
Epilogue: All's Well That Ends Well

It is not to be thought that all these weighty matters could be settled in a moment. Explanations had to be made and objections overcome; but the ladies, who love a wedding, not to mention two weddings, carried all before them and plans were soon afoot.

The Misses Prawne and Mrs. Henderson entered into the spirit of the celebrations wholeheartedly, but Mr. Henderson allowed himself to be persuaded only after some earnest talk with Mr. Simon Pontefract and several frank discussions with his spouse. That good lady impressed upon him the undeniable fact that it was time Drusilla had a household of her own. Mr. Henderson was inclined to feel that he would miss his daughter so far away in Bristol, but Drusilla promised to visit often and the prospect of grandchildren at some point did much to reconcile her parents to their imminent loss.

Drusilla herself was quietly determined and, owing to Mr. Pontefract's pressing circumstances, the wedding was arranged for mid-September, with Anne as bridesmaid and Sir Mortimer as best man.

Miss Letitia and Mrs. Henderson greatly enjoyed shopping with the young ladies for their trousseaux, as Anne's wedding was to follow in October. Meanwhile, Miss Ippolita pursued more cultural endeavours and struck up a friendship with Georgiana Upcroft, much to the benefit of that lady. Jack Davenport agreed to stand

as best man at Anne and Mortimer's wedding and
Stephanie and her husband accepted their invitation
with delight, as did His Grace, the Duke of Wellington.

The weeks before Drusilla's event passed happily.
Anne found great satisfaction in the development of a
warm relationship with Mortimer's sister and her family,
who accepted their prospective new member with
unfeigned enthusiasm.

One day in late August Mortimer took his betrothed to
visit her prospective new home in Sussex, accompanied
by Lady Montfort. On the drive, Hester told Anne how
they had lost Shawcross Manor for a while, as a result of
their father's debts, but Mortimer had been able to
reclaim their ancestral home when he inherited from a
wealthy uncle and now the estate was flourishing. As they
wandered round the gardens, admiring the fountains
and flowers, the dahlias at their best after some heavy
rain, Anne realized how fortunate she was to have such
pleasant prospects. When Mortimer was lured beyond
the ha-ha, designed to keep animals in the park at a
distance from the house, to inspect some fencing with his
gardener, Anne expressed her contentment to Hester.

'We are fortunate to have you too, my dear,' replied
Hester. 'I began to fear that my brother would become a
bachelor-recluse here. He was very much at loose ends,
when he returned from the wars.'

Bravely, Anne voiced the small doubt which still
troubled her. 'Was Mortimer very cast down by Lady
Tremaine's marriage?'

Lady Montfort smiled reassuringly. 'That was many
years ago. But you should ask him yourself, Anne. Let
there be no secrets between you. There has been enough
misunderstanding already. See, here he comes. I will
leave you and go in search of refreshment. I'm sure Mrs.
Beddowes will be equal to the occasion. She is an
excellent housekeeper.'

Hester retreated, leaving Anne alone by a small fountain which contained a statue of Cupid, wearing an impish expression. The water trickled merrily and a well-fed goldfish leapt towards the sun in a graceful, curving arc. She laughed aloud and Mortimer, hearing her as he crossed the wide lawn, hastened his step. The expression of love and joy on his strong face was such that Anne's lingering misgivings vanished. Consigning Lady Stephanie to oblivion, she reached out her hand. Mortimer grasped it and pulled her to him. They sank down on the low parapet which surrounded the rippling water and for a moment all was still, but for the hum of bees and the twittering of birds.

'Idyllic,' murmured Mortimer, brushing Anne's hair with his lips.

Anne sat up. 'In the summer!' she agreed, as memories of winter desolation in Somerset rose unbidden in her mind. He followed her train of thought without trouble.

'Will you like it here?' he asked, in swift concern. 'I know Sussex does not have the same associations for you as it does for me, but we could buy a house in Town and live there for part of the year, if you feel Shawcross will be too quiet and lonely for you. Would you consider selling Fernditch? I do not want you to feel obliged to escape from me again.'

Anne relented at once. 'Dearest Mortimer, pray don't look so uneasy. I only wanted to tease you a little. The manor is beautiful and tranquil. There is not the least necessity to have a London house, but perhaps, if you think it wise, we will sell Fernditch. It holds few happy recollections for me and it is so remote. We could always visit Brighton to make purchases or seek a change of scene. Hester has told me what a lively place it is and I am always refreshed by a visit to the sea.'

She chattered on. 'Besides, in my experience, village life is rarely as somnolent as it may appear to an outsider. Hester is a mine of local information; she described for me some of the adventures you had the year that she and Hugo were married, when a smuggling ring dominated the district. Why did you never mention it, I wonder?'

'So much has happened since; I had other things on my mind,' he responded dismissively. He gazed at the little Cupid, vividly recalling that summer ten years ago when he had courted Stephanie de Beauclerc in the raffish seaside resort of Brighton and been rejected. It had been a year of excitement and adventure, a year of threatened French invasion; of spies and danger, of military parades and balls. But Stephanie had been right, he now reflected. They had had little in common beside a mutual love of horses and he had been army mad. It was better this way. At peace at last, he closed his eyes and raised his face to the sun. The breeze ruffled his hair and he sighed blissfully, then spluttered, as Anne, who had been trailing her hand in the pool, sprinkled some drops on his upturned countenance.

The deed done, Anne made as if to spring up and run off, but Mortimer's hand shot out and caught her wrist in a vicelike grip. 'No so fast, my lady,' he drawled, shaking the drops from his nose, 'You shall pay a forfeit for that piece of impertinence.'

With easy strength, he forced her back, so that she was suspended above the sparkling water, her bonnet ribbons floating limply. A curious fish swam up to investigate this unusual phenomenon and Anne twisted and wriggled, shrieking indignantly, 'Don't let me go, you brute. I can't swim!'

Grinning, Mortimer swung her to her feet and caught her in his arms. The past was forgotten; the future awaited them.

Lady Montfort, appearing unseen on the terrace steps, retired again quietly to drink her tea in solitary state.